MARS NEEDS BOOKS!

Borgo Press Books by GARY LOVISI

Driving Hell's Highway: A Crime Novel
Gargoyle Nights: A Collection of Horror
Mars Needs Books!: A Science Fiction Novel
Murder of a Bookman: A Bentley Hollow Collectibles
    Mystery Novel

MARS NEEDS BOOKS!

A SCIENCE FICTION NOVEL

GARY LOVISI

THE BORGO PRESS
MMXI

MARS NEEDS BOOKS!

FIRST EDITION

Published by Wildside Press LLC

www.wildsidebooks.com

DEDICATION

For my young and lovely wife,

Lucille

CONTENTS

"When governments fear the people, there is liberty. When the people fear the government, there is tyranny. The strongest reason for the people to retain the right to keep and bear arms is, as a last resort, to protect themselves against tyranny in government."
Thomas Jefferson

"In a democratically free society, everything goes, but nothing matters. In a totalitarian society, nothing goes, and everything matters."
Unknown

"Books?
They are nothing more than antique and quaint, primitive information storage devices. They have no meaning today."
Simon

"No one on Earth reads anymore. Books are lost things from a lost past. But on Mars, all we do is read, and all we read are the old crime and hard-boiled paperbacks from last century."
James Ryan

CHAPTER ONE
SIMON

He went by the name of Simon.

Just, Simon.

But that one name encompassed power unimagined by lesser rulers and despots throughout the history of the old planet called Earth. The few people who mattered all knew the name—and they feared and obeyed. While the vast majority of people who did not matter hardly knew he even existed. To have that knowledge could be a death sentence for them. In a sense, most citizens were lucky in their ignorance, but it is a damned dark way to go through life.

Simon sat back in his chair luxuriating in the sheer ambience of the naked power he possessed and so often wielded, and in what he had become.

Just what had he become?

The man who controlled everyone and everything.

It was that simple.

He was an old man these days, gray hair, but with a body that was still lean, taught, hard. His mind was still sharp and just as merciless as ever. His cruelty was legendary among those who knew *of* him—for no one actually personally *knew* him, except one slim slip of a girl. So few on Earth even knew of his existence at all. Nor did anyone know officially of the existence of the organization of which he sat as head—the Department of Control. Unaffectionately known and feared among those in the worldwide government Authority as the DOC. Still and all there were hints galore, crackpot conspiracy theories veiled in fearful whispers in the underground Net about him, and about the DOC, in many dark stories. The people—the citizens—had heard rumors but no one ever spoke of them openly.

If they did, they simply disappeared, never to be heard from again.

It was that easy.

It was that fast.

It was that final.

Simon surveyed the massive expanse before him—looking upon the magnificent vista that was his controlling headquarters and his home. He sat at a long circular desk linked by dozens of high-resolution view screens. Through them he could contact anyone in the world, find out anything he wanted to know. Through his system he was linked to a trillion-power servers that held all the data in the world. Information was power and Simon could access information on any subject he desired instantly, and any person as well.

Of course, this was all connected to dozens of orbital satellite blanketing the Earth and armed with the latest killer lasers guided by pinpoint GPS tracking. Through his system, Simon could locate, lock onto, and destroy any person, anywhere, at any time. It was a neat "toy" and one he used frequently to rid himself and the world of any hint of opposition to his rule. Simon and the DOC never needed to arrest or imprison their enemies; those enemies did literally disappear.

Poof!

Nothing was ever left behind. Then the target was immediately deleted from the digital record, and it was like he or she had never existed at all. It was all so neat and quick, never troublesome.

Simon reveled in it.

Simon's headquarters—what he had made into his own private world—was surrounded by one-way protect-glass that allowed him a totally secure environment as he kept track of his staff who worked feverishly on the massive workroom floor below. They monitored and put into place his plans. *His* plans, Simon corrected. He smiled. In this instance it wasn't a conceit he had stretched too far—though God had been erased from the digital record long ago—Simon felt he was a more than adequate replacement. Simon knew the word *His* was used to refer to the deity. But *He* was the deity now. *His* plans, Simon's plans, were all that mattered. Simon's world had no God or devil in it, only Simon.

Simon ably fulfilled all aspects of both.

The DOC originally began by incorporating the old CIA and FBI and later added top secret departments of the fabled NSA and other very Top Secret agencies. After the terrorist attacks of September 11, 2001, commonly known as 9/11 in what had been the old United States, from last century—or LastCen—DOC evolved and secretly came into existence. Once all security and information agencies were merged under one controlling legal authority, DOC had its impetus. DOC had been a minor governmental office back then ruled under a benign nondescript bureaucrat. Later it was merged with 200,000 other federal government employees into the new Homeland Security Department. The Patriot Act, renewal in 2011 and Patriot Act II, III, and IV in 2016 under President Jackson Taft, expanded its power in all areas. In a few years, as their mandate and reach grew, a new Director named Simon came to power. He took direction over Homeland Security and all such agencies and eventually ran them as his own private domain. J. Edgar Hoover had nothing on this boyo!

Ten years later, though few were watching, and less even noticed, Simon under DOC authorization actually took over day-to-day management of the United States of America. He was not a dictator or even a leader, and he was certainly not President. America still went through the motions of self government. Simon was wise enough to maintain the fiction of electing presidents and even allowing diverse political parties— but he ran the show behind the scene as the head of the DOC. Simon had become the real power behind most transactions and most policies involving government and national security. From then on he only expanded his powers worldwide, growing them exponentially year by year.

Five more years and Simon and the DOC broadened their influence around the world. And few in the know knew it. Less cared, none understood. And certainly no one spoke a word about any of it.

Most informed people around the world living in the system of traditional nation states, saw the DOC as a myth, some crazy urban legend, unknown and not believed by sane people as if it were one of those "out-there" conspiracy theories. The kind of things nuts and the mentally defective drone on about endlessly. A corrupt media shielded citizens from conservative and traditionalists complaints, people who feared the huge concentration of government power and authority, as well as those on the left worried about large concentrations of political power. This was exactly what the DOC wanted. Only this time those last few on the right—and the left—had been right.

But no one really listened.

As the years passed, political leaders and their nations rose and fell, but Simon always remained in control and the DOC rolled on from one success to the other—from one power grab to the ultimate power grab. World-wide domination.

Simon molded the DOC to his will, and the DOC molded Earth and its people to his specifications. Eventually outmoded democratic governments and ineffective nation-states were disbanded and redesigned into the new, more effective, Security Districts. This was to fight international terrorism, enhance trade, make government more responsive to the "people"—now called "citizens"—as everyone was a citizen of Earth—but it was also to better effect tight, concise, effective *control*.

Eventually the DOC put in place a new planetary government, the worldwide "Authority" that ruled the Earth—for the DOC—and for Simon.

Early on, the move had been a darling of political leftists and socialist internationalists, who simply gushed lovingly over it; the idea had been loosely based on the defunct United Nations—or the Soviet Internationale. The Authority came into existence under the theory of benevolent big government being able to help everyone with their special needs and to ensure their every want.

The Authority became a worldwide totalitarian government dressed up as a smiley-faced super Mommy State, but underneath it could be hard and harsh. It soon became a master with not such a smiley face at all. By then the old nation states were gone, now everyone was a citizen of the world. Equality and utopia had arrived, and no one complained—*if they knew what was good for them.*

To accomplish this and keep it in place every form of media manipulation, unconscious message implanting, and propaganda was used to control the masses. Psychological control centers and reeducation 'camps' were established to get people thinking *correctly*, so they would cooperate and accept all the good things the Authority was bringing into their lives to make it better.

Utopia had, in fact, arrived!

The goal for the Authority was to keep power and extend power. They did it by controlling the people into absolute obedience.

Control was key.

Control in every form imaginable, and many forms not imaginable.

It had worked better than Simon had ever anticipated.

Yet not all was perfect in *His* paradise.

There were a few difficult cases that still persisted. They called themselves "individuals" and while they were scorned as uncooperative, inflexible, and troublemakers, even subversives—and when necessary, traitors—they still persisted. They were of course dealt with accordingly. But killing didn't always work. There was no real satisfaction in it after a point. You can not kill *everyone*. When one of these so-called individuals was killed, another seemed to be born to take his or her place. Simon realized that something had to be done to breed this taint out of *His* humanity.

In cases where citizens were merely troublesome, they would be dealt with in a variety of ways. In the early days, some citizens seemingly couldn't get their fill of protests. They protested everything. After the DOC took control all that nonsense stopped. In cases where protests were organized, or like-minded groups acted, key members would be brought back under control by a variety of means. Sometimes these organizations would just cease to exist. As if they had never been. Often members disappeared altogether. An unusually large number seemingly committed suicide, voluntarily or forcefully. It made little difference. Others awoke to discover they were being arrested for a variety of trumped up crimes they had never committed. It did not matter. They were always convicted. It was even rumored that the worst of these had been shipped out to Mars and the other planetary colonies. All media and educational outlets were used to enforce absolute compliance— technology guaranteed success in a way no other totalitarian government had ever achieved before in human history.

Truth was always the greatest loser, of course. However if you didn't like the particular truth spouted today, just wait until tomorrow, or the next day and there will be a new version you might like better. But probably not; because the one thing you could always count on is that things will always get worse.

* * * * * * *

Arabella Rashid walked into the room. Her sharp eyes quickly scanning all the images on the screens that glowed in front of Simon's desk. She looked at him intently, carefully, trying to hide her fear. "I see you're really going to let them all leave, after all."

"Yes, we need workers on Mars and some of the outer colony planets," Simon said quietly.

She used to have an Anglo name, but five years ago she had

taken the name of Arabella Radshid. She never told anyone why. Not even Simon. Especially not Simon. She was thirteen years old now and an acknowledged genius. Her IQ was said to be the highest in human history. It had naturally caused her to become noticed by DOC scientists and eventually, Simon *Him*self. She was being groomed as the Assistant Director of DOC. One of his most special creations.

Like the ancient Roman Emperor Tiberius with his creature and successor Caligula, Simon often said he was nursing a viper for the citizens of Earth!

Arabella Rashid had also been Simon's mistress for the last five years.

She was only thirteen years old but she had learned much from her mentor.

Her master.

Simon often told her he was big on mentoring, especially with young, often under-age girls. One could hardly call them women, when they still had years to go to attain even their teens.

Arabella had been disgusted by all of it. However, it was all she knew in her short life, even as she hated Simon with a hidden passion that was unquenchable, one as righteous as the old gods of myth. The forbidden gods of her Ancestors. Simon was the only god allowed now.

However, while Simon was a monster in many ways Arabella Rashid didn't let that bother her, or misdirect her, from her own goals.

Yes, she had her own special goals, even at thirteen.

"You surprise me," she said softly. "Letting a group of troublemakers get away so easy. They'll only be a problem for you in the future...."

Simon gave her one of his all-knowing smiles. It wasn't arrogance; it was power supreme and cruelty incarnate, only tempered by vast knowledge and experience, "My darling, that is the plan. They'll be a problem—I dare say it, perhaps even a challenge—for us to crush. And thus, their demise will make us even stronger."

Arabella Rashid nodded. She thought that she understood. The knowledge made her wince. Simon's devious cunning was as if it had been given birth by Satan himself. She looked at the man closely; an old man now, but her superior in so many ways. He was her mentor in all things, her lover, her master, a monster incarnate she realized. An inner shudder ran through her that she could never express openly.

Of course she'd never been told about the Devil, or even God, nor much of anything that was from any of the old religions, all of which was strictly forbidden. Religion had been relentlessly attacked, degraded, ridiculed, and finally sent away by the government. The government saw it as a threat, a dangerous pluralistic voice to its all-encompassing laws and regulations. All religions, and so much more, had been erased from the culture and society many years before her birth. None of it existed in the digital record, and since that was the only record that mattered....

Even in her special position, she'd seen truth covered by lie upon lie, so she'd had to dig furiously and dangerously for every truth or fact she ever discovered. Nevertheless, if you looked hard and deep enough, it was still possible to uncover truth.

Sometimes.

Some of the ancient information storage devices known as "books" still existed. Antique hard copy texts printed and published many decades past. Of course, most unapproved texts had been expunged years before. Billions of books had been destroyed outright. Gathered up and burned. Now all modes of media were tightly controlled. Obsolete media, such as TV, video, CDs, the Internet, and even the latest full cortex implants and brain inserts—were all heavily edited, corrected, abridged, or changed. The digital record was the approved text for everything these days and it came straight from the DOC through the worldwide government Authority.

It began long ago when they put secret chips in phone devices, computers, even video screens to tell what you were doing, watching, saying—along with your location data. All personal messaging was on file for access by the government too, so there was no privacy even on your most personal devices. All media was interconnected and any government agency that desired the data had access to it.

These days it was called by a special name.

Oneness—one voice, one set of facts, one truth—one way to think and act for everyone.

She hated it.

These days all information and history in the digital record was audited and amended instantaneously. History and facts changed as the DOC decreed. People fell out of favor, or ceased to exist with a keystroke. Yesterday's hero, might be forced to become today's suspect, then could become tomorrow's non-person. At that point he or she would be erased from the digital record and cease to exist. No record would ever be found about them, anywhere, not ever.

But just as "Arabella Rashid" had been born on that dark and terrible day five years ago when she'd taken her new name and new her persona—upon that first rape by Simon—she had known she would fight to win her freedom if it took her a hundred years. She was still a slip of girl but she steeled herself to her new life. She learned, and she grew in power and intelligence. And boldness. Her fear drifted away from her as she planned her revenge on Simon...and upon the world that had betrayed her.

Then she found the old books.

When she found those old books five years ago she naturally began to read them, in secret, for all were forbidden and unapproved. She learned their secrets. She learned their stories and messages. She saw the hidden worlds the words on paper told her about. She felt those words deep in her heart and she was able to see their truth. She knew then that "Dear Simon" now "Dear Old Simon," her superior, her mentor, and her lover, was the devil incarnate and she began to make her plans.

She smiled lovingly at Simon right now, all the while keeping up the pretext, but he did not return her smile. Did he suspect?

That could mean her doom. Strangely, now she did not care. She hated him, hated what he had done to her, and what he had stolen from her. She hated what he had done to the world too. It was the Old World that spoke to her now, the Old World she read about in all those old books. The books told her that the world had been such a wonderful place before Simon and the DOC controlled everything. Well, maybe not *exactly* wonderful. To be sure, it hadn't been perfect, there had been severe problems in those old days, but at least people back then had been free to make their own choices. Free to fail, even. *More* free, she corrected. Today the concept of freedom was dead on Earth, the heart of Man had become blank and empty, the mind of Man closed shut. And that was just the way Simon and the DOC wanted it.

Arabella Rashid was growing older too. In fact, at just thirteen, she felt so old; for she had experienced so much. She had seen too much darkness. Truth be told, she was now also too old for Simon. *He* preferred his "mistresses"—as if they had any choice at all in what befell them—quite a bit younger. Though no person but she knew this most intimate truth about him. It was, in fact, the most secret of all DOC secrets. She was too old for Simon now. She knew his eyes had already wandered to others. She didn't regret this at all, she only felt pity and fear for those others. She was determined now that if Simon had in fact destroyed all freedom on Earth, there would be one place where it would not be destroyed.

"Simon?" she asked sweetly.

"Yes, my dear?"

"Will you let me set up Mars? Let me set up the outpost and the colonists. You want it to be a dumping ground for incorrigibles and troublemakers, well I think I could help cleanse our planet of these undesirable elements. Putting them all on Mars is a good idea. Then we can deal with them all later as we like."

"Easy, Arabella, I have my plans for them. DOC scientists have done endless studies, reports, extrapolated future crisis data from current trends. There is a method to my plan. I ask you, why has every great empire in the history of this world—why have they all eventually fallen?"

She was quiet and did not answer; it had been a rhetorical question, his way to allow her an inner glimpse of his wisdom, knowledge and power.

He told her, "Ancient Egypt and Greece, Rome, Britain, Soviet, American, Red China, it does not matter. The reason they each fell, is that they rotted from within. They lost control. Control is what is important; it is the only factor that can stop this inner decay from occurring in our own time. Total, complete, uncompromising Control. Control over every aspect of life, of thought, of being. Now we have achieved that here on Earth. Complete totalitarian control over every aspect of the human citizen."

Arabella Rashid acknowledged his truth, "Yes, the Department of Control is the total master."

"And I am the master of the DOC," Simon laughed with a sinister power he knew only too well, and held so tightly to his being.

"That is true, Simon," she said finally.

"So we have achieved total control on Earth. For now. But that is not enough, Arabella."

"How so?"

"Total control must be achieved for all time—forever. And there lies the rub, my dear. I want myself and the DOC ingrained in this world and its people unto their very soul. To do that our scientists have determined that unless certain challenges present themselves at certain nexus points in our history in the future—all this, all I have built here—will eventually collapse."

Arabella Rashid felt a brief surge of emotion, actual joy at the prospect, but she camouflaged it well. "So Mars is part of your plan, master?"

She knew he loved it when she called him master.

"Yes, these incorrigibles and troublemakers—men only—they will not be allowed any women to procreate and enlarge their vile numbers—will be set up as a future enemy. An enemy for DOC to destroy and be victorious over. These are to be my straw men, Arabella. Their existence and rebellion will ensure the DOC's supremacy forever. They will become the great bugaboos of our Earthly citizens, we'll brainwash all to accept our truths about the men on Mars. They will become the enemy of us all. Feared, hated, despised. And it will work. And because of that, I shall live forever as the master of it all."

Arabella Rashid stood stoic and silent but within her soul was anger and fear. This man—this monster...so twisted by hate and power.... It was not sane. It could not be done. Nevertheless, she knew the combination of his ultimate power, mighty intellect and relentless drive for conquest made him supremely dangerous. Anything could be possible.

"Are you familiar with the term—the antiquated term these days to be sure, Arabella—of God?" Simon asked softly.

"No, I...."

"Come now, I know you read, even some of the old forbidden hard copy texts. Those paperbound books from a hundred years ago. It would take all day for me to have your brain transcribed and then whipped clean of it all, but then you would loose so much of yourself, so don't try to play dumb with me, girl!"

"Yes, I am familiar with the term—I mean, the concept of—God."

Simon smiled divinely and it was horrible to see, "Well, Arabella, I can tell you with all certitude, that *I* am now God here, young lady. I am the new God of our Earth, a new God to reign forever. Our science has ensured that I shall live forever... as a God...."

Arabella Rashid was stunned and revolted by his arrogant words but she could ill afford to let him see even an inkling of her true feelings. She had played this game for years, had learned it when she'd been so much younger—at the feet of the master.

Instead she smiled sweetly and nodded pleasantly.

"How little you truly know or realize, my child," Simon added in paternal disdain, now leaning back in his huge chair, all-knowing, all-powerful, laughing all-insolently....

"What?"

"My dear, you have no idea. Our science, our technology, the DOC—we have learned so much from the past. It is all ours for the taking, for the using. Billions of memories, and the manipulation of those memories, facts, all that data—all of it to give us the outcome we want. It really is quite amazing. It is all now in the digital record, just electronic impulses, bytes and bits, nothing more, nothing less. Electronic impulses to be manipulated as we see fit, whether in a machine...or the human brain."

"Simon, what are you trying to tell me?"

"Hah! That's why I chose you, among other reasons—so sharp, so inquisitive, so perceptive! And you mean to tell me you really have no idea at all?"

"No idea about what, Simon?"

"Your dreams, child? Why, your very dreams?" he chided her softly.

Arabella Rashid tensed, a chill swept over her soul. It was a more private area than any mere physical place that Simon had already raped and plundered within her years before. Her dreams were sacred, personal, special, even mystical. They were the most secret part of her inner being. They were not for being known to anyone. Especially not by Simon.

"What are you saying?" She held down her panic.

"Come on, girl, don't tell me you do not even have an inkling. You must. You have the dreams, don't you?"

"Yes, I have dreams...," she agreed carefully, softly, fearful of what was coming. What new monstrous device was up Simon's wicked sleeve?

"Hah! But not just any old dreams, eh, my dear?"

"I don't know...."

"Did you never suppose...?" Simon asked softly.

"Suppose? Suppose, what?"

"Memory, it was all cloned. See, I know all about you, child, more than you even know about yourself. I searched for you, I found you. I created you."

"What do you mean, Simon?" she was becoming fearful now, but held herself in check, at the peril of her sanity.

"I bred you, girl. I know you took the name of Arabella Rashid after that night when I first took you, but before that you were...."

"No, don't say it!" she screamed.

Simon laughed. "Now then, what was your name...?"

"No! Simon, no!"

He laughed heartily, she'd not heard him so happy in years—the vile bastard! He was enjoying every moment of this torture.

"Yes, your name.... Do you remember that little girl? I remember her well."

Arabella Rashid froze with fear and loathing. She was not that other girl now, that weak girl who had been abused by Simon. She was someone else now. She was Arabella Rashid. Someone stronger, more powerful. Smarter. Different. Like in the book.

She hoped she was. She prayed.

"Yes, her name, dear girl—your name—it was Cathy... Ryan...."

She didn't say a word.

"Acknowledge it!" Simon demanded loudly, brow-beating his thirteen-year old girl lover/victim as she stood so powerlessly before him.

"Yes," she answered meekly.

"Well done! You have accepted one basic truth at least, Cathy—Arabella," Simon said it as if he were twisting a knife into the young girl's vitals. "Well, anyway, our DOC science has made magnificent achievements. Stunning achievements! Progress, that will be most useful...."

Arabella Rashid tightened up inside but could find no words. She was at Simon's mercy, she had always been at his mercy.

"You are a clone, child. A clone of that self-same Cathy Ryan who lived way back in the 1950s—far away in last century, You are one of many I have had reconstructed for my own aims. Personal and political. You see, we can not only clone the physical body, but we can delve deep into the inner psyche and soul. We can retrieve and duplicate memories and personality from our special long-ago original stock of people."

Arabella Rashid was stunned but at this point in her life she was ready to believe any evil that the minds of men like Simon could conceive.

"You and James were the first. Agents, spies, and killers that proved most useful. A matched set. In my opinion, you two were the best as well. Of course there were some others. All amazing early prototypes. Eventually, once the process is perfected for mass production, we'll be able to bring them back in large numbers—shock troops for the new order. We will create amalgams of the worst of the worst, the Huns, the Old Guard soldiers of Napoleon, KGB killers, the Gestapo and SS. Isn't that delightful? And of source, we will bring back their leaders as well—the most excellent killers of all time—Adolph Hitler, Joseph Stalin, Mao, Pol Pot, and even Saddam Hussein and those two lovely sons of his. Now those two boys surely died far too young—so much potential so sadly wasted there."

Arabella didn't say a word.

Simon nodded, smiled, "Good boys, so young. Terrible to be cut down before they had achieved their full potential. Well, that shall be changed. Corrected!"

Arabella scarcely knew what she was hearing. Was it the ramblings of a mad man? Or the promises of a monster with the will and ability to carry out those promises and make them come true?

"Of course, they shall all rule under me, in my future directorship of the DOC. They will not exist under their original names, but the DNA, their memories and personalities, will all be the same. Exact! My angels, playing the parts—I, as their God—shall decree for them."

Arabella Rashid knew now that Simon wasn't just an oppressive ruler, a rapist, and a monster—he was the Devil himself. His once massive mind had deteriorated into madness and an evil deeper than any other human being in the history of the race. He had to be destroyed. Now. This instant. Before he took one more squalid breath of pure sweet air. Simon had to die and Arabella Rashid was the only one who could make it happen.

"It will be glorious," Simon mused.

"Yes, Simon, it will," she said, moving closer to him.

"And you shall rule by my side," he said, with a twisted smile that she knew was false, even mean in its false promise.

But now Arabella Rashid smiled back, as she bent down to kiss Simon's cheek. She did it with a great gentleness, a warm softness, a delightfulness that she knew Simon felt irresistible. She smiled again at the thought of what she had to do.

Then she did it.

CHAPTER TWO
THE DEPARTMENT OF CONTROL

Simon was dead.

The world was free!

But Arabella Rashid found herself more enslaved now than ever.

For the Department of Control, and the world totalitarian government headed by the hated Authority and all its minions personally picked by Simon, still went on and on and on. To not accept that reality would mean death and worse. So she must continue with the fabrication. She must continue to play the game. And the crushing, binding, and enslaving of minds and bodies—as no government, no cult, no organization in human history had ever done before—must continue seamlessly. With Simon never seen, but with his presence always felt, and when necessary, even heard from. With Arabella speaking for him, and giving the orders in his name or through virtual image holos. And in so doing she attained complete control over society and the world via The DOC. And at the head of it all now—was Arabella Rashid.

* * * * * * *

How had it all come to this?

Arabella Rashid sat quietly with only the corpse of Simon for company beside her. He looked so quiet and peaceful in death, a little aged man, perhaps someone's funny old grandfather if you didn't know any better. You could never imagine all the damage he had done to the human race.

Now what was she to do?

She shed not a single tear for her former mentor, nor one tear for her present position. Instead, she decided to use that superior mind that Simon had created for her to examine the situation and find a way to put into operation a plan that would free the world and some day bring back human dignity.

She wanted to set in motion some kind of revolution—but she knew the world was not ready, nor able to understand that concept yet. The fear was too ingrained. It ran far too deep.

So first things first. The germ had to be planted, and nurtured, ideas had to be kept alive and spread. She had to be careful and plan for the long haul. She was good at planning. She took a long overview of the present situation. It was grim. Earth was out as a source. It was too tightly controlled and monitored. The people had been too deeply neutered. But Mars was another story. It might be the perfect place. It was a world full of incorrigible, pain-in-the-ass troublesome men, all non-conforming individuals.

Mars might just do the trick!

She realized it was necessary for her to now assume leadership of the Department of Control. As much as she hated the very thought of it, she must assume control of this monster Simon had created. She must keep the DOC and Authority in place, maintaining order, even as she planned to crash it all down into the dust heap of history on one fine glorious future day.

First she'd have to get rid of Simon's body. The evidence of her crime, if discovered, would surely doom her and all her plans if discovered. Then she had to construct a story to explain her assuming control of the DOC. She realized that here, in this type of organization, a rumor might work best. A rumor from Simon's own office, presumed to be from Simon himself. It would be an order for her to assume daily control of the DOC. The only person who reported directly to *Him*. It would require her to monitor all departments, oversee all personnel, give orders and decrees in Simon's name to the leadership and all the staff. Holograms of Dear Old Simon would help. Thus she would become the impenetrable layer between Simon and the DOC. And all would obey, or else. Then, for all intents and purposes, as far as anyone at the DOC knew, the new realignment would be in place. She never used the word coup, but such intent might be implied. It would never be whispered openly. DOC secrets remained secret.

Simon was *out*.

Arabella Rashid was *in*.

And that was that! The new order of things continued seamlessly.

The King was dead, long live the Queen.

Everyone throughout the vast bureaucracy of the DOC, the worldwide governmental Authority and the various security districts they controlled, would accept the fact. The new reality was indisputable—or disputable at your peril. Questions, she knew, that would never be asked.

But first to dispose of Simon's body. That bit of physical evidence, the evidence of murder, had to disappear. Forever. It had to be done correctly and quietly. And she realized that here, she needed help.

The only person she could think of to call for such a duty was another of the clones, the one by the name of James Ryan. She thought it strange that she remembered his name and image so clearly now from an earlier life. She began to wonder just what Simon and the DOC had done to her memories. Had Simon, in fact programmed her? Had he told her the truth? Was she even now, somehow, following his orders? Orders that were not her own? The thought chilled her and she immediately dismissed it—but doubt still nagged at a dark place in the back of her thoughts for she knew Simon and his evil ways only too well. So questions only posed more questions.

Arabella Rashid placed the appropriate request for Ryan in the usual manner, as if Simon himself was still the Director. It was an order no one would ignore, an order that must be obeyed immediately upon pain of terrible consequences.

* * * * * * *

James Ryan heard the call and obeyed. He quickly put the old paperback book he had been reading back in his pocket and stood attentive and waited. Soon two DOC officers approached him and he was told to immediately take the private elevator up to the Director's personal level.

The mansion-like edifice atop the World Tower was a maze of a hundred luxuriously appointed suites of various size and function. Ryan was lead along cold chrome hallways by armed replicant DOC house staff, bodyguards in essence, former DOC shock troops who had proven their value and loyalty. He was brought before two huge engraved wooden doors—they looked as if they had been taken from some ancient cathedral in old Europe—and then he was told to wait once more.

Ryan sweated, fearful, as he tucked the old paperback—a forbidden and subversive media—down his pants and hoped it would not be discovered. He wasn't obsessively concerned about it now—for being called to the Director's office was much more serious and potentially deadly than anything that could result from being discovered with some old book. Be it forbidden or not. He tried to calm himself as he waited, but the fear was roaming inside him wild and bright and it threatened to push him into full panic mode. However, Ryan held himself firm and kept his nerve. He waited and he prayed, not knowing what would befall him in the Director's office on the other side of that ancient engraved doorway.

When the wooden doors automatically opened, Ryan was ordered to enter the room. He took a few hesitant steps forward and went inside. The guards did not follow him. That in itself seemed odd, and made him curious. Then the doors suddenly slammed shut behind him with a resounding boom, and James Ryan thought it was just like the sound of doom.

"You can come, James Ryan. I will not bite you," a young

woman's voice—she actually sounded like a girl or teenager—said with forced friendliness from above him through a hidden speaker. She did sound young, maybe just a girl at that. Strange. Ryan didn't know what to think or what to expect. He would have been surprised at how young Arabella Rashid really was, had he been able to see her. Young in appearance and years certainly, but not in experience and intent. In fact, he had no idea how formidable and dangerous this wisp of a girl could be when it became necessary.

Ryan moved forward as instructed, one more tentative step deeper into the Director's sanctum, his eyes slowly adjusting to the light. He couldn't see a woman, or girl anywhere, to connect to the voice he'd heard, but he did see an old, white-haired man slumped over a long circular console of screens and monitors. These flickered with the light of various images as scenes shifted; showing what appeared to be selected surveillance locations in the building, the city and around the planet. It was amazing, here was the control center...for everything.

"James Ryan?"

"Yes," Ryan replied nervously.

"I have work for you," the voice said in a tone that brooked nothing but obedience. Ryan was sure now that it was indeed the voice of a young girl, a teenager most likely—certainly not a woman. Most strange, he thought, but he was wise to keep his curiosity to himself and his mouth shut.

His only reply was, "Yes."

"I am the Director of the Department of Control," her voice proclaimed with a matter-of-factness he immediately accepted. "Simon is no more. There lies what it is left of his mortal remains. You will dispose of the body as per my instructions."

James Ryan didn't know what to say or even think. This was incredible and explosive. He took a quick look at the body of the old man slumped at the desk. So quiet, so peaceful, so dead.... Ryan nodded, looked down and said, "Sure."

He waited, there was no response from the girl's voice.

Then he looked over at the corpse of the old white-haired

man once again. So that was Simon. The monster himself, or so rumor went. He, like all who were part of the organization, feared the legendary Director of the DOC. Ryan took a deep breath and released it slowly, hoping to calm down. Hardly anyone inside the organization ever saw the man in the flesh, and certainly no one outside the DOC had ever heard his name.

Ryan smiled, so this had been the feared Director he had heard so many rumors about. The man legend said was the most evil man in the world, and the most dangerous. He didn't look so deadly now....

But if he was dead? Then this girl...?

"I am the Director now," the mysterious girl's voice said from the secrecy of some overhead speaker, and Ryan's attention was brought back to reality and his particularly uncomfortable and dangerous place in it. For he realized now that as bad as the rumors about Simon had been, it now appeared that he had somehow been overthrown or murdered by this woman—this girl. If such was the case, then how much more dangerous and deadly must she be than the man she had replaced?

Much more ruthless. Much worse.

Ryan steeled his nerves. He feared what he must do and what his future would hold for him after he did it. A brain wipe for sure. Perhaps even a deep unmarked grave in a far away place where he would be dumped in and forgotten forever? The thought didn't comfort him. Nevertheless, there was nothing he could do about any of this, other than obey. He was owned by the DOC and the DOC had given him an order. You did not ask questions. You just did as you were told. And, if you so desired, very quietly so no one noticed...you prayed.

"I will tell you later precisely how to dispose of the body and you will carry out my orders exactly as I give them to you," the girl's voice said with a force of steel he could scarcely believe possible from one so young.

"Yes," Ryan said. There was really nothing else he could do or say, and still continue to exist on this side of heaven or hell.

Then he did as she told him.

* * * * * * *

Later, after it was all done, Arabella Rashid sat back in Simon's chair and allowed herself to appreciate the utter exhilaration of unlimited power as it washed over her. Simon was gone, she was free. It was delicious. Almost infectious. Her eyes locked on the surveillance images playing out on the screens in front of her.

She smiled, looked down at the man on the table being worked on by the DOC scientists, as per her orders and said softly, "Well, Ryan, when you wake up tomorrow you will not remember anything about Simon, or me, or what you did with his body. Instead, you will have an entire new set of memories and desires...some of them you would never have thought possible in your wildest dreams...."

She picked up the old book now. From her own forays into forbidden texts she knew that it was what was called by people from the old days as a "paperback." That was evidently because of the soft cover wrapped around the pulp paper hardcopy pages. It had been on the console beside her and now she thumbed through its pages at random. It was old, from LastCen, last century in the 1990s. A long time ago. Before the DOC, before the Authority, even before Simon—but just barely. It was something that proclaimed itself "a future science fiction classic"—whatever that might be.

It had the title *Mars Needs Books* and seemed to be about the future—but not the future as it was now, as it really was here today, but one extrapolated from the past through rational conjecture. It seemed to be some alternate reality story, some primitive wish-fulfillment fantasy about a world that *might* be. Or, perhaps one that *should* be? But that was not *this* world at all.

Arabella Rashid looked at the garish cover and smiled. There was a stalwart hero with ray gun and some sexy space-suited vixen with large breasts.... How trite? Funny, really. So quaint and how totally irrelevant. She threw the old paperback down on the console and looked back at the still form of James Ryan as the marvelous DOC mind machines pumped him full of desires, memories, and duty that had never been his own. Yet soon, they would be as much a part of Ryan as was his very soul. If he had one.

"You're taking a trip, Ryan. You're going to Mars. And you're going there to accumulate and collect old mystery and crime paperbacks. Preferably hard-boiled private-eye novels. Yes, that's correct. And I'm going to send you shiploads of them, and many men—all settlers—will be transported out there and they will read and treasure them too! Troublemakers, malcontents, and fools, all with their brains fixed—just like you. Every one of them will be a fanatic just like you—obsessed with collecting paperbacks, buying, selling, trading, and above all *reading* the damn things! You won't be able to help yourselves; it will be ingrained inside each of your minds. Then you will be mine. My modern equivalent of the Irish monks of our Dark Age, keeping the knowledge from books alive—the stories and the humanity they possess. But not scientific and technical data. That information is changeless and available unfettered in the digital record—for how would our society survive without it? No, what I am talking about here is fiction. The stories and novels that sing their songs to the human heart. The art of the storyteller to bridge that indefinable gap between life and truth and dreams—and yes, even nightmare. The haunting dreams and nightmares of men—and women—that is what is at stake here. These shall not be lost. And though the DOC has caused Truth to perish from this Earth—it shall not perish from our history. One day it shall return. Unfettered. These old mystery and crime paperbacks hold truth in their stories with individualistic heroes, and their many shades of good and bad. You shall protect and preserve them."

She watched Ryan closely. He did not move. He was in a stasis field. He had no idea what was being done to him.

"You'll all be fanatics. It just wouldn't work any other way. You will be terrified, full of fear and hate. You will be programmed with a fear, an unreasoning paranoia about using any media other than hard copy paperbacks. You'll be terrified of mind control from vids, any form of implants, all mass media in any form at all. You will never trust it—you can *never* trust it. Instead, you will be *readers*. You will read the old and trusted hard copy paperback books of LastCen. These hard copy editions, printed and bound in their own day are the only words you can trust. I will have it engrained and programmed within you all. This is the only mode of information storage device which has not been changed since it was published decades ago. Ryan, you and your fellow 'Marsmen', will only trust hard copy text because it can not be altered without discovery. You will hate the Authority. Some day, you and your band of misfits and malcontents will lead the revolution off-planet, on Mars, and then finally, on Earth."

CHAPTER THREE
THE WHEELS ARE SET IN MOTION

It took twenty years for her plan to come to fruition. She had been careful—she has had to be so very careful. She used Simon's DOC science. However, instead of bringing back the monsters of the past as Simon had planned—freaks like Hitler, Stalin, Usama Bin Laden, and their insane evil ilk—she had cloned the personalities and minds of truly great people—men like Gandhi, Martin Luther King, Albert Schweitzer, and Albert Einstein—women like Ayn Rand, Margaret Thatcher, Corazon Aquino, and Golda Meir.

Then just for pragmatism purposes and security concerns she rounded things out by including the psyches of great warriors like George S. Patton, George Washington, Robert E. Lee. Moshe Dayan, and Arthur Wellesley, the Duke of Wellington. When all these outstanding minds and personalities were combined, the amalgam was placed into a human replicant and named Moses Sage.

Then Moses Sage was set to lead the revolution for human freedom and dignity on the Earth.

Some day.

Arabella Rashid called it the Janus Project. It was named after the ancient Roman god who had two faces. The two-face. She smiled at the idea. She liked the duel purpose of it all. When she explained the Janus Project to the DOC scientists and DOC Board, she did so as if it were merely the continuation of Simon's genius plan. That plan had been to milk the DNA of the worst past masters of murder and mayhem in order to create a group of future DOC soldiers and leaders unlike anything the human race had ever seen. All working for Simon, and the DOC, of course.

"Simon's grand intent," Arabella Rashid told the members of the DOC Board through secure link holochannels, "his Janus Project, was to offer through the bodies of a new generation of clones, the DNA and actual minds of some of the most ruthless men in history. These would serve the DOC and become the new shock troops of the empire. The new leaders for a new era of the world and then outer planetary domination. These were Earth's most ruthlessly talented, and now from every past era of human history, they will be brought together again to work for us."

The applause from the Board members was staggering, the smiles and nods from the scientists was all the approval Arabella Rashid needed to secure her position as the new Director of DOC.

"We see that now the proper choice has been made for Director," Emilio Chávez said over a secure link from his region of planetary control in the North-South American Security Sector.

"You will prove a worthy successor to Simon. This Janus Project is sheer genius," Mildred Millian added, offering the younger woman a fist salute, a term of respect lately popular in the Southern European Security District, her area of planetary dominion.

"The Janus Project," Arabella Rashid continued, "will transform seemingly innocuous young men to grow up and become educated as per our direction. Their minds and thoughts bent with purposeful design to your every want and desire."

There was immediate and resounding applause from the Board members. They liked what they were hearing.

Arabella Rashid smiled glowingly at them all. Yet inwardly, she shuddered and prayed that none of them would ever suspect the deadly dangerous game she was playing.

For it was well known by those in the know, the Janus Project would create a group of the worst monsters culled from human history. Artificially bred and created, with memory and obedience implants. These clones of the most dangerous people who ever existed, were set to change human history forever. They were just what the DOC wanted, just what the hated Authority needed to further tighten its grip on everything human. An army of truly murderous monsters without one scintilla of humanity to stay their hands.

Arabella Rashid clicked off her view screen and sat back comfortably in Simon's old chair. Her feet were perched upon the console in front of her as she picked up the old science fiction paperback she had taken away from James Ryan days before. She sighed, thinking of him again. He would be on his way to Mars soon, with a cargo of a few hundred men who would become new settlers. They would be miners, many would work themselves to death in the mines. On the ship with them were crates of old paperback books. She smiled. What a cargo! Human reprobates and crime paperbacks. They did seem to go together. Ryan would never be able to figure it out. He would never even imagine such a plan, and whether he suspected he'd been tampered with or not, he'd perform as he'd been programmed. They would all perform as they had been programmed and that was all that mattered.

The girl who now called herself Arabella Rashid looked at the garish cover art on Ryan's paperback copy of *Mars Needs Books*. The spaceship and supermen motif was colorful and quaint. The sexy girl in very abbreviated outfit, was crass and exploitative, and the old paperback book she held was so....

She just laughed now, remembering one of the characters had been named Arabella Rashid. She'd taken her name from that powerful young woman in the book. She'd seen a copy of the book long ago, years ago, maybe this was even the very same copy she'd seen back then? She looked at the old paperback carefully. The entire package was antique. Certainly obsolete as an information medium. For a second she thought she should do a search/scan for info on the author. The book was credited as written by someone named Philip K. Dickson. Perhaps a pseudonym or a play on words? She decided it did not matter. The author did not matter. Not now. What did catch her attention was the sentence printed in bold print at the top edge of the cover. These phrases she knew now had been called by the unlikely name of "blurbs," back when actual hard copy books had still been published. Arabella Rashid was drawn to one sentence on the cover. It said, *"The story of Moses Sage—the Superman who brought the promise of revolution and freedom to Earth and the spaceways...."*

"Moses Sage?"

Arabella thought of the Janus Project. Now it seemed there might be even more to Janus than the DOC Board and even she knew about. Arabella Rashid's secret part of the Janus Project—its other face—had been more two-faced than the ancient Roman god's namesake could ever be imagined. Instead of the clones being implanted with the DNA from the minds of monsters—she had managed for one replicant to be implanted with all the forbidden data of the saints and heroes. That one single replicant was now to be called Moses Sage. His mind would contain the DNA combinations from the minds of the best men and women in human history. Including some of the greatest military leaders and strategists of all time to ensure the success of the revolution.

Meanwhile, next to him in the vats, dozens of monster clones would continue to grow and evolve, but they had already secretly been infected with a timed self-destruct virus. Those Janus clones would all mysteriously die upon the attainment of their twentieth birthday. All but one. All except Moses Sage. But he will be gone and in hiding long before his sibling clones began their death dances.

"You will grow into manhood unfettered by the world to learn and develop into a great leader. Then, decades from now, when all is ready, you will take the name Moses Sage and lead the underground and its revolution against the Authority and the DOC," she said, gently putting down Ryan's old paperback.

Arabella Rashid knew she had planned well but it was a complicated plan. It was a long plan of many years duration and anything could go wrong at any time. She had just passed her thirteenth birthday. She would be a woman well in her thirties once Moses Sage presented himself to the citizens of the world and began his revolution to free Earth of the DOC. Meanwhile, Ryan and his group of malcontent mining settlers would be gone from Earth and safe on Mars. Where for the time being, they would be reading paperbacks and dreaming of revolution.

She smiled, the wheels were set in motion.

Arabella Rashid picked up the old paperback from the console again, flipped the paper pages. *"Mars Needs Books*, indeed!" she said with a shake of her pretty head. "We'll see where this all leads us, one day, James Ryan."

Then Arabella Rashid placed the book in a plain manila envelope, writing upon the outside of the envelope, "For James Ryan, Eyes Only!" and placed in gingerly in her outgoing mail slot for immediate delivery.

CHAPTER FOUR
THE YEARS DO PASS US BY

For a thirteen-year-old genius girl-child, Arabella Rashid knew that the game she was playing was devious and deadly. But it was also fun. It was her way to change the world that Simon had built all around her since she had been a mere innocent. She hated that world, and she hated Simon. His death had been a true pleasure for her. It meant he would never hurt her or anyone else ever again. Death gave a certain insurance, a reassuring certitude for the living that such evil monsters would never get at another victim.

But she still had the nightmares.

Those never went away. Even when she had become a woman and understood it all. The little girl child deep inside her, was still terrified. That little girl, was always scared. But she was brave and strong and overcame all that life and Simon had thrown at her.

The years passed, and Arabella Rashid grew into womanhood. She became a stunning young lady, but remained aloof and always guarded. She was guarded in her self and thoughts, and of course, literally, being guarded by the top security shock troops the DOC had to offer. And through it all, she never forgot Simon's ill use of her. She never forgot all she had learned from him as well. She hated Simon and damned him to hell every day for what he had done to her and all the others. Yet even as she tried to fight against everything he represented she was fearful that she was becoming more and more like him every day.

Relentlessly the years passed by. The old Earth flew around the old Sun, and Arabella Rashid thought sometimes of the man called James Ryan. Images of his rugged good looks flashed in her mind. She was saddened at what she had caused to be done to him. First had been the brain wipe, then the implanted memories and instructions. She wondered just what kind of a new man he had become. James Ryan had been a DOC special agent, as cold-blooded and ruthlessly efficient as any the Department of Control and Simon had created in their early clone program. Much like that little girl, who had become Arabella Rashid.

There had been war at the DOC in the days before she had killed Simon. All of Simon's various early creations having grown up, educated by Simon and the DOC, becoming nice little monsters. So ambitious. So ruthless. They had fought each other behind the scenes in a long clandestine war, teens and pre-teens in a dirty high-tech *Lord of the Flies* battle for survival—and Simon's favor—which was after all, the very same thing back then.

Those had been hard days. Arabella Rashid remembered them now with a shudder. These more modern days were different, colder still, after all hope for her was long gone. However the DOC was still unaware of her actions. Though the Authority ruled all, she now realized it was...vulnerable.

Even then she still kept James Ryan in her thoughts. She allowed herself a small smile of joy as her mind imagined his strong face and handsome form. Ryan was older than her by ten years. It was nothing like the age difference with Simon. Her thoughts of Simon caused her great anger but her thoughts of James caused her to smile—almost like a little girl again. He was magic for her soul. She realized now that she had a crush on the man. She'd been only thirteen when she'd first met him but he had not left her thoughts and her dreams since then. She often wondered about him. How was he getting on?

The last contact she'd had with Ryan was when she'd seen to it that an old paperback book had been delivered to him. She wondered what he thought of it. She wondered what his new programming would make of him now. His old personality was gone. Now he was a new person with new memories and programming. A totally different person from the man she had sent for to do some sensitive body disposal work years ago. Nevertheless, he was still a DOC agent even if his memories had been all erased and replaced with new ones. As a DOC agent he must have been brain wiped on many occasions. Now his mind was full of made-up memories and new personality traits. Now he collected and read old hard-boiled crime paperbacks. Obsessively. It was quite ridiculous on the face of it, and Arabella Rashid laughed almost cruelly, but it was an important part of her plan. Meanwhile, poor Ryan's memories of her and DOC, and the death and disappearance of Simon, were all gone now. Erased forever.

Arabella Rashid smiled. Ryan was an agent of the DOC, like she had been. Still was, in fact. He was not as high up in the hierarchy as she was certainly, but she realized, everyone these days was an agent of DOC in some way. She wondered where Ryan was now. What was he doing?

She wondered where he had come from, what he had done in his long career for the DOC? It must have been many terrible things. Now Ryan's new implanted programs were all in, and according to her plan they would kick in on the long trip out to Mars. But Ryan wouldn't be going to Mars for a year yet. In the meantime, she'd had him placed in the general DOC special agent assignment pool. He would be given jobs like any other DOC agent. And he'd perform them like a DOC agent was supposed to perform them. With ruthless efficiency. Doing just as he was told.

Arabella Rashid's mind kept coming back to that old science fiction paperback. It was with Ryan now, or it would be with him soon. She had given express orders he was to have it on his next assignment and that it was to follow him and be his personal property until he was placed on the ship to Mars. Then it would be taken away from him and on the long trip out to the Red Planet, his new programming would kick in—and he'd become a reader and collector of mystery and crime paperbacks.

She smiled, wondering what Ryan would make of it all, had he but known. But of course, he wouldn't know. He wouldn't know anything. No matter that his brain had been wiped and re-implanted, Ryan was still an intelligent man. He'd surmise something was up once he saw that book. He wouldn't remember it, of course, nor anything else concerning Arabella Rashid or Simon, but he'd be very curious. The old science fiction paperback would spark his consciousness, he would know that it meant...something.

But what?

She wanted to give him that hint, just to keep him thinking.

The new Director of the Department of Control read the secret files about the progress of the cloned children of the Janus Project. It told about each clone and who it was based upon—Adolf Hitler, Idi Amin, Jeffery Dalmer, John Wayne Gacy—the list was endless and ever more horrendous. She read the "Biographies" and "Accomplishments" sections of the host subjects and was truly appalled by one after the other, as atrocity piled upon atrocity.

She signed sadly, "These people aren't even human beings. They really are something else, something non-human. Simply monsters, each and every one of them, and they shall never see the light of day."

When she came to the next to last subject, a large "X" had been overprinted. Here it was noted that the host DNA was supposed to have come from Simon himself. Arabella Rashid smiled, and whispered, "Not this time, Simon. You may have saved enough of your DNA for this project in advance of your timely demise, but your clone will never live long enough to use it. You know what that big red "X" means?"

Simon could not answer her, so she told him.

"It means, the fetus was born dead. You see, Simon, I had one of your more amenable DOC scientists insert a deadly virus into the mixture. The fetus developed, but as it developed it was also dying and it was finally born dead. As you should have been."

Arabella Rashid turned up the screen, clicked on the next file. The name didn't matter, the contributor of the DNA was listed as Napoleon Bonaparte. She smiled at that, Napoleon tempered with Mahatma Gandhi, Albert Einstein, Martin Luther King and Albert Schweitzer added to the mix would be beneficial, among with many others.

She said, "Many years from now this one will drop his given name and take up the name Moses Sage. Then he will begin his real work. His work for the freedom and dignity of the human race—which will need him more than he can ever know."

Arabella Rashid then smiled as her thoughts turned to the man she had sent out to Mars. "Right, Ryan? You know it too. Someday, Ryan, we shall meet again and maybe the world will be a better place for us."

CHAPTER FIVE
MEMORY CAN PLAY YOU

Ryan was lying naked on the cold floor of a small cell-like room. Alone. Dark. Thinking.

He didn't know when it all began. He didn't know when it would end. Or how it would end. In fact, he didn't know much of anything at that point.

Here's what he did know.

Something deep inside him told him all about it. There seemed to be some little voice inside his mind. It told him about how there's always been this struggle in the world. It is between people, sometimes individuals. More often it is between groups, governments, political theories and ideologies, even sometimes crackpot ideas expounded by morons and maniacs. Seemingly with all of them at each other's throats. In the end it is the individual who always turns up the loser. The little guy and gal cut down another inch. Made an inch shorter each day. They are pounded down into the ground, some of them sunk in so low they have no place else to go. Some of them down so low their eyes have to look up just to see level ground. Sometimes they think they're looking up. In reality they're just standing down deep in a ditch they know they're never getting out of. Kind of like a grave.

His thoughts told him that these days the individual is the biggest loser of them all. While any individual skilled enough to become self- sufficient has become the scariest person of all to the system. To the hated Authority who run everything and thus to the rumored DOC—The Department of Control. The DOC, that controls everyone and everything, though few even know of its existence. But those that truly understand the word fear, are terrified to hear that name even whispered.

Even now Ryan wonders if it all really exists. The DOC? Some say it's worldwide. Others say that it originally began as a way to monitor the Internet or fight international Islamic terrorism after the attack on the old United States of America on September 11, 2001. Regardless, in no time it seemed the DOC was soon not only monitoring but controlling, and not only the Internet. It was soon influencing, then controlling our government, then foreign governments, and not soon after, damn near everything.

Their hand was felt heaviest when they began rewriting history. They altered all texts and laws, changing everything online until no one knew anymore what the original facts had been. Most citizens didn't care though, as long as they were given programs and government giveaways. A lot of it was mind-numbing, glitzy entertainment, bread-and-circus thrills. They were offered and accepted a vast wasteland of mindless entertainment: originally beginning on what had been called "television" far back in the early days, then on the Net, later with live inputs plugged directly into the brainpan. They infected the minds of millions of these "wireheads" with powerful subconscious suggestions and propaganda protocols that controlled their actions and thoughts. It was all crap to deaden the mind, making them pliant and obedient. Head slots for disks became conduits for instant downloading of mindless music, sex and violence, so-called "entertainments," that went directly into the brain. The young especially loved it and were especially vulnerable. They were encouraged in school and at public events to form "group link-ups" when each had a direct brain-link input slot in their neck. Then they could all be on the same program. Literally. Of course everything was heavily dosed with Gov-prop lies, sly distortions, and ably focused suggestions that you had no choice but to obey. Orders to conform. Directives to do as you were told. And warnings about how dangerous and wrong it was to *ever* question authority—especially The Authority.

It wasn't long before most people didn't even know how to think rationally at all.

And history? Facts? There were so many versions. Which version did you want? No one remembered now just which version was actually *true*. Few even cared what events were authentic or *real?*

What was reality after all?

Facts, truth and rational thinking had become the greatest casualties of the high-tech future. No one was even sure if the leaders were actual people anymore, and not just made-up holograms of idealized persons in virtual format. Who were they really? No one actually ever met any of them. What did it mean, when what they said or stood for changed by the hour. There was no way to check anymore with actual written records, hard copies. Most had been destroyed. There was no way to go back now, no way to discover what laws were actually written and on the books. There were no books. The books were gone long ago. Laws changed daily, even hourly now. The digital history was revised by a stroke on a keyboard. No one knew about this, and worse, no one seemed to care.

That's just the way the future was.

But how had it come to this?

Ryan heard a while back some rumor that The DOC had gone interplanetary. That it had agents, maybe even offices and reps on the mining colonies of Mars, Luna, and all the other planetary colonies and stations. He figured, why not? They wanted to control everything, and it seemed they sure as hell did.

Rumors abound about everything of course. Facts and truth don't exist. Most of the bad rumors, the worst of them all, concerned The DOC. Most of them were started by The DOC too. But of course, everyone knew The DOC didn't really exist. Surely it couldn't exist. Or so everyone said. You see, no one is supposed to know it exists. And in truth, almost no one does.

Except Ryan.

He knew.

At least, he thought he knew.

Unless it's all a bunch of crap he got out of that old science fiction paperback he'd been reading lately.

Or out of his dreams.

Or nightmares.

He was not so sure anymore.

They play with your mind here.

Truth means nothing to these people. The truth is, he was not sure of much of anything these days....

He tried to think back on things sometimes, but it was hard when he realized he couldn't even trust his own memories or senses.

Memories.

What do they really mean? What are they? Really.

Memories are cold, frozen, and it hurts real bad to think about the past, but if he tries real hard, and if he can stand the terrible pain, sometimes he can free up a few bytes from the granite block that's inside his head.

Sometimes he thinks his mind has been tampered with, his thoughts processed for him. Programmed. Altered. Sometimes he thinks he's crazy. Sometimes he's sure of it. Other times, he's just not so sure.

What if he is right? About being crazy.

Well, that might be true, but deep down inside he didn't really believe that.

Well, what about being programmed or altered?

That would be the scariest thing of all!

Sometimes he'd laugh, thinking he was the only sane one! Then he really had to laugh. Sometimes he'd even cry about it. Of course it's not true, it can't be true. He couldn't be crazy but it's been known to happen. It was hard to explain.

The world today is a very screwed up place, and if you happen to be very screwed up yourself, then you actually might fit into it very well. Maybe he was a "normal," at least according to the parameters of his world. And conversely, living in this sewer of a world, maybe he was just plain crazy.

Or at least he would end up that way before his time here ran out.

One thing he did know is that whoever really runs the show here, has control of it all. There's all kinds of subliminal, and not so subliminal, messages in vids, neural implants. Most people pop them into their head slots like eating candy. All the software and info has been manipulated and loaded with brain-wash mind-controlling, behavior-modifying codes, and political propaganda. That had been going on for decades on Earth. No one with half a brain—or who has half a brain left these days—can trust any neural software, vids, or implants. No one who wants to keep their own mind free can ever trust any of this modern media. It has all been compromised.

However, there were some die-hards who stay away from all modern media. They say it is poison for the mind. Some say it is poison for the soul as well.

These few hard-core "individuals" only read books. Actual books in hard copy. Old books are best. They're deemed safest. Those cannot be easily infected; meaning manipulated or tampered with. While they certainly can be compromised, it is not cost effective. So hard copy books remain relatively safe and the older they are, the safer they are. Preferably books from LastCen. Last Century. These are almost always paperbacks. These are best. Paperbacks have no screen, no neural implant, no virtual reality disk, no memory chips. There is no interference or interface at all. Nothing but the actual book as written by the author and printed on paper. There is only the paper and ink, and the reader's eyes and mind.

Paperbacks from LastCen were common once, relatively inexpensive, and still held truth and honesty in hard copy. The old ones are best, before POD—print on demand—began. From that moment on text could be changed, amended, altered, corrected, or revised even in hard copy, just like what has been going on for decades with electronic media that make up our digital memory today. So the oldest paperbacks were always the safest; those from the pre-POD days of the 1980s—and the best and safest of all were dated from the faraway days of the 1940s to the 1970s.

In the beginning, the Authority told everyone they did all changes, updates, corrections—for the good of the people. It was done to better society. It was done for only the most noble and virtuous reasons. In the beginning, it appeared they were correct. That was what was so chilling about the changes. People accepted them so easily. That's how it began.

Whenever government tells you that what they are doing is "for our own good"—you'd best run for the damn hills!

Ryan knew the best stuff was published in paperback over a hundred years ago. It had been written back in pre-computer days, during the 1950s and still written and published up until the year 2020. That is when the last actual physical books were published as mass-market hard copy paperbacks. Hard cover books had long before ceased to exist except in the most rarified academic circles and never for fiction. Those LastCen old days sure had been a time when people remembered freedom, and how to live free. It had been a time of wonderful ideas, expressed in delightfully odd little books with amazing and idiosyncratic subjects and content, all lovingly created with effective cover art and design that made each and every one of them special.

Ryan suddenly screamed in agony.

There it went again, that pain in his head.

The pain was powerful. It always came back when he tried to think. Maybe the pain in his head was from trying to access his old memories? He knew they probably had put a psychblock implant to stop him from thinking certain thoughts, accessing certain memories, trying to figure out certain truths. It was a way to block things they didn't want him to know or remember. They could usually stop you from remembering. His own true memories could be twisted or transformed into things he had never known existed. Truths he thought he knew down deep inside him were now things his mind could be forbidden to access.

They can do that. They can do anything to you they want. Of course he couldn't remember much of it now. Maybe that's why he was here.

Wherever *here* might be.

But every once in a while Ryan was able to free a strand or so from the cobweb that made up his mind. And then, he had a memory. Then he could remember and even think about those memories. He savored every one of them. It's wonderful to have a memory. But he always wondered if it was truly his, or not. Was it his or had it been planted into his mind? He wondered if it was something he was actually remembering on his own, something of his that had come back to him after so many years? Or was it something they'd programmed into him? Something they wanted him to remember? Something that was not a part of him at all. Something they wanted him to *think* was a part of him?

Ryan thought about that now.

He thought about the old days.

He thought about the man....

He'd been called, "The Man Who Can."

Ryan thought that they had called *him* that name once.

Someone did.

Somewhere.

A long time ago.

In another world.

In another reality.

He didn't know if it was his reality or not.

But the memories came back now.

They flooded into his mind.

The Man Who Can!

The Man Who Can.... *What?*

Ryan was afraid to think about *what.*

Afraid of what *what* might mean.

He closed his eyes and dreamed.

He wished he was on Mars.

He wished he was feeling better, just sitting down and able to relax, maybe read that old paperback.

But that was not to be.

The old memories came back now.

The Man Who Can.

Ryan could see the man standing there. Tall, strong, handsome and much younger. Tough and sure of himself. And it was someone he thought he knew.

He thought it was....

CHAPTER SIX
THE MAN WHO CAN

...him!

They told him two things. Don't talk. Don't think.

They enforced it with revocations of privileges, beatings, solitary. He liked solitary. Actually, for someone with his unique personality, it wasn't half bad. Later on they put him in genpop, general population, and tried the gang rape thing. Four cons. They didn't get very far, but it was the principle of the thing. He wasn't fair game. For no one! Everyone should be made aware of that. They were. He wasn't worth their trouble either. It didn't bother him. He had time. He waited. Afterwards he got two of them. Slit their throats. Cracked the third guy's head. Made the fourth guy fly. Right off the 3rd Floor tier. That guy hit the ground landing face-down—splat on the concrete. None of them four would ever bother him again. No one else did either.

When the new kid came in Ryan told him to watch his ass. He didn't mean it figuratively. The new kid was young, inexperienced, chicken-shit pure. At least for this hellhole. Sure, he was big and bad out on the street, but in here he was just so much fresh meat. Porterhouse steak. He told the kid to watch his back. Anyone mess with him, he told the kid to do all he could to hurt the guy back as much as possible.

"What do you want me to do? Kill him?"

"Kill him?" Ryan said shocked. He couldn't believe the kid. "Damn right! Kill him three times if you gotta! People will be watchin'. Think you're one crazymother. They'll stay away from you. That's fine. That's what you want. You stay away from them too. Don't talk. Don't let no one get a chance to know you. Find out you're human. Never, ever smile. Unless, of course if you're beating out someone's brains. Then feel free to smile all you want. You can even laugh if you like."

The kid nodded, understanding for the first time now.

Ryan added, "And never, ever, let anyone do you a favor or give you anything. Do not ever accept a gift. Of any kind. Don't ever take it or you'll regret it later!"

Now, no one messes with Ryan. Or the kid. They read books. Paperbacks. All kinds of science fiction stuff. Robert A. Heinlein, Edgar Rice Burroughs, Poul Anderson, Philip K. Dick, Harlan Ellison, Eric Frank Russell, Frank Herbert— all the legends. All kinds of great stuff about people on other planets, other worlds.

Any world.

As long as it isn't *here.*

Here is a maximum security prison.

They talk in whispers.

They are the only two insiders.

Everyone else is an outsider.

There's another guy in another cell. Don't know what he's in for but the cons are giving him a hard time. Ryan lets it be known he's his friend, and a friend of the crazy kid. They don't like their friends to be messed with. That stops the man from being messed with. The guy is grateful. The three of them talk. They talk about a lot of things. They want a lot of things. The most important thing they want, is *better.* They want things to be better. Better things inside. Better treatment. Maybe to get *outside?* That's the best thing they think of, but of course it's an impossible dream within the walls of this very special prison.

There were two others. They bunk together. Ryan knows they're doing it to each other. But that, in and of itself, doesn't bother him. They're honorable, they keep it to themselves. It's their private business. They're getting hassled by some of the younger and newer cons. Ryan goes to talk with them. Then the five of them talk to these young cons, in the yard, behind the pump house.

It goes real fast.

Real hard.

There is no other way really to "discuss" this type of thing in here.

A half dozen teeth on the ground. A couple of broken bones. The face of the chief wise-guy troublemaker kissing the bricks. Again and again and again, his new address now is the prison hospital ICU.

The five of them form a club. A mutual protection society. Anyone can join. More do. It gets bigger and bigger. They don't start trouble. They don't take sides. They don't care from Mafia, Muslim warriors, white Aryan supremacy guys, faggots, drug addicts, two-bit criminal moron losers with shit-for-brains. It's all the same in here. The dregs, the most violent, the most wicked offenders this society could produce. And that's saying something! The seven percenters. It was his job to bring them all together.

Ryan did.

The club grows.

Others join them. More and more. Time passes. They manage the cons now. They keep things cool. No fights. No rapes. No stealing. No trouble. Otherwise you get trouble back ten-times as bad as you tried to give. A couple of guys feel the heat. Their deaths are fast and hard and serve as dire warnings to all others.

That stops any confusion or competition.

It's not long before they work with the warden. They cooperate with the guards. They mingle, network. It's not easy, it takes a lot of changing of old stereotype ideas. All around. It also takes a lot of time, but they're in the nation's newest maximum security prison, and all they have is time. No one's ever getting out of here still sucking air. And they all know their next destination is a ride on the belt into the incinerator, and a handful of dry black ash thrown down the toilet by some relative back home they never knew they had.

So they plan.

They plan like brainy little mothers.

The new warden is lax. The guy seems to be the last of the bleeding-heart political-correct libs from some long ago fanta-syland that used to be the United States. It seems like he don't really understand what the truth is here. Criminals are crimi-nals. It's plain and simple. That is who they are, and that is what they do. Don't expect a snake to act like a puppy dog, that is outside its nature. Ryan and his guys don't explain it to him either. The guards are lax too. Some have been bought off, some are no better than the scum they guard.

Ryan and his group are all so friendly. Attitudes are peachy. The cons get calm. The guards are cool. No serious trouble for a long time. The atmosphere is good. Ripe. Getting riper by the minute.

The big day finally comes. They've been planning for months. Complicated shit. Like when Ryan got the Entertainment Committee to show that Steve McQueen film, *The Great Escape*. Usually, everyone would be cheering, joking, shooting the breeze during a film. Not them. Not during this film. Everyone was quiet. Thoughtful. Real serious. Serious as hell. Planning—dreaming serious, about getting *out*.

This place was the first of the old MSPS Centers (Maximum Security Prison System) for hard core violent criminals. It housed the worst of the worst, the most vile predators our society had to offer. It boasted the hard-core 7% of violent, evil, serial killers, mass murders, home invaders, child rapers, and others that commit over 70% of all violent crimes. They also had a large percentage of what were termed "special politicals." That's really where Ryan came in.

They were all here. Collected like Satan's Hit Parade. His very best, warehoused in this newest of Max-Sec prisons. Here there was no attempt at rehab. No programs. No early out. There was no *out* at all. Ever. For anyone. Except death—natural or otherwise.

And that's the one thing everyone wanted most—even more

than life itself—to get *out!*

Even for a day.

Even for an hour.

Even for a few damn minutes!

And Ryan had a plan to make that happen.

He knew they'd probably all die doing it. He even told them so. They understood it, and still all of them signed on. It didn't matter. They were all waiting to die anyway.

He'd been working on The Plan for months. The other cons treated it as some kind of sacred project. It was the closest any of these freaks ever came to an actual feeling of holiness in their miserable lives, that they hadn't perverted terribly. Nothing was spared for the success of The Plan. Everyone was in. After all, they had nothing to lose and everything to gain.

What's life in a Max-Sec prison compared to even one day of freedom on the outside?

Some citizens outside the place might say it wasn't worth it. Some cons inside might say it wasn't worth it either. But when you've served ten, with life to go, the days are long and there are just too many of them to spend caged like a rat in a box. Sure, prison was entirely what every one of them deserved—or worse—but they still wanted out at any cost.

When you're in prison for life and you know you're going to die there—there isn't anything more important than one thing....

Getting out!

It becomes an obsession.

They all had the same obsession.

They had it real bad.

* * * * * * *

The Warden decided to watch the old-time program on his private office view screen once more. Quietly, thoughtfully. It always lifted his spirits when he was a bit down to view this simple old program.

He smiled. The cons finally had a chance to watch *The Great*

Escape. He'd allowed it this one time. They loved it. It was the kind of film that spoke right down deep into each con's gut. It was their favorite film.

The Warden had his favorite film too. A film all his own, that spoke down deep into his own gut. It was a one-hour episode of an old-time Vid-tube show...what used to be called a television program, originally telecast way back LastCen. It was an episode from the Golden Age, when the Vids had been called "TV." This particular one went way back to the classic era of the 1960s. It was in old-style black and white. Strangely enough, the primitive lack of color lent it an arty look that gave it a severity and impact that color never could. But none of that mattered because it was so incredible. So full of his own particular truth. It was Spec-Fic. Or speculative fiction. What had been called "science fiction" back then. That was when citizens believed there was a future worth dreaming about instead of the nightmare that existed today.

Now that they were actually *living* in the future it wasn't so pleasant. Science fiction had lost its meaning.

The Warden's favorite story was from an anthology program called *The Outer Limits*. The particular episode was titled, 'The Zanti Misfits'. Even now its cold logic gave the Warden chills. So right, so true, so full of crystal clear justice that it sang its song right into his ever-loving warden-heart.

Ostensibly it was a simple story about ugly monsters from outer space or some such silly notion. Alien invasion by the Zantis, a race of horrible insects with human-like faces. The actual story however was about what the Warden believed to be a bold and innovative way to deal with the worst hard-core violent criminals. What did a civilized society do with them?

What do you do with your worst misfits?

The Zantis had found a solution. So had the Warden and the Governor.

The Zantis sent their misfits to Earth.

To be executed by the humans.

The warden and the governor had James Ryan to deal with

their Zantis.

It was all thanks to the DOC and approved by The Authority.

It was quite simple really. The old TV show clearly gave them the answer.

KTA.

Kill Them All.

The cons were planning to break out; serial killers, mass murderers, multiple rapists, child molesters, contract killers, out-of-control psychos, and hundreds of mass-murder terrorists, Mafia, gang killers, and dangerously violent politicals. Too many damned politicals. They were the most dangerous to the system. They were the ones the system really wanted to make go away. The others just offered the smoke screen.

Ryan was helping to make that possible.

How were these men going to be properly handled, dealt with, taken care of, and punished for their crimes?

It would be done just like the Zantis did it.

KTA.

The Warden smiled.

He shut off the disk.

All was right once more in his world.

* * * * * * *

Ryan had the cons declare themselves an independent government in exile. A government of the oppressed and downtrodden. They never even mentioned the fact that they were outlaws, murderers, convicted incarcerated criminals. They declared independence from the worldwide Authority, and from the Eastern Security District of what had once been the old United States of America.

They were not criminals at *all* they told the world news media, they were prisoners of war against an evil capitalistic, imperialistic system. They never mentioned that in every case they were the evil in that system.

They proclaimed open revolt against the hated government

and openly opposed The Authority.

They even had their own flag! Ryan thought that was a particularly nice touch.

Ryan set up a Central Committee based upon quaint old communist guerilla warfare planning. It was all doomed to failure. He was there to ensure failure. He became the President and con leaders were cut in on prime slots such as Secretary of State and Secretary of War. They even had a Treasury and Treasurer. That guy was a former corporate bigwig who had embezzled half a billion dollars from stockholders and retired employees of his own company. Ryan had them all work it like a shadow government. When the time came they would take over the prison and declare themselves independent of all authority. They would immediately petition the United Nations for recognition of their independence and national status. The fact that the old UN was practically defunct now didn't dawn on these geniuses, nor that the new worldwide Authority would never stand for such a rebellious act.

It was all a sham of course. Most of the morons Ryan was in with couldn't plan a hot date with a pre-paid hooker, much less pull off this serious revolutionary crap. But it gave them focus, it bent them all to his will, and it shut them up and stopped them from thinking too much about what he was *really* doing.

Ryan's job was the most dangerous of all. He was the Judas goat—or maybe, just plain Judas. If the cons ever got wind of what he was really up to he would be skinned alive. Slow. Then cooked—roasted over an open flame. He was rightly concerned about that part. He knew he could bet on that becoming a serious reality if he was ever found out, and the skinning part was no exaggeration either. Even worse could happen—if the cons could think of something that could be worse. Which was always possible. In that area, at least, there was no lack of imagination or originality among inmates for those kinds of things. Some of the sadists were even specialists in their own way of torture and mutilation and took great pride in it.

But they'd never find out. It was all set. Planned. This was a cut-and-dried, tried-and-true operation to manipulate the group mind. And as in all things, the media would be their conduit from the group to the public. It was a new operation run by the Department of Control. The DOC had become more proactive than usual, but pretty much the same kind of thing that had gone on since the formation of the Security Districts years earlier. Now DOC was hitting their stride. This operation was one small example of what it was doing all throughout the world regarding security matters.

The cons would never find out. They were too stupid to do anything but go along. These were the worst of the worst. They had no hope, no purpose. Ryan had given them some hope now. Even more, he'd given them a purpose. Unite—work together—and get *out!* They'd do whatever he said. They were all suckered in by his game. They had no choice. And anyway, they deserved what they were going to get.

Of course the prison authority cooperated. Only the worst of the crooked guards were working the blocks on that fateful day. If any of them were offed it would be no great loss. Just like with the guards over the Zanti prisoners. Security would be lax. Some of the cons—they called themselves troops now—thought it might be a set-up. Ryan told them to forget about that. They had their own CIA, and things had been prepared for them in advance.

Not to worry. Ryan waited, patient, then it happened.

The cons took over the prison in one hour. It went smooth and fast. According to plan. Ryan had special squads ready to make sure inmates didn't go berserk. Everyone knew the rules and obeyed them. There were standing orders to kill anyone who broke those rules. The enforcers were some of the worse offenders, but they also were the ones who wanted to get out the most. They, like everyone else, had things they were itching to do on the outside. Some were very evil things. So everyone stayed calm. Real business-like. Time enough for craziness when the fireworks really started. It wouldn't be long to wait, he promised them. First he had to do one more thing. It was pretty important.

He had to get himself *out*.

They'd declared themselves an independent prisoner's government. They voiced all kinds of outrageous demands through the ass-kissing media. The media being only too happy for the story, waiting for the blood to flow, anticipating it and the high ratings as they decried all violence, but too thought-policed and politically correct to ever admit it. Or to report the truth. So the cons demanded money, cars, total immunity from prosecution and repercussion. They wanted reparations from the State. Their records cleared. Apologies from the Governor. New idents. Women. Pizza and beer. All the drugs they could do.

Of course the Governor refused it all, but he did say he would be willing to negotiate.

The cons threatened.

The Governor said he'd talk to their leader.

One man, the leader.

That was fine by Ryan.

He was their leader.

This was his exit move and he was ready for it.

Ryan said good. It's a first step, he told his troops. Not to worry, we'll all get what we want. Eventually. Just be cool. He left with the Secretary of State and Secretary of War for a ride to the Governor's Mansion to discuss the problems with the big man himself. So they could come to some sort of agreement. The Cons thought it was cool. Just a matter of time.

It was.

Time that was running out.

On *them*.

A limo picked them up at the prison main gate. The limo had their flag waving from two tiny antennae on each front fender. Like some damn diplomat's car. Which it kind-of was. It was a nice detail the cons all noticed and ate up. It looked real impressive on the news vids. Ryan knew the troops back inside the joint would get a real kick out of it. They'd be talking about it all day. It would help keep them in check.

A National Police Trooper opened the limousine door for Ryan like he was a visiting dignitary from an actual government. Like he really was the president of some stupid made-up prison country. Ryan knew what he was doing, though. It had all been agreed, planned, that this play at formality, however ludicrous, must be strictly adhered to. This was, after all, a play in one act. It had to look and feel exactly right.

The two bozos with Ryan were suitably impressed. Neither of them were big brains, of course. Ryan didn't want guys like that too close to him. These were violent offenders. Murderers. They'd gotten life from soft-bellied judges so far removed from reality that they couldn't even tell the difference between a person being "sick" or being "evil."

Do *you* know that difference?

Well, Ryan *knew* the difference and his guys were just plain evil.

That's one reason why it was all so easy for him back then. He could never have played out this game with citizens, like some of the other DOC agents do now, but these criminal boyos had made their beds many years before he ever met them. They deserved what they got. It didn't bother Ryan at all. It was a job to him like any other, and not as bad as most.

When they reached the Governor's Mansion Ryan had his escort get out of the car first. Then he picked up the gun from under the seat where he knew it would be waiting for him. Ryan called out to the two cons, and when they turned around he shot them both stone cold dead. They never expected it.

Ryan sauntered up to the Governor's Mansion and rang the front bell.

A liveried butler met him there instantly. He was a very young man and smiled at Ryan in recognition, "Mr. Robinson," he called Ryan by the name he knew him by. "It is good to see you again, sir."

"Hello, Jenkins," Ryan said to the butler, smiling, holstering his weapon. Everyone on this operation knew him as Blake

Robinson.

"The Governor is waiting for you in the study. Please follow me."

Governor Leland Jackson sat watching the reports on six large screens in a comfortable book-lined study. Ryan hadn't seen real books in years. Actual, hard copy books. These were all paperbacks of course, and they all looked new. Ryan figured they had to be many decades old. They had been very collectable antiques even then. Many were actually forbidden. There were even a few old-time hard cover books from before LastCen. All were priceless collectors' items. LastCen they had been so common. Like everything else in Old America had been.

Like freedom had also been.

The Governor got up, he came over and shook Ryan's hand, happy to see him again.

"Dammit, Blake, it's good to see you. And look at the mess you've made for me there. Now we'll just have to go in and clean it all up, I guess." Governor Jackson smiled knowingly, then laughed heartily, "Good job, my man! Good job!"

"Well, it looks like a real bad prison riot, sir. May be one of the worst this year," Ryan said, sitting down in the big chair he was offered. He took the drink the Governor handed him and one of those great Cuban cigars he foisted on his most important guests. It was the only thing left of that island since it had been nuked back in 2015.

Ryan said, "Well, Lee, I did it. They've declared themselves independent of the old US of A—and of the worldwide Authority—which of course is far worse. They are in direct rebellion against the Eastern District Security Government and by the way, actively advocating and fighting for its overthrow."

"Yes, it's a marvelous situation, Blake. Much worse than the typical bellyaching for porno and conjugal visits. This is armed open rebellion against our nation. Or what's left of it. A department of The Authority is behind it all, of course, but no one knows that. Nevertheless, we can't countenance a violent overthrow of government. Can't have that, now can we? Of course not. That can not be tolerated. It must be put down with max-force according to the law. It's a great day for law enforcement—or justice, Blake."

"I imagine not one of them will survive," Ryan added.

"I'm sure," the Governor replied with a knowing smile. "In fact, I think I can guarantee it."

They watched with interest the close-up of the final images of tanks, 'copters and heavily armed and armored shock troops mowing down the prisoners.

The prisoners had some small caliber guns—a small amount Ryan had smuggled into the prison to lend credence to his authority among them, and to make their revolt seem legit. They didn't have enough firepower to do more than annoy the hundreds of trained officers in bulletproof body-armor pouring into the prison after them. Ryan and the Governor watched with interest as the cons were easily mowed down. Slaughtered. No quarter. No surrender. Just as had been planned at DOC headquarters by the Director.

It was over quickly. It did not bother either of them afterwards. The cons were finally getting what they deserved, and truthfully, it was all a lot more merciful than what many of them had done to their innocent victims. Each one of them had taken part in terrorizing a docile citizenry for decades. Now was payment day. It was a massacre for sure—but this time it was right back at *them*. And they deserved it!

The politicals that had caused so much trouble—now were lumped in with common criminals and shared their fate. These were libertarians and small-government democracy lovers, so-called independents and patriots who fought against the world-wide government Authority. Free speech types with big mouths and cried out about things like the old U.S. Constitution and the Bill of Rights. In the end, they'd been lost in the mix— which had been Ryan's actual mission in the first place. A shadow political eradication job, typical of the DOC.

The Governor said it best to the media in his touching victory speech: "My friends, a society that can not protect itself and deal with its most violent and chaotic criminal element doesn't deserve to survive. And it won't. Not for long. This tiny seven percent minority of monsters are responsible for over two-thirds of all violent crimes and many far worse political crimes. Their eradication lifts the heavy tax burden off the people of my Security Sector, and gives back some measure of justice to people who have been made victims for the rest of their lives."

Ryan watched as the prison was consumed by flames and the buildings began to fall in upon themselves. Some of the inmates were still inside. Their revolt had ended. Every once and a while a burning inmate would run out toward the government troops and ask for mercy. He'd be shot down dead while the media panned their camera angles with close ups for the evening news. Not one of those convicts had ever shown their victims a shred of mercy. So not one convict would survive the final devastation. The fire also helped to get rid of a substantial amount of evidence. Soon this group of cons would be just a bad memory—and all the politicals with them forgotten as well.

"Good riddance to bad garbage," The Governor said. He switched off the vid screen, then switched on an old video. It was an old VCR tape. Ryan was surprised his ultra modern system was also equipped with such obsolete media devices. He watched as opening credits appeared on the screen. Ryan smiled, he knew what it was. He had seen it before. It was that old *Outer Limits* episode, "The Zanti Misfits."

"A very good show," Governor Jackson said. "Far ahead of its time. It's one of Warden Wilson's favorites."

Ryan just nodded, "One of my favorites too, Governor."

CHAPTER SEVEN
SOLITARY CONFINEMENT

That's basically how it started.

The Eastern Security District used Direct Action Groups, or Rapid Response Teams, that paved the way for them to mold society. They initiated events via undercover specialists, agitators and provocateurs—like Ryan. Or Blake Robinson. Or was it Robinson Blake? It didn't matter. Ryan can't even remember much of it now. They've done so much to him over the years. It began innocently enough. He even had pride, once, at being an agent for them. Then The DOC came in and changed everything. The DOC, The Department of Control. From out of the chaos, came...control on Earth—and a hellish future.

Now Ryan was locked away in a metal can of a cell who-the-hell-knew-where. Naked. Nothing in the cell but four empty gray steel walls, a high gray ceiling, a cold gray steel floor. No bed, no commode, no sink, no window, no slit in the door. No ventilation system he could see. It seemed like he was breathing the same old stale air but it couldn't be.

They'd thrown him in here some time ago. He didn't remember when. Or why. He didn't remember much at all. He just woke up in "here." Nude and cold. Confused and scared. Alone except for an old paperback book he found on the floor beside him. He didn't know why it was there. He didn't know anything about it. It looked like some kind of old-time science fiction novel. A paperback with no cover. The title page said, *Mars Needs Books*, and it was by some obscure one-shot writer from LastCen named Philip K. Dickson.

Sometimes memory does come back. There were other agents doing other things. All kinds of things. Most were bad things. A lot worse than what he did. Ryan just killed killers and politicals. He knew the others killed innocents. He couldn't remember why or for what reason, though. Most of these agents did all kinds of bad stuff for The DOC. All of it was for The DOC now that he thought of it. Now that he thought of it, he probably worked for The DOC too. Somehow, through some complicated mix of various cover corporations or government agencies. It was hard to tell. It's hard to tell anything from back then.

Even before any of them knew there was a DOC running things, Ryan knew something had to be up. There seemed to be a plan. Somewhere, someone had a plan, and it was working. For them. But not for everyone else in the country or the world. It was working against citizens. Against the country. Against freedom and justice. But no one knew it for sure, there was just no evidence and no one knew how to identify it and stop it.

It hadn't only gone on in the old United States either; it affected or infected countries throughout the entire world. There was sabotage, bombings, sensationalistic murders, riots, terrorism, chaos, all set up to destabilize. Terrorism became an all-out war after 9/11. It was going on in every country in the world. Terror was used to destabilize the world. Or at least the industrialized world. The various financial panics were worse. The Third World and the Developing World really didn't matter much. They were hardly even players and certainly never stable. In this drama, they were the booty. The plunder. Their crap was all under control. They weren't going nowhere they weren't told to go.

The industrial world was something different. But even the nations of that world were all becoming unglued. Ryan just wondered who would be there to pick up all the pieces and glue the entire mess back together again into some semblance of order—and what that order might look like.

CHAPTER EIGHT
JUST ANOTHER SUICIDE

He was locked away. Under their control now. Whoever *they* were.

He was thinking about things again.

Thinking too damn much.

The dirty bomb used in the Chicago bombing had killed over five thousand people. Much worse than Oklahoma City or even the terror of 9/11. But the tactical nuke that was detonated in a shipping container at the docks in Red Hook, in Brooklyn was the worst of all. It took out half of New York City. Four million dead and the country's economy in ruins. After that, the United States effectively ceased to exist, even though the fiction was maintained for another dozen years or so. In the end, it dissolved almost as fast as its old Cold War nemesis, the Soviet Union had. He remembered it in a flash of memory now, coming back to him. It was scary. Real. Serious. Bad. A guy named Ryan had been involved in it somehow.

The guy they got for it was a guy he knew. But it wasn't that Ryan guy, it was another guy. This other guy had been an agent also, and he had been into a lot of nasty business. However, Ryan didn't think that guy was capable of mass murder, and he didn't think his string-pullers, Americans like him, would be capable of ordering something like the mass murder of millions of their fellow Americans. But anything was possible when there was a point to be made, a political career to be enhanced, or a cause to be advocated. No matter how crazy. Or how evil. So the bomb blew, the people died, and Macky was set-up as the fall guy.

Maybe he really was responsible? Who knew for sure?

Ryan remembered that for two weeks before he died the vids and media reported how depressed Macky had been, how despondent and shameful—full of guilt for his horrible dirty deed. Dirty deeds, done dirt cheap for sure. Of course no one ever spoke to him other than the federal cops, no one ever interviewed him, you never saw him on any vid or program actually say he was depressed, shameful, or especially guilty. You never saw or heard him at all. Macky never said a word. That was kind of unlike Macky.

Something was going on.

So his suicide wasn't totally unexpected.

They cut him down in his cell. The twenty-four hour suicide watch had been lifted for the Christmas holidays. Nice touch, that one. The media played it up big and Citizens saw it as a Christmas present from the Big Man himself to citizens everywhere.

Ryan wasn't buying any of it.

Thing was, Macky was a sharpy. He may have been set up, but he wasn't taking the rap. He wasn't no patsy. Even in death he spoke loud and clear.

After the doctors and ghoul-squad cut him down, they immediately determined that—for sure—it really was suicide. What a surprise! Then they had the body taken away for autopsy. Purely standard stuff, cut-and-dried to back up the official determination of suicide. Nice touch, smoothly done, except Macky wouldn't keep his mouth shut even in death. Though no one noticed it, Macky had something to say even as his fully clothed body hung there in his cell right before Ryan. When he was cut down before the corpse was sent to autopsy, Ryan made sure he was there when Macky's body was stripped of its clothing.

Ryan saw the message. It had probably been cut with a razor, cut right into his skin before he died. The resulting scabs formed words—words written upon his stomach and chest that were quite easy to read. They said,

"No Shame. No Guilt. NO SUICIDE, EITHER!"

More words were cut into the side of his abdomen. They read, "Innocent. DOC did me! DOC did IT!"

After seeing that, Ryan knew he had to get away. He had to get as far away as he could, some place where the long arm of The DOC could not reach him. Off-planet maybe. As far as possible. Ryan had to get somewhere they could not touch him. Fast. Maybe Mars? He had seen something he was not supposed to see. Those words were his death sentence. The same for the doctors who performed the autopsy. You should have seen their faces. They knew the score. They knew they'd get a visit soon— their families too—just in cased they'd blabbed. No one would find any bodies, people just disappeared like that all the time now. They say there are a lot of serial killers, but Ryan didn't think so. If there were, they were working for the government! It happens too much now. Like in old Argentina in the 1970s, like Russia in the 1950s, like Germany in the 1930s. They disappear—gone forever!

It went fast. The doctors just disappeared. The autopsy photos? Well, it seems that none had ever been taken. So they could not possibly exist either. Ryan knew different. He'd taken some of the photos himself. His copies disappeared as well.

Macky?

Just another suicide.

Ryan?

When he woke up he was here.

Wherever *here* might be.

Solitary confinement. Lost. Forgotten. Alone. He wished he could escape, get to Mars. At least those were what he thought were his own thoughts in his head. But they can play with your mind here, program you into whoever they want you to be. Did he really want to go to Mars? That's what he thought he wanted to do, but he was not even sure of that anymore. Maybe it's just stuff he'd read in that old paperback?

Mars Needs Books.

Was there even a human colony on Mars?

Ryan remembered years back when the third President Bush had begun the project. Then when the fourth President Bush, his nephew, initiated settlement and the second President Clinton began colonization. But of course, that was all so long ago. Decades really. In the reckoning of present history it was ages ago to the current digital world.

He didn't remember it that clearly. He didn't know how long he'd been here. Weeks? Years? Decades? He felt old, but he couldn't tell if he was old or not. He couldn't tell much at all.

Ryan picked up the copy of *Mars Needs Books*. The old battered paperback had blurbs on the back cover that began:

> A rousing novel of interplanetary intrigue and adventure as a slip of a girl, Arabella Rashid, seeks to change the world and set it free....

He turned to Chapter One and began reading....

> "Everywhere he went on Mars they were always asking him about the paperbacks...."

Ryan wondered what the hell this was all about?

He never realized it then, but he was already on his way to Mars.

CHAPTER NINE
MARS GETS BOOKS

Everywhere he went on Mars they were always asking him about the paperbacks.

"When are the paperbacks coming in?" he heard a voice ask.

"What's in the next shipment?" he heard another voice call out to him.

Ryan looked around him astonished by the huge dome, the red-brown mountains in the distance, the two moons hurling by overhead, and the men who were talking to him. Rough-looking characters all. Miners.

Was he really on Mars?

"Ryan, have you heard anything yet?" another voice asked, it was a miner named Williams. Ryan somehow knew the man's name. A miner? On Mars? How Ryan knew this he was not sure, but he knew it—Williams was a miner on Mars—and Ryan was on Mars now too!

Ryan could not reply. His mind raced, trying to fill the void posed by a hundred questions.

He looked around him; finally he nodded knowingly, accepting it all.

Well, that had to be it. He was Ryan again. Okay, then he would be Ryan and he'd play his part as Ryan in their new game. He began speaking to the man standing there in front of him as if the words had always been ready to come out of his mouth. He knew the signs of programming.

"Well?" the man asked him impatiently.

"Well what?" Ryan asked trying to gather his thoughts.

"The paperbacks? Are they due soon?"

James Ryan looked at the man and suddenly found himself saying, as if it were the most natural response, "I put the order in a year ago and they should be on the way out here on the next supply run."

He was Ryan now. He was here on Mars. That was his new name. Or was it his real name? Probably just the name he was using here. It did not matter. He was James Ryan now. So be it.

Other men were beginning to crowd around him. They were rough, they looked like...miners of some kind.

Another of these miners, one named Alvy, just shrugged and said, "I expected it. I was out on detail for two months, hell of a desert run, but I hoped when I got back the ship might've come in."

Ryan didn't say anything. Somehow he knew that all these men, everyone here, was waiting for the latest shipment. How he knew this he could not say, but it was an incontrovertible fact he knew deep within his mind, way down deep within his psyche. Programming for sure. But why? He realized that it was knowledge that must have somehow been implanted into his memory. It was scary really; them messing with your memories and thoughts like that, but links and implants were done all the time on Earth these days. Why not out here? You just had to learn to go with the flow.

He was some kind of agent again, apparently. But was he really here, on Mars? It all seemed so unreal, even surreal, but his mind seemed to know exactly what thought to think, which way to think it, and the right words to say. He was James Ryan now, an agent, after all. So he decided he'd go with the flow, at least for the time being. Until he figured out just what the hell was going on.

The miner named Alvy pulled out an old battered paperback from his back pocket, thrust it forward. "Look, Ryan, I've got a really great Raymond Chandler here, *The Big Sleep*. I'll trade it for anything by David Goodis, Jim Thompson, or that other guy, Bruno Fischer. I got all the Dashiell Hammetts, and read all the Hal Masur's that you turned me onto last week. That Scott Jordan is the lawyer that Perry Mason should have been! I finished up all the Daniel Woodrell's—terrific! The James Crumley's were tops too! Great stuff, but I'll pass on those others."

Ryan shook his head, came back to reality, or what passed for reality now.

Last week? It must also be part of the programming, detailed background memory. Now he found himself pulling out some primo condition paperbacks from his pouch. They were like new. Even being over a hundred years old and made out of cheap browning pulp paper. It was amazing that they could still look like they did when they were new. They were thick, tight copies. Old editions from way back LastCen. Some of the best examples of hard-boiled paperback crime. One was a James Ellroy called *Clandestine*—bleak noir corruption and violence; the other was just titled *Flood*, by Andrew Vachss—hard-boiled action and attitude from a heroic advocate for child safety—and the last was a real golden oldie—*Black Wings Has My Angel* by Elliott Chaze. That one seemed to be in the original 1950s Gold Medal paperback edition. It was rare. It was impossible to find. How the hell did he know that? How the hell did he even have it? And when had he read all these books? Because Ryan suddenly realized that he had vivid memories of all the titles, authors, characters and plots of each of these books and many others. How could that be? And if he understood how—through brain implants and programming—then why?

Ryan remembered some of the best of the books he had read on the way out to Mars, or so his memories told him. There were many in the old yellow-spine Gold Medal series. These included the hard prison novels of Malcolm Braly like *On The Yard*, so true and intense. He could relate to those books right down onto his soul. There were other books by guys like Edward S. Aarons, aka Edward Ronns, Stephen Marlowe, Dan Marlowe about hard men who were spies and special agents.

Emmett Grogan's, *Final Score* was his one crime novel and a masterpiece that had been forgotten much as he had been sadly, but his other book, *Ringolevio,* was also very hard-boiled—all about his hard life experiences. Maybe true, maybe not, always fascinating, as it stated "a life played for keeps." He fondly remembered reading copies of old crime digests like *Trapped, Guilty, Manhunt,* and others of that ilk full of great short hard crime stories. He smiled when he thought of the stories. Then his mind stuck on that E. Howard Hunt guy, who early on wrote as Robert Dietrich turning out paperback originals in his much-underrated Steve Bentley crime series. He did outstanding memorable work. Then there was Brett Halliday with his Mike Shayne private eye books that could always be counted on to be entertaining crime and noir reads. The Dell paperback editions of Mike Shayne all had cover art featuring lovely, gorgeous women by master artist Robert McGinnis. They were true beauties—the gals—and the books!

Alvy drooled. He wasn't a collector, he was a reader. A reader who loved to read. Who needed to read. He couldn't explain it really, but he was like most of the men on Mars, they were all seemingly compelled to read. Like it was an innate part of them, or some obsession.

Although Alvy had never read either of these authors before, he said he'd heard all about their stuff. They were some of the best. Miners would do whatever they could to find their books, or pry them out of the hands of other readers. Or some other dead miner/collector, who would have no use for them any longer. One of the most righteous things for a man to do on Mars was to pass on books they'd read and enjoyed to another fellow miner.

Ryan decided to make Alvy a happy man, he traded away the Ellroy book and took the Raymond Chandler in its place, putting it deftly in his pouch. He kept the Vachss and the Chaze. Those books he could always trade for more substantial matter, like food or shelter later on.

Ryan innately knew that some paperbacks were better than

money out here on Mars. It was a strange truth but how he knew that fact he couldn't exactly say, he just knew it was true.

There were no consumer goods on Earth any more, only relics leftover from last century. Everything on Earth now was ultra high-tech virtual, or holo. The bottom line was that it was all fake. It was all lies within lies within lies. All wrapped up in a neat little package of still more lies.

It was a funny thing how the settlers and frontier men here on Mars had evolved their own strange society. It was so separate from Earth. Not only in distance but in orientation and outlook. So very different. While it mirrored much of Earth, it was not the Earth of *today*, it was the Earth of LastCen. What had been termed 'The American Century,' back when there had been a separate America—a United States of America, that is. Before the one-world government dream of the internationalists had come true and created The Authority. Well-meaning but naive and dangerous socialist wet-dreams of power and social justice which had come true after decades of struggle, finally— which paradoxically meant the death knell to human freedom. All the well-meaning one-worlders accomplished was to make it easy as hell for a world-wide authority to control them and everything and everyone. A new kind of digital-tech totalitarian government that had never been accomplished before in human history and had become entirely successful.

In the old days on Earth there'd always been another country to run to, a fast ship to sail away on, or an "America" that could be a haven across the ocean. Even an Australia, somewhere down under. Today even the faraway colony planets were under the control of Earth's worldwide Authority and it was rumored the terrible DOC was lurking behind it all pulling the strings.

Paperback books were a key component for the men on Mars. They were not only throwbacks to an earlier and better age, they were the only existing methods of information storage that were free of any kind of mind control tampering, implanting, or manipulation. Hard copy can not be revised on a daily basis without evidence of the tampering detectable. Even in the event of reprints, comparison of different copies could show changes if they had been made. That was not true with the digital record. That can too easily be re-programmed, pre-programmed, and altered, and never show any evidence of tampering.

The Marsmen (what the men on Mars liked to call themselves these days) existed in a hostile, demanding, primitive, cruel world. They survived, and made it bearable only on a diet of luck, hard work, and individualism. They had few vices or pleasures, they just wanted to be left alone. In their very limited leisure time, they would read books. However, all they would read were mystery novels and hard-boiled crime fiction. They'd read a page here or there, catch a scene or chapter when they could, and they loved the damn things. They would talk about them—the stories, the characters—incessantly. Like they knew them. They trusted and loved the old books, the characters in them and the people who wrote them. But they only trusted paperbacks published on Earth during LastCen. Because they were published before any of the modern media existed. Before all that digital crap they hated and did not trust came into being—before there was complete control.

"Put that crap in your brain and it will change you forever," they told each other passionately about all other information mediums. They believed it like a religion. They didn't like much in the form of entertainment, except reading. None of them ever used an input slot or brain link, though most every citizen seemed to have been born with them these days.

But these Marsmen sure loved the old paperbacks. They loved to read the harder stuff—hard-boiled crime was their meat. Usually the harder the better. So-called mainstream fiction; romances, westerns, horror, and even fantasy porn left them stone cold. So-called Science fiction, was just a joke to them. Science fiction was seen as phony crap anyway. To them more lies. They saw it being as unreal as the vids, implants and software that too many citizens on Earth thought was only too real. A media believed to be truthful by the masses on Earth. That stuff was not even considered worthy of turning on and viewing here on Mars.

The miners all agreed there was something special about the old paperbacks. Those books spoke to them. They got inside them. In their hearts, in their minds, in their souls. The stories, the writing, and the characters bored right into their inner being like a laser and the stone cold truth of the stories had a real impact on these hard and lonely men.

Perhaps it was because of the hardship of living on Mars. The desolation, the danger, the cruelty of existence and the utter isolation. The best hard-boiled and noir fiction spoke to this so eloquently and realistically. There was the down-and-out, tough-guy private eye fighting his heroic war by himself, and living precariously by his own moral code among all the cheap lies and betrayals. There was the noir femme fatale each man dreamt of meeting. That was another big part of it.

See, there were no women on Mars. But the men hoped. Some day.

Then there was the aloneness in a world where every man and every bit of luck seemed to be against them. It was something the men on Mars understood only too well and the books told them they were not alone. That counted for a lot.

Or perhaps it was because the stories gave an accurate view of Old Earth the way many settlers had heard their home world had once been like—or the way they wanted to remember it. Both the good and the bad. The so-called 'good old days'. Crime and hard-boiled fiction dealt with people like them, situations they could relate to, the day-to-day struggles of hard, tough, everyday working men. Every story was about an individual trying to stay afloat and hack out a life for himself against all the odds. Their love of private eyes in hard-boiled fiction was also a manifestation of their fanatical desire to see justice done in a world where none existed.

Who could really say why the men on Mars loved the old paperbacks so much—but they surely did. They read them, they collected them, and they talked about them endlessly. Some thought about them too damn much. They seemed to think about them all the time. Of course these books weren't produced—the word for it had been "published" in the old days—on Earth any more. They hadn't been produced since the days just after LastCen, before 2020. The old copies that survived from then and earlier were avidly collected on Mars. The older the better, to most men's way of thinking.

Ryan didn't know how he knew all that history, nor why and how it had happened. He just did. All he knew now was that he'd given up a primo James Ellroy for a classic Raymond Chandler. Traded the Chandler to Fat Jack for a pulpy Carroll John Daly Race Williams novel in a 1984 International Polygonics paperback edition with a great Nicky Zahn cover. It was a nice collector's item. He then traded the Race Williams for a meal at The Martian Chronicles Café, with all the imported Earth beer he could drink. It was a good deal. Earth beer was scarce, but paperbacks were still worth more.

Later in the evening Ryan picked up a Harry Whittington crime novel and traded that for a beat up 1953 edition of an old Lion paperback called *Bourbon Street* by some guy named G.H. Otis. It was one of only two books by Otis, a whirlwind hardboiled crime read. He'd never even seen the other Otis novel, *Hot Cargo*, rumored to be an even more obscure Lion Book. This was Ryan's best trade all month and a great discovery for him personally as a reader and collector. Lion Books were hardly ever seen anymore.

Manny, the barman at the café was also the owner of *The Book Snook*. Snook being an early LastCen slang word for a kind of obsessional fool. Many of the book guys knew they were a bit odd, but what the hell, they reveled in that individualism. Anyway, Manny had tried all evening to get the Chaze book out from Ryan's grubby little fingers without any results. Manny pleaded, begged, he even threatened. Sort of. Ryan laughed at that.

Manny shrugged, tried another tack.

Ryan was no fool. Ryan wasn't giving anything up. Not just yet. Especially not that Eliott Chaze noir classic.

* * * * * * *

For more than twenty years, since he'd first come out to Mars—or so his memories now told him—Ryan had marveled at the insatiable interest in private eye, noir and hard-boiled crime fiction shown by the settlers and pioneers. The men loved to read the stuff. They were fascinated, even obsessional about it. But only in the old paperback format. It was interesting, that with all the stuff on vid and available in neural implants—absolutely none of it took root with these men. None at all!

No one on Mars trusted that stuff. Everyone knew, or at least was totally convinced that it was all corrupted with mind-control commands and secret programs they hated and feared. That made it dangerous stuff. Stuff to stay away from.

There was no such risk with the paperbacks. To the men of Mars there was nothing like an old paperback from LastCen. A real book! They each had their own feel, even scent. The cover art, the type, the company logo, even the paper and binding were often noticed in detail by the men. It was a personal kind of thing, the book speaking to each man as an individual. Vids couldn't do that. It just wasn't the same. Implants and disks with virtual reality fantasy dreamscapes maybe seemed real—in some cases more real than reality itself—but those could never be trusted. Hence, never fully enjoyed. The men feared them all.

It was said by some that paranoia had become the national sport on Mars and they were probably right.

The men really appreciated the cover art on the paperbacks also, especially the older books. Sexy girls, often half-dressed, abounded. They were beautiful, lovely iconic images of gorgeous women and they were shown with strong, tough, virile men. The Marsmen saw themselves as being like the men on those covers and some of them were right. They saw the women on those covers and they each wanted a woman just like that.

The artists—whenever the guys could make out the miniscule signatures on the covers of the books—or the rare time the artist was actually credited on the book—made those books even more collectable and prized. Books with covers by the master artists of noir and dangerous femme fatales like Robert Maguire, Robert McGinnis, and Walter Popp were sought after by all. Covers by greats like 'The Three James': James Meese, James Bama, and James Avati were avidly traded and saved. Artists such as Bayre Philips, Peff, Reginald Heade, Robert Bonfils, Harry Barton and Harry Scharre among so many others were praised for their sexy, often dangerous women, and held in high regard by the men on Mars. Each man had his own favorites. But each man loved the cover art and what it said about that particular book.

However, not every man on Mars read the old paperbacks.

The worst thing to be on Mars was a brain-fried wirehead who did not read. There weren't many of these, but there were a few. And there was nothing worse than a political or self-righteous wirehead with a brain full of pre-programmed political mush he actually believed to be his own thoughts and ideas! Most of these men were sent out to the desert where they stayed and thankfully lived alone. Many were believed to be undercover DOC agents. They were strictly monitored and exiled to a small ghetto on Northside. They were dangerous and not to be trusted—but they were more harmful to themselves and they existed in their digital dream world alone and lost.

Reading books, was important, but actually *owning* and collecting books was a pursuit which seemed to have died after the turn of the century and the advent of the Authority on Earth. Now, decades later, it had become a really big thing here on Mars. The personal connection between reader and author, the physical feeling of holding—and actually owning a copy of the physical book was a last remnant of personal power and freedom in a world with none left in it any longer. It was important. It meant a lot, in a world where nothing meant anything anymore. Those old books were glorious priceless relics from a time of freedom, independence and individuality. The men on

Mars cherished them. To own them, to actually possess any of those great old relics, was a privilege, a sacred duty, an honor that each man felt deep down in his being. They had no religion to speak of, but they had the old paperbacks. And that was enough for them.

James Ryan had experimented with some of the novels on the vids, but like everyone else he knew, he found he just could not get interested in anything electronic or digital. To be truthful, he hated all damned entertainment software. He knew all of it was full of manipulation and revision. There was a certain feeling on Mars, a backlash really against digital media and all that was hi-tech, but since practical reality and pragmatic survival necessitated the use of this technology, it only came out in quirky personal things like clothing, food, and of course reading matter used for entertainment. Or so the men of Mars had surmised when they discussed their strange fascination with paperback books.

Ryan remembered it had all begun years ago, or at least his memory told him that now. It had begun when friends had seen his small collection of mystery and hard-boiled crime paperbacks after he'd first come out to Mars. That had been in the early days, two decades ago. Or so his mind told him. From that day on, the interest had taken hold of everyone. Now it showed no end in sight.

Ryan shook his head, wondering just what memories were real and which ones had been planted into his brain. It was perplexing. He knew he had been somehow programmed. There was no question of it. The paperback obsession was just too weird a kink to be natural even in one individual, much less all the Marsmen. He also knew he had better figure it out before it all came back to bite him. Because it denoted something serious. It wasn't only this paperback obsession, it was the paperback obsessions of almost all the men on Mars.

Now that meant something big. But what?

Ryan couldn't worry about it now though. He had other things on his mind. He had traded away most of that original personal collection over the years. He was now left with just the Elliott Chaze book, an old Gold Medal edition from the 1950s, what had once been called a "paperback original." That meant it was not only a first edition but the first time ever that work was printed in any form. He knew from history that in the old days stories and novels would sometimes first see publication— or novels would be excerpted—in magazines. What had been known as periodicals. A lost hard-copy form now, he imagined.

Anyway, his Gold Medal paperback was in gem shape. It was the only copy of that particular book on Mars, and it was a legendary novel in hard-boiled circles. It was an honest-to-goodness actual book from the middle of LastCen. A total treasure! Even from that era back a hundred years ago scarce copies sold for a thousand dollars or more. But mostly it was a good book people just wanted to read, an incredible hard down-and-out tale of a small time hood and a brutal femme fatale bad girl who led him down the road to grim horror and deep destruction. Darkest noir at its very heart and soul.

Ryan had even thought once about reprinting it. Making some copies in the local print shop. It wouldn't be too difficult to do and the expense was negligible. But somehow it seemed wrong for him to do so, almost a perversion, or something close to being unholy. He feared that might bring him too close to being like the people he hated—those who controlled, manipulated and changed everything. No, he didn't want to become an editor or a publisher at all, and neither did any of the other Marsmen. Ryan's desire was only for the original books, the true items that were sacred to him. It was the same with all the other men on Mars. Reprinting copies was out, it was actually loathed. So they never reprinted anything. Ryan knew it was illogical. Another indication of DOC programming, he was sure. They printed material all the time; newspapers, advertising items, notices, reports, tons of technical data. But never fiction. They never touched fiction that way. There seemed something special about fiction. It had Ryan puzzled but he didn't have enough data to even create a half-baked theory about what it all might mean.

Early on Ryan had come up with the idea of having old paperbacks sent out to him from Earth. Crazy idea, and he did not know where he'd gotten it, but he seemed to remember he had a brother back on Earth who always bought up whatever old paperbacks he could find. There wasn't much. Then his brother would send them all out to him. Ryan would even send his brother "want lists" of particular titles and authors to look for and purchase. The older the better. His brother sent the books out to him in bulk lots on the monthly supply ships. When he could afford them, or so the short notes his brother included in the shipments implied. The books were not easy to find, but they still showed up from time to time. So many billions had been printed and distributed all over the world for so many decades. Some of the older stuff actually went back to before the 1950s! That was over a hundred years ago! It was funny that Ryan couldn't even remember what his brother looked like, but that long-lost brother still sent books out to him on every supply ship like clockwork. Ryan never forgot him and his shipments and he was excited because he knew a shipment was due soon.

Of course, a lot of it was incredibly delicate stuff, and expensive to ship out, and Ryan could only afford a small box of a few hundred paperbacks each trip. But that was enough. Now twenty years later, the arrival of new books had mushroomed into an incredible event in the social fabric of the men on Mars who read and collected the things. They were all readers. They each craved new books, more books, better books!

"A book-jones is a powerful thing to see once it takes hold of a person," Toothless Joe had told him with a twisted grin.

Now Ryan was waiting on his latest shipment. The biggest and best one ever.

So was everyone else on Mars.

One of the miners of long-standing named Alvy got his attention. "Come on, Ryan, I'm dry, man. Read the Lawrence Blocks and Donald Westlakes, and that damn Richard Stark is a wow! I even read the Charles Willefords, now that guy painted some nasty dudes with his words; loved that Wayne Dundee stuff too, his Joe Hannibal is just tough enough, but I need something new. Something special. You know? I can't get Fat Jake to part with Paul Cain's *Fast One* and *Seven Slayers*, so what am I to do? Can I just borrow your Chaze book? I'll be like, real gentle with it. You know how I am with books?"

Ryan looked at him closely, said nothing.

"I just want to read it, then I'll return it to you, in perfect shape." Alvy continued. "I won't dog-ear a page, I swear. I won't crease the cover. I won't crack the spine at all. Rather crack my own spine, Man! I'll even give you all my Lawrence Blocks and Loren Estelmans."

Ryan shook his head no, but smiled nevertheless. Actually, it was an excellent offer for just one quick read. He knew Alvy was desperate. He could see it in his eyes. The guy hadn't had a "great read" in a long time.

Guys read a lot of books, most of them were okay, a lot were good, some very good, but when you got your hands on a book that was a "great read" that was truly something special. It could be life-changing. It was something to celebrate, to pass on by word of mouth to everyone you knew. It was the ultimate for a reader. It was a book that could change that reader. Every reader is always looking for the "great read" fix, that's why they read in the first place!

Ryan knew like everyone else Alvy had a lot of what he'd call "good" or "okay reads"—but it was the great ones—great books—like great women—that made life special. It was a sad shame to see Alvy going so long without that great read he craved so much. That was a big thing to these men. To any reader. It would also be a good deal for Ryan because he would get his grubby hands on a lot of primo trading stock that he could move without much trouble. After all, he'd still get his copy of Chaze's *Black Wings Has My Angel* back. Probably in pretty good shape, too. Alvy did treat his books with respect. But Ryan just couldn't go through with it. *Black Wings*...why, it was the one book he had that he hadn't even read yet himself! It was not Chaze's only book, but it was an acknowledged master-piece, even in its own lifetime. Ryan just couldn't let it out of his hands. Not yet. Not until he'd read it himself and experienced it firsthand. It was a great one—and the great ones don't come along every day.

Alvy understood, "Sure, man, I know. I'd do the same thing if I was in your place. It's hard like hell even to trade books I've already read. I love them so much. I always want to keep 'em all. Something in me makes me a little crazy that way. You know? I like to read 'em again. You know? The real great ones.... They're like...."

"I know," Ryan said quietly, he understood.

"...yeah, Ryan. They're like...my friends, maybe more, maybe family."

Ryan smiled. For him the books were not only friends, they were his family, maybe even his parents. It was simple really. They'd been more mom and dad than his real mom and dad had ever been to him. More than the flesh and blood mom and dad who had left him and his brother when they were just infants. Deserted him. Deserted his brother too. Or so his memories told him now. He wondered off-hand, how much of that might actually be true. Maybe some of it? Maybe none of it?

Ryan looked at Alvy, he knew the signs. Alvy was going through reader withdrawal. Nothing new to read, no hard-boiled, no crime, no private eye stuff, no noir or bad-girl femme fatales, no tough-guy detectives, no bent cops, no kick-ass atti-tude. Nothing around at all. He was dry. It was tough booking days on Mars, for sure.

Fat Jack said, "Alvy don't look too good."

Manny brought Alvy a drink, sighed, "Hey, I got a copy of Mike Avallone's *The Tall Delores*, Alvy. It's even signed by Avo himself. At least I think it's his scrawl. But I guess you've read that one."

Alvy nodded, "Yeah, long time ago. Read all the Avo. All except...." His eyes brightened. "You wouldn't have a copy of *Death of a .300 Hitter*, now would you?"

"His own-self bio? The one where he really opens up and spews a gut full? You kidding man! I wish! That old small press edition from 2020? Why that's scarce as hell, man! Some people don't even think it exists—like all those other rumored small press titles. I think it was because the print runs were so tiny. Only hundreds of copies printed instead of tens of thousands, or millions."

Manny just laughed. He had also heard it didn't exist, like all the other books said to have been published by that smallest of small presses out of Brooklyn, New York. Wherever Brooklyn had been.

Alvy sighed, the look in his eyes was sad to see.

Ryan said, "Rumor says only 500 copies printed, I'm sure even less sold. Rare as hens teeth, for sure!"

Fat Jack blurted, "I think I read somewhere there was this guy once on Earth that collected books long ago, and he said he had an actual rare 'unsigned' Avallone?"

A couple of the guys laughed. It was affectionate, however. They all knew about Avo—as he'd been called. He had lived a long life, and signed a lot of books for any of his loving fans with great pleasure. He was a good guy from the old days, from what they had all read about him. He'd signed so many books for his fans that it was said an actual unsigned Avo paperback might be rare. He was known as one of the kings of the paper-backs, having written hundreds of the things in the last half of LastCen.

Alvy ignored Fat Jack and turned back to Ryan.

"Look, Ryan, you're our source," Alvy said bluntly. "You got the connection. You gotta come through for us. I can't take it being dry like this no more! I'm going out next week and I just gotta have a new stack of paperbacks I've not read before to take out with me!"

Tommy Buffer, who was known by all as a block-headed fool, and probably the only miner on the entire planet who did *not* read mysteries and hard-boiled crime stuff said, "Come on, Alvy, why don't you just break down and read some science fiction?"

The moan of annoyance was loud and powerful.

It came from every voice but one. Tommy's own.

"Oh Christ!" Alvy barked, "No way!"

"Science fiction?" Manny laughed. "Are you like, kidding us?"

"Well then, what about fantasy fiction?" Tommy added, trying to be helpful. But being the direct opposite.

Ryan just shrugged, it was a real shame to see this. Tommy being serious and all about what he was saying, offering guys to read science fiction and, even...ah...fantasy fiction. Unfortunate, too. For him.

But Tommy Buffer was nothing if not persistent and he continued to try to convince Alvy. "Come on man, after all, science fiction is the literature of ideas."

Alvy did not appreciate any of it and just flipped Tommy off.

Tommy persisted prattling on about all the great ideas—never mentioning that every one of them had been proved so very wrong by present reality.

When he mentioned fantasy fiction, Alvy finally lost it.

"Give me a break, Tommy! Science fiction is a joke. Irrelevant with a capitol 'I'. But Fantasy? Are you serious? I know all about that crap. Elves, ogres, fairies and all that unreal shit!" Alvy shouted, annoyed for real now, pushing Tommy out of his way. "I don't have to stay here and listen to this. Be insulted like this. Who the hell would read that propaganda and garbage anyway? Sam Spade? Philip Marlowe? No way! Sure as hell not Mike Hammer? You hurt me, man, you really hurt me talking like that!"

Science fiction, fantasy and horror fiction of any kind, in any format did not go over well with the men on Mars. And even though it was a science fiction writer, the great Philip K. Dick himself, who foretold paperbacks would become future collectable artifacts in his classic novel, *Do Androids Dream Of Electric Sheep?*, that didn't change a damn thing. Anyway, most of the Marsmen felt Dick's book was actually a future crime novel. In fact, *Androids* had more in common with hard-boiled fiction and noir than science fiction anyway. So there! The same could be said for Alfred Bester's masterpiece, *The Demolished Man*, about a murder in a future society where all people were telepathic and there had not been a murder in 500 years!

Most of the guys felt what they called the Dick-head stuff was super good stuff. So was Bester. The problem with it was the men on Mars were now living in that future. It was a future all the old science fiction writers wrote so well about *but* had been so *wrong* about. They never dreamed it would come to pass the way it had. They'd had it all figured wrong. So science fiction was out now. It had become totally irrelevant—men on Mars considered it...*boring!*

Tommy Buffer left to go back to work alone. Despondent. Surly.

Nobody missed him.

Ryan finished his drink, bought a round, then got a call on his cell from Base.

It was from Buzz-Brain McConnell, he ran the supply depot. "Hey, Ryan? You there? Listen, the supply ship just got in. We're holding a big package for you. *From Earth!*

Alvy heard. He looked at Ryan carefully, anticipating, his eyes bright. His lips moist. He whispered, "Do you think it's the books, Ryan?"

"Yeah, Alvy, I think it might just be the books."

Well, that emptied the bar out right quick. Every miner and old hand followed Ryan down to the Base. Even Old Manny, hung up the "Closed- Gone Booking" sign over the window of *The Book Snook*. Overweight, even for Mars, he trudged behind, trying to keep up with the others.

"Remember, Ryan, I paid you last December. I have an option. I get first pick after you. I get any book I want, any book I can pick out, all for my own. My own personal book."

"After I pick my five!" Ryan told Manny reminding him of the full deal.

"Sure, Ryan," Manny said, defensive. "Sure, no problem.

You take yours, then I'll take mine. I'm not worried. I know I gotta get something good from that box. There's gotta be.... What? Twenty? Fifty books in that box?"

"I don't know, Manny," Ryan said, walking quickly. Anxious now also.

Usually there were just a hundred or so books, the freight being so expensive, but even that amount would be enough to bring a smile to Manny's fat old face. And Ryan's too. He'd sell or trade the stuff away for cash and food and if done wisely, it could keep him flush with cash or credit lasting him months.

"Think there'll be some more Ellroy? I like that guy's stuff. What about that Daniel Woodrell? I hear tell his *Give Us A Kiss* is just too incredible! What about James Crumley? That Terrill Lee Lankford with *Shooters*? He's *sooooo* good! Then there's that punk noir, *Dial 999* by the mysterious H. Raven, I hear that's a keeper! I still got a jones for Hal Masur's *Bury Me Deep*, his Scott Jordan is a hard-boiled lawyer better than Perry Mason ever was, or William P. McGivern's *Rogue Cop*—now that was harsh but true. I also hear that *Red Rain* by Michael Crow is good, and that his second, *The Bite*, may be even better. I hear rumors that Crow wrote a third also. Anyone know who he is? Was, I mean. I mean, didn't he write under a pseudonym? Stuff by any of these guys would fix my fix. Ed Gorman's Jack Dwyer books are tough through and through, highly recommended. What about some of those S. J. Rozan, Charlie Stella, or Ken Wishnia books?" Alvy said, babbling now, his eyes aglow and all wishful-like about books he'd never read and author's he'd only heard about. He had that glazed-eyes look, thinking, dreaming, mostly to himself. Each man was kind of immersed in his own thoughts and fantasies on that long hot walk to the depot.

Quietly Alvy added, "Hey, Ryan? Man, I sure hope there's something there for me. I still haven't found out what happened to Buzz Meeks after *The Big Nowhere*. Or maybe there'll be some of them Max Allan Collins' Quarrys or Nate Hellers I heard tell about? Those are supposed to be real kick-ass killers!

What about some of those cool Hardcase Crime retro paperbacks. Just when you think all the great stuff is long dead and gone a guy like that Charles Ardai—aka Charles Aleas—reissues them all and they live again. Amazing! Beautiful books! Do you know how many came out in that series? What do you think about them? I love 'em, man! You love 'em? I Just think they're the best! Shit, I'm babbling again. You think any of them will be in this batch?"

"Could be," Ryan said, smiling, but noncommittal. He had no idea what could be in the box sent to him from Earth. No idea what his brother may have found—gold or junk? Of course, Ryan was like everyone else on Mars just then, hoping to get his hands on some good stuff. Having a jones for that next great read. Especially books that no one had ever seen before, like *Box Nine*, *Concrete Blonde*, or even *The Black Echo*. He didn't even have author's names for these yet—but later found out that the first book was written by Jack O'Connell. The last two were by Michael Connelly and had actually been big bestsellers and early books in a long-running series of outstanding crime novels about Harry Bosch, LAPD cop, a problem maker and solver. A popular series when they came out in the 1990s and beyond, and just as popular here on Mars almost a hundred years later. Both those guys went on to write a lot of fine stuff.

"What about those Nameless books by Bill Pronzini? They're great! There were a lot of them, I hear, but I can't find them all, either," Fat Jack said with enthusiasm. "I liked that Nameless guy, kinda reminds me of when I worked the volcano mine on Olympus Mons with Jonny Scroggins. Them was sure good old wild days. We did a lot of reading in the off-hours."

"Bad old days to me, if you gotta know," Alvy interrupted, "Scroggins is long dead, and life ain't any easier for all our hard work. But you're right about some of them old books!"

"Yeah," Fat Jack said, dreamily. "It was great fun stuff. What do you think, Ryan?"

"I don't know, it was okay. I think a lot of these authors wrote great stuff, they're some of the best kept secrets in hard-boiled crime. In writing, generally."

Ryan walked on, a trail of miners following him. He was wondering what was in the box. The anticipation building and threatening to burst at any moment.

They reached Base Ten soon and entered the depot. By then Ryan had almost a thousand guys around him. Word had gotten out fast. A new shipment of books was in! They had followed him all through town like some damn parade lead by the Pied-piper.

Old Baxter Moneybags—no one knew his real name and no one much cared either—offered Ryan $100,000 OldDollars to buy the entire box and all its contents, straight-up, sight-unseen. Unopened, and uninspected, of course. He might have known something. He was a Wiley old coot. Ryan knew it was a great offer, but he kindly declined it. He couldn't accept. He just couldn't give up the books like that, sell them sight unseen, it would be like giving up his birthright.

The crowd cheered Ryan's decision. It meant they wouldn't be denied seeing what

was inside the box. And maybe...going home with a little something themselves?

Baxter next offered Ryan any ten paperbacks from his own personal collection. The good stuff. Baxter probably had the best private collection of Dashiell Hammett and Raymond Chandler paperbacks on Mars. He had genuine vintage era paperbacks like Avon digests and even a lot of the later Ballantine, Vintage and Dell reprints that were never seen on the open market these days. They went into a collection, they stayed in that collection. Never sold.

"The ten books can be your choice, Ryan," Baxter cooed softly, as soft as butter melting on hot toast. The crowd moaned in awe at the audacious offer and wondered what Ryan would decide.

Ryan wondered if he should take the offer. It was big. Maybe too big, but he just finally smiled and shook his head. He knew better, so he kept his thoughts to himself.

There was another gasp from the crowd as they realized that Ryan might actually be thinking of accepting the deal. Baxter had over two thousand of the best hard-boiled and mystery paperbacks on Mars. He even had digests for Christsakes! No one ever saw those anymore! He had near complete runs of all the Hammetts and Chandlers but he also had paperbacks by many classic writers from the Golden Era.

These included paperbacks of the Mike Hammer hard-hitting classics by Mickey Spillane; the poet of the lost David Goodis; the mysterious Cornell Woolrich (and his harder-edge alter ego pseudonym, William Irish); along with classic masters like John D. MacDonald; horror-crimester Richard Matheson; Howard Browne, who could almost out-Chandler and out-James M. Cain (those two masters) in his own fine works; Richard Prather, creator of cool and fun redhead private eye Shell Scott; Robert Bloch, of whom *Psycho* was just one of his many masterworks; books with the real nasty heroes of Charles Willeford; the hard-as-nails Joe Puma paperback originals by William Campbell Gault; Bruno Fischer's noir crime thrillers; Charles Williams' brilliant thrillers; the great Chester Himes and his wonderful Coffin Ed and Gravedigger Jones policers; Evan Hunter as Ed McBain and *his* 87th Precinct policers.... The list just went on and on.

Baxter even had a few rare 1950s British gangster digests by really obscure guys such as Ben Sarto, Grey Usher, Griff, Ace Capelli, and the amazing Hank Janson. All incredibly rare. He even had the rare 1951 Lion Book paperback edition of *The Cheat* by Don Tracy—one of the first books made into a great noir film *Criss-Cross*—"Nothing stopped her, not even a husband!" Baxter smiled, he also had the Lion paperback of *My Flesh is Sweet* by Day Keene—"a woman goes astray!"— which was also on the block for trade. He figured he had Ryan just where he wanted him. Then he dropped the kicker and told everyone he had a complete set of 1950s Falcon digests, even though no one ever said they had seen those. Those digests were locked away in a safety deposit box in MarsBank. The Falcon

Books series included Evan Hunter's hard-boiled drug book and first novel, *The Evil Sleep*. Baxter had the only known copy on Mars. Baxter's collection was just too good to be true. He also had *Honky Tonk Girl*, an incredible Jazz and murder noir by Charles Beckman, Jr. Men on Mars actually paid good money just to view Baxter's collection. His place was the nearest thing to a museum on the planet for the average guy. However, there were rumors that persisted of a vast secret library that even dwarfed his huge accumulation. Or so some men had heard tell. It was rumored to exist like the Resistance was rumored to exist. Ryan just smiled to himself and kept quiet about what he knew of that.

Baxter told Ryan he had complete runs of all the late age guys and gals. He had a complete run of thrillers by John Grisham, James Patterson and John Sandford. He even had some Bernard Cornwell crime thrillers. The old guy hoarded books by writers as diverse as Eugene Izzi, Joe Lansdale, Richard Lupoff, James Ellroy, Larry Block, Tom Boyle, Sue Grafton, Cindy Rosmus, James Lee Burke, Stan Trybulski, Ken Wishnia's Filo books, Bill Pronzini, James Crumley, William F. Nolan, Will Sanders, Allan Guthrie, C. J. Henderson's Jack Hagee books, Mike Black, Wayne Dundee.... The Lees Sisters—Arlette and Lonni... and the latter's incredible first novel from 2011, *Deranged*.

In a special alcove by one wall in his house he had his own favorites which included key and powerful works that had actually been signed by Jason Starr, Dennis Lehane, George Pelecanos, Victor Genschler, Max Allan Collins, and one of the greatest crime authors of all—Elmore Leonard.

Then there were runs of Agatha Christie, Craig Rice, Mignon G. Eberhart, Josephine Tey, Charlotte Armstrong, Ngaio Marsh, and Lisa Scottoline. His set of Patricia Cornwell, Kay Scarpetta novels was the best on the planet. He had hard-boiled, soft-boiled, and almost everything in between. He had a complete set of the Hardcase Crime books—1st and 2nd series!

His offer to Ryan was an incredible deal and full of wonderful possibilities.

But Ryan knew Baxter was a sharpie. The man wouldn't make such an offer unless he had a sure thing in the works and maybe knew something no one else knew about the books that had just come in.

Ryan just couldn't allow himself to accept Baxter's offer. He finally shook his head spouting a determined, "No. Sorry, I can't do it."

It killed Ryan to turn down that offer, but he knew that he had no real choice. You see, more than anyone else there, he wanted to open that box himself, to see what was inside himself. He wouldn't sell that right for any amount of cash or trade. No matter how much it might be.

A lot of guys in the crowd approved of his decision but not all.

Manny blurted, "You're crazy, Ryan! Baxter has Thompsons! Matheson, Goodis, Robert Blochs for Christsakes! Man, he's even got all the original Spillane paperbacks from the 1950s in them lovely wicked Signet paperback editions! I heard he's got one of the damn things even signed by 'The Mick' himself!"

There were a few 'ohs' and 'ahs' from the crowd. These days old paperbacks signed by the actual vintage era authors or cover artists were truly rare, and Spillane's work was looked at by some as the Holy Grail of hard-boiled-dom.

"Forget him, Ryan," Alvy said, dismissing Manny's words with a brush of his hand. "Take the box. It's yours. No matter what's in it, you can't pass it up. Especially sight unseen."

Ernie Cigarettes, smoking up the room shouted, "No way you can give it up sight unseen, Ryan. You know that. Not sight unseen."

Ryan knew Ernie and Alvy were right. He had to know what was in that box and he had to be the one to open it himself. It was his, after all.

When they brought the box over and called out Ryan's name he was dumbfounded. He never expected this. The box was huge! It looked more like an old style steamer trunk, and there was an awed gasp from the crowd around him too. Workers, old hands, miners, they'd never seen the likes before. They all kept up a steady stream of chatter interspersed by frenzied whispers of speculation about what wonderful paperbacks must be within that box just waiting to get out into their eager hands. It was a tense, exciting moment, if you were a reader. However, these guys weren't just readers, they were book *lovers*. They lived and breathed the old stories. A cache like this was a godsend to them, a dream come true, as exciting as digging up buried pirate treasure.

Ryan looked at Baxter and gave the old man a wry grin.

Baxter shrugged. He had tried, after all. He said, "Well, I suppose you're going to open it all by yourself."

Ryan nodded.

"Ryan?" Joe the Pro added, from behind the parcel cage, "Here it is. I got a hell of a big box here for you from Earthside."

Ryan stepped up, claimed it. Signed a slip for it. Marveled again at the size. Hefted the box, it was heavy. I mean *heavy!* He recognized the feeling. It was full of paperbacks! Stuffed to the edges!

Ryan spoke to the mass of men in the depot office, and to all those crowded outside in the street that could hear him, "You all tell me almost every day how Mars needs books! And you're right. We do need more books. Well, here they are!"

A cheer went up from the crowd.

"Open it!" a chant began.

"Open it, now!"

"Yeah, Now!"

"Yeah, I just can't stand it no more, Ryan. I just gotta see what's inside! Come on!"

"Any Spillanes in there? *I, the Jury, One Lonely Night*? Maybe, *Primal Spillane*? That last one contained some of his earliest work, cool stuff and it had Maguire cover art I've heard. You got one of them? Come on, let me see," someone shouted from the back of the room straining to see over the heads of the crowd.

"He didn't open it yet, moron!" someone else shouted back

to him.

"Oh, sorry. What about classic stuff from *Black Mask*, *Manhunt*, or even *Hardboiled*? Any of those crime digest magazines in there?"

"He don't know yet," another guy yelled out exasperated, "He told you, the box ain't opened yet!"

"Then open it!"

"Yeah, open it! Now!"

"Come on, Ryan! Open that damn box!"

"Yeah, stop stalling!"

Ryan nodded, carried the box over to a table near the window where everyone could see better. Faces were pressed against the glass looking in from outside as another crowd pressed in surrounding him by the table. He set the box down. For a moment Ryan, and seemingly every member of the Mars colony was silent, just staring at the box. Almost dumbfounded. Taking it in. Examining it from every angle. Savoring every detail. Thinking. Wondering. Dreaming. It was like a Christmas present for people who had never had Christmas, which of course had been disallowed and forbidden since before they were born by The Authority and The DOC.

There was no Christmas on Mars, no holidays of any type. Life was just too hard here, it demanded all your time, your total attention just to stay alive. Reading was the only solace, paperbacks the only portal into imagination. Reading these books was their form of entertainment, the doorway to their dreams and desires.

Alvy ran his hand over the box, touching it lightly. Almost lovingly. He said, "It feels like there's good stuff inside, Ryan. I can tell."

"I know, Alvy. You got a nose for books. A feel for books. I hear you. I feel the same thing."

Alvy looked at him and smiled. Ryan nodded. It was time.

Someone shouted from outside, "Come on now, open that damn box!"

Everyone laughed nervously, apprehensively.

Ryan took out his pocketknife. He gently pried off the lid. The box was an old style wooden crate. The lid came off with a loud screech as the nails holding it down so tightly now gave way ever so slowly.

Slowly. Slowly. *Screech, screech, screech!*

Finally, Ryan had the lid pried off. There was an audible sigh of anticipation from the crowd as it pressed ever more tightly around him. Each man aching to get that first glimpse at what lay within. What wonderful books might be seen on the top of the pile, the first time to be viewed by eager Marsman eyes?

Ryan removed all the foam packing material that seemed to fill up most of the crate. Then he pulled out a large block, wrapped in plastic, heavily taped with cardboard for added protection.

"The books!" someone whispered.

"It's them!" someone else echoed.

"Yeah!" another guy said in obvious awe. "Just look at them!"

Ryan nodded, it was an electrifying moment to these men. Of course, you couldn't see much the way the books had been wrapped, but that didn't stop anyone from commenting on what they *thought* they saw . Or what they *hoped* might be there.

Ryan set the large block down on the table in front of him as everyone crowded around. They stood silent watching him use his pocket knife as delicately as any surgeon to carefully take apart the block to get to the books wrapped within.

Ryan worked carefully. Fast but careful. All the time wondering about the contents of the package. It was a really big square block of books. Something that size could hold perhaps 240-350 paperbacks. His heart skipped a beat when he saw there were five copies of the rare and final hard copy 9th edition of *The Paperback Price Guide* from 2020. The last year when paperbacks, or books of any kind, had still been actually allowed by the government to be published in any hard copy format before the "going green" nonsense had taken a fanatic hold on the publishing world. That was so long ago, after the United States of America had broken up into the new Security

Districts, when The Authority took over and started making laws for *our* own good—as they told us constantly.

The news didn't stay quiet for long. Someone yelled out, "He's got a Guide!"

"2009?" someone barked his question.

"No, 2020!"

"Damn!" I think that was the last year for the Guide, a terrific book to have," someone else said.

Up to that time there had been no copy of this book at all on Mars. It was worth a king's ransom alone just for the hundreds of rare cover illustrations it displayed of books never seen before. It was estimated that 60% of the books listed in the guide, most not crime or even hard-boiled at all, did not even exist any longer. No copies were available at all for most of those ancient treasures. Thousands of different editions, of thousands of different books, were gone forever. Lost forever. It was tragic.

Ryan worked feverishly now. He saw something else. It was an illustration on the cover of one of the books. It showed what looked to be the face of an Earth government Storm Trooper, but in reality it was the face of a State Policeman in mirror shades from LastCen Earth. Ryan pulled away more of the wrapping and discovered what he had was a scarce Quill paperback edition of *The Killer Inside Me* by Jim Thompson. The book had been common LastCen, rumor said, but these days any copy was incredibly hard to find, even this later reprint from 1984. Surely an auspicious date, in and of itself.

"I see a copy of *Killer,*" someone said out loud.

"Not the Lion edition?" another asked hopefully.

"No way, man, you gotta be kidding about that! No, it's the Quill reprint." someone else replied. It turned out to be Ernie Cigarettes. He was smoking up a storm as he strained his eyes to see what Ryan was pulling out of the package.

Most of these guys knew about the rare paperback original of Jim Thompson's *The Killer Inside Me* from Lion Books in the 1950s. It was never seen these days. It was only rumored to exist so that's why this later copy was still a good find.

"It's the later Quill edition. It's a scarce and very collectible LastCen reprint," Ernie added, in his best Mr. Know-it-all tone.

"Well, it's a good start."

"What else you got?"

The excitement of opening the package was evident to Ryan and surged through the crowd as well. It was like opening the biggest and the best present during the biggest and best Christmas. Or that's what it must have been like. It was always the same feeling every time Ryan got a shipment of books and opened it but this time the size of the block of books had everyone transfixed. It was wonder, awe, wild mystery all rolled up in one huge box filled with the treasures of the unknown. It was glorious.

Finally Ryan got more of the packing off and pulled out more books. He was pulling them out three and four at a time now. Then carefully piling them high all around him on the table forming a wall. There were gasps and mutterings from the crowd, faces pressed to the glass in front of him, jostling, grunts, groans, then applause as men tried to read author names and titles from the colorful spines.

There turned out to be over three hundred wonderful old paperback books, and they seemed to span all eras of LastCen. They began from the incredibly ancient Eisenhower and Ozzie & Harriet era of the 1950s—all rare stuff today more than 100 years later. There were 1960s spy books, even a rare 0008 Clyde Allison spoof porno spy novel. That would be a keeper, Ryan noted, putting it in his pocket before anyone saw it. He had heard these were great fun and excellent reads. They were sexy James Bond spoofs. Then there were some actual James Bond books themselves by Ian Fleming. And better yet, some incredibly hard-boiled early Gold Medal paperbacks by Donald Hamilton. The first one in his Matt Helm series was there, *Death of A Citizen*, and it was a masterpiece of intense tough-guy writing. He also saw a *Man from U.N.C.L.E.* old-time TV tie-in paperback, again by the prolific Mike Avallone. It was the first book in that series. There were even some Ted Marks! These last were also wonderful spy spoofs featuring the Man From Orgy. Sex mixed with spying and satire by a master Cold War author and raconteur. Ted Marks, who was actually Ted Gottfried, who also wrote lesbian novels as Leslie Behan! Get it?

There was a good smattering of what was known as urban horror, righteous revenge, vigilante books, all authentic 1970s LastCen male-oriented action and adventure stuff. These included heroes like The Executioner, The Destroyer, The Butcher, and a couple of rare Lone Wolf books by a guy named Mike Barry. He was actually some long-ago and forgotten science fiction writer, but this stuff was hard-boiled murder and mayhem; and as such right up their alley. Wonderful fun. The Marsmen cut the author some slack because of his science fictional meandering's under his true name and forgave him those sins. They were not so forgiving of most other work in the science fiction genre.

There were even some militaristic novels from the 1980s, popular during what had been called the Reagan Era. The history texts were blank on this leader. So much had been erased, but it appears there had been a great American president named Ronald Reagan once. He had been an icon of honor and integrity, a leader of virtue and honesty. He was responsible for the collapse of the hated old Soviet Union "Evil Empire" and the fall of the international communist totalitarian empire that it supported. The DOC naturally hated him, its hierarchy despised everything Reagan stood for and did all it could to discredit him and his many achievements. Finally they had all but erased him from collective memory, he had been totally erased from the digital memory, but his legend still lived among the people in whispers. Reagan was even mentioned in some of the old anti-commie Cold War paperbacks from the 1980s. America had changed and was long gone, but Ronald Reagan was not forgotten. He would never be forgotten. He was remembered with reverence and love, like the legends of King Arthur, Robin Hood, or even George Washington himself.

The contents of the box also contained some of the great last-gasp of hard-boiled stuff from the 1990s and the turn of the century up to 2020. Works by the best of those sometimes known as the Last Wave noir writers. It was all hard crime, violence and sex but with good stories and excellent characters. There was even some small press stuff, from a time when small press outfits had actually been allowed to publish independently. These small outfits sprung up like mushrooms, glowed brightly, then too-often quickly expired. In the meantime these crazy individuals, partnerships, dedicated groups and collectives published the books they loved. They published them just because they loved good books. What a concept! What a time to have been a writer, a reader, a collector or book lover!

In the end, hard-boiled fiction had made a whopping comeback at the end of the Millennium. Later some writers for the small crime magazines even made it big with books that eventually became bestsellers. Some had been made into "films." Of course, even that was all old stuff these days. Obsolete, but sometimes actually antique-cool. They didn't actually make "films" anymore. Hollywood was long gone. The area in Los Angeles where all the movie studios had once been, had received a small tactical nuke in 2015 from Muslim fascists even as the stars who once lived there were holding a fund-raiser to promote peaceful understanding and dialog with jihadists. Go figure!

Today the new technology of the present century was all computer-generated and designed, few actual humans had any input in it any longer. And government during this PC, or Present Century, had become the ruler of everyone and everything.

Or, so the people were told, and so the people believed.

Mars was different. Here men read paperbacks for entertainment. They even collected them. That older stuff seemed to have been written just for them. It was gut-wrenching, tough-guy or gal crime and private eye stuff, rugged individualistic hard-boiled fiction. Stories about guys like the guys who had conquered, colonized, and now lived on Mars. Stories about guys like each and every one of them!

Meanwhile, reading kept them all sane and free and away from the corrupted digital record. All the subliminal Earth programs that could influence or control your mind and life had no effect on them. Paperbacks helped keep these men free from infection and control. Or so they had been programmed to believe so many years ago, before they had ever come out to Mars, and so they believed now.

No one would have ever thought that Mars could turn out the way it had. Ryan sure wouldn't have believed any of it, even though he was one of the chief reasons for it. It all seemed so strange to him as he lay the books gently out on the large table before the pushing, excited throng of men. He put down one book at a time, letting everyone get a gander at the cover so they could all see just what had come in. Each would soon be available for sale or trade. The men drooled as they looked at the covers, anticipating, making deals, dreaming dreams.

They looked like a crew of hungry scavengers, semi-starving, lusting frontier rascals. Which is what they actually were. Eyes glazed with book-lust. A special kind of lust all its own and known only to serious readers and collectors. All kinds of talk was brewing about important points like value, condition, cover art, and of course, the wonderful stories between those covers. Especially the stories. For they all actually read all these damn old books. They lived them too. They were serious men. A little crazy. Well, maybe *more* than just a little crazy. Nevertheless, they were serious about the books. And they knew what they liked and they knew what they wanted.

Ryan knew that was all true. It was good too. Out here there was absolutely no trust of the Earth government. Or Earth culture. But there was no way to get the government out of your life, your thoughts, your very mind! Unless you left the planet and went out to one of the hellhole mining colonies. It was dangerous. It was full of terrible hardships. It was also the only way for Earthers who still had their own mind, their own thoughts, and their own dreams, to live their life on their own terms and be left alone.

The Earth government slogans were all so friendly, so patronizing, so elitist so "for-your-own-good" and so big-brotherish. So politically correct. They said the reason why they did things was, "For everyone—for their own good." The very words sickened the tough, staunchly individualistic Mars miners and pioneers. They had left a world they'd grown to despise—to come to an inhospitable world that seemed to despise them. And yet, Mars had not taken away their humanity, nor their freedom of thought, like Earth had. The government here wasn't against them like it was on Earth. In fact, there was very little, if any, real government on Mars at all. Which was just fine and dandy with everyone.

Furthermore, the miners of Mars hated and feared the way holograms and neural implants used by Earth pop-culture melded and imbedded themselves deep into the mind of the user. It caused total subconscious submission of the mind, control of a person's thoughts. The blatantly biased news, the government- propaganda media, the PC philosophy of outright lies all done "for your own good," the subtle subtexts for obedience and complacency infiltrated into every part of life on Earth. Secret messages and subliminal suggestions for kids in their toys and games told them to inform on their parents, teachers, siblings and friends. After all, it was once again "for their own good." In truth, the media and pop culture on Earth had been secretly manipulated and subconsciously designed for decades to attain and maintain control of each person's mind, thoughts and desires. The Authority controlled everything. And the people didn't even understand the difference anymore. Those that did, didn't say one word about it. Mind erasure could "cure" all those ills and if not....

If not—death could "cure" them permanently.

Earth had turned into a planet of sheep controlled by a police state.

"Never question authority" was one message publicly stressed with pride and expensive ad campaigns. It was advocated with a heavy-handed, almost religious zeal. In the old era of PC— which LastCen had stood for 'politically correct' but now stood for "present century" the terms seemed to have become indistinguishable to all Citizens. Everything was digital. There were no books. No tamper-free, revisionist-free information-secure storage devices existed. Everything was open to revision, change, and to tampering by the Authority and the DOC. And everything was changed. On a daily basis. Old truth was written out, while newer truth written in. Always different, sometimes totally opposite. Heroes were written out, or became instant villains. Most of these "persons" never actually existed in the first place, except in some holo image or implant. Nothing is ever what it once had been, or what it was remembered as being.

And the books, all those wonderful, glorious old paperbacks; those colorful, sexy, hard copy packages were all outlawed, but they were still sought after by some. Carefully. The books themselves, as physical objects, were special things. So cool, each with their own individual design, publisher, logo, cover art, author, politics, style. Each had their own special look! They really stood out. They even had their own unique feel and smell. The glue, the paper, were even individualistic. They were not just some cold plastic disk or chip; paperbacks were like a personal letter to you from another human being. Something personal from another person just like you. For *you*. The miners understand that, but they didn't think about it much. They just loved reading, and they loved reading the old paperbacks.

Ryan's memories gave him inklings that he had been responsible for some of this over twenty years ago. Since he'd come out to Mars he'd been a reader, collector, book trader. At least that's what his most intimate memories told him and he had no reason to doubt them. Not yet. Though he was suspicious, for sure. He could remember how little by little over so many years, he'd got that whole damn planet-full of ornery miners and hard-headed rascals reading the stuff too. As it turned out, surprisingly to him, it wasn't that hard to do at all, once he showed the books to them they all loved the old paperbacks as much as he did.

He could never really figure it out. Maybe it was because of all that hard-boiled reality and tough-guy attitude. It really spoke to the men. Ryan even briefly entertained a passing thought that perhaps the entire planet of men had been implanted to read and collect these old paperbacks? Surely one of the strangest notions he'd ever had. Silly really and so totally unrealistic an idea that he had dropped the thought immediately. Still and all, he wondered. There was a certain book he remembered having read a long time ago. It was not hard-boiled at all, in fact it *was* science fiction. It was something about paperbacks and Mars, but he couldn't remember it clearly now, it seemed so far in the past, in another life really. Maybe another persona? He just didn't know for sure.

Anyway, paperbacks and Mars just seemed to go together to Ryan's way of thinking. Ryan couldn't even ponder the "why" of it. He did not know why it all worked so well either. It just worked here on Mars. For whatever reason. Meanwhile, everyone on Earth thought the men on Mars were crazy and a bunch of freaks and troublemakers. And maybe they were. They kind of had to be, didn't they? To leave Earth and accept all the danger out here? Most Earthers thought anyone leaving the home world to come way out to Mars of all places, just had to be crazy. That was putting it diplomatically, of course. Then again, the "crazy" men on Mars weren't murdering each other wholesale like the so very "sane" and "free" men were doing down on Earth every single day. Every single minute.

Ryan sighed. Too many thoughts lay heavy upon him and he tried to brush them all aside as he laid out the books on the table. He counted them. There were 348 of them. Five of them were price guides from 2020. All the books were in good shape, and man did they look and feel beautiful! Garish covers, bright colors, beautiful sexy women, stalwart male heroes. Wonderful images of a happier and freer long-lost twentieth-century America blasting their way into the eyes of the lucky beholder.

The five price guides Ryan would put up for auction next month. Marsport had a monthly collectable books auction broadcast over the POD. They might just bring him enough cash or credit to get him to early retirement. Those books were like gold on Mars. Actual hard copy reference books full of bibliographic information, were never published anymore. These were crucial and valuable. Ryan would hold the auction next month because he wanted to give all the miners and farmers out in the fringes time to get in their messages and bids. That'd mean more bidders, higher prices realized. That would also mean he wouldn't get bush whacked by some lone crazy collector all upset that no one had told him about the auction. Kinda silly, but Marsmen were serious about their paperbacks. Things could turn deadly sometimes.

Ryan remembered the story about Jack the Whack. He found himself whacked just last year for holding out on returning stolen goods to the rightful owner. The stolen goods had been an impossible-to-obtain, rare set of Coffin Ed and Gravedigger Jones crime novels written by Chester Himes. The Marsport judge ruled the killing justifiable homicide, and then he promptly borrowed a copy of *Cotton Comes to Harlem* from the owner to read as part of the Court's compensation in its decision on the case.

Ryan had the 348 paperbacks laid out on the table so everyone could see them. It was an impressive display. All covers were face up. They included a variety of items: two Bill Crider Sheriff Dan Rhodes novels, a John Eagle Expediter novel and the first book in the notorious and violent Butcher series. Both of these latter books also written under pseudonym by the prolific Mike Avallone. These were paperback originals (PBO's) from Pinnacle Books, from old-time USA, way back in the glorious 1970s. They were almost 100 years old now and still looked unread. Their original cover price had been just seventy-five cents! That would change soon out here. There were even more crime paperbacks from the 1990s up to about 2020 when paperbacks (as well as all manner of books in hard copy) had finally gone the way of the Dodo through government edict.

"Come on guys, give me some breathing room here, will you!

You're acting like a bunch of bloody lunatics," Ryan shouted to the crowd.

"Hey, Ryan! I ain't never even been to Luna, so don't go callin' me no lunatic!" a short guy with red hair named Komanski shouted back.

Marsmen might be a touch crazy, but the people on Luna, known as the Lunatics, in some cases had become *actual* lunatics. They were just plain screwed up and dangerous. A few had even become cannibals, for starters, secret members of a bizarre sect called The Last Ones. That didn't help their image much. So to be called a lunatic on Mars was a heady insult. It could even result in a duel.

Komanski and everyone forgot about all that however, once their eyes fell on a copy of *Devil in a Blue Dress* by Walter Mosley. That was Mosley's first kick-ass crime novel. There was also a copy of another Mosley title, an even harder crime book called *Fearless Jones*. He also saw the haunting Jack Ketchum crime thriller, *The Girl Next Door*, based on a true crime case as monstrous as anything real life could throw at a young girl. He also pulled out the three scarce Hardy crime novels, Popular Library paperback originals from the mid-1970s by Martin Meyers. Each of the three old paperbacks had cool Walter Popp cover art. These were never seen these days and were very underrated reads. Good stuff. The big redhead looked back to Ryan dolefully. It was evident he wanted those books very much.

Ryan said, "Sorry, Komanski, sorry guys. Just give me a bit of room and I'll start to parcel these out to you very patient and long-deserving readers."

There was a loud cheer.

Alvy laughed and said, "And don't forget us serious collectors and scholars of the mores, values, and social systems of the late American twentieth century on Earth."

"Ah, yeah, certainly. Damn Alvy, we got scholars and bibliophiles here now!" Ryan said with a laugh.

"Oh, shut up, Alvy," someone barked to a general chorus of

more laughter.

Alvy smiled. It was always like that when Ryan got a shipment of paperbacks. It always drew in the hard cases and old coots that hadn't seen another human being face to face in months. Some, even for years. And most of them liked it that way just fine. Others wouldn't speak more than a dozen words a month while working—but when it came to the books and the stories within them, they became damn chatter boxes. Then it could be impossible to get them to shut the hell up. Mars was rough on men. It hurt them. Serious hurt. It was hard on their bodies but worse on their minds and spirit. Unrelenting. Like the stories of the old American West. Far worse, though. Too many of these men had been hurt much worse when they'd lived back on Earth. Emotional cripples, social misfits, loners and paranoids that extended the meaning of the word "individualist" to sometimes foolish, if not insane, excess. There were political theorists of all kinds, capitalists, free traders, entrepreneurs, right-wingers, Trotskyites, old-time commies, with loads of nihilists, anarchists, socialists, libertines and bohemians. Also just a lot of people who just did not trust anyone or *anydamnthing*.... They were often cranky, sometimes religious, gun-toting as could be, generally anti-crime, pro-drink and anti-drug. Too many were fools, knaves, cretins, hardheads, and hard cases. Some were even glorious madmen. They were all readers. Readers, thinkers and dreamers, to a man. Mostly they dreamed about being free and staying free. Mostly they read the old paperbacks to remember what freedom had once been like. The life of freedom, the feel of freedom, the very taste of it.

Alvy smiled, it was always like that on Mars. A glorious family of misfits, but a true kind of family, nonetheless. Survival dictated the terms. Paperbacks and their hard-boiled, tough, individual, violent, truthful words made it all understandable. They made Mars a bit easier to deal with.

Alvy and Old Manny were the first ones in line. They stood fidgety and anxious. They presented their chits to Ryan. Alvy picked up the copy of *Box Nine* by Joe O'Connell, a first paperback printing of this fine tough female private eye novel from the early 1990s. Dark noir in a made-up town a hell's drive south of Boston. Whatever "Boston" had been.

Old Manny walked away on a cloud with a rare copy of Chester Himes' *The Real Cool Killers*—Coffin Ed and Gravedigger's best and most brutal adventure. Two tough African-American or Black detectives plugging away in an ancient ghetto called Harlem. The book had them fighting the bad guys as well as their own bosses. White bosses. Sometimes back then, the worse guys could be other cops. Himes' two cops were some of the best of the best. Rough stuff but so true for its time, delving deep and hard into the dark racial mood of the era. Most Marsmen couldn't believe that color had even been an issue once on Earth long ago but apparently it had been. Sometimes. Sometimes too often. Paperbacks with Black heroes by Gar Anthony Haywood and Gary Phillips were popular with readers. Older books dealing with race and crime by Iceberg Slim, Odie Hawkins and Donald Goines were also much sought after, but those old Holloway House paperbacks were just so damn scarce.

Little by little the paperbacks were parceled out. Trades were made. Ryan took the five Paperback Price Guides and did a quick grab of an ancient 1950s Pocket Book edition of *Rogue Cop* by William P. McGivern. That guy was so underrated. Then there was the B. Traven novel, *The Treasure of Sierra Madre*, so cool, so good Bogart made the film of it. And all the great James M. Cain noirs—that man understood noir and femme fatales in classic novels like *The Postman Always Rings Twice*, *Double Indemnity*, and even with *Mildred Pierce*. Ryan also grabbed up a set of Hank Janson crime novels written apparently, by old Hank himself, said to be a tough Yankee newspaper reporter whose cases took place in the post-World War II era. In reality the series had been started by a UK lefty author name of Stephen D. Frances, who actually self-published the first rare books in the series—in, of course—paperback. Simply amazing! Ryan looked over these carefully. They were British, and old, but they had some of the best sexy bad-girl covers anyone had ever seen, all by a guy named Reginald Heade. These were, of course, the later UK Telos Books reprints from far back around 2004. No one had ever seen any of the original 1950s British Hank Janson paperbacks these had been reprinted from, but the introductions by a guy named Steve Holland explained it all. These were even rare. These books would sure be treasured here on Mars. Ryan could already see guys dying to get their grubby fingers on these as soon as they came within reach.

"Come on guys! Move back! Give me some breathing room!" Ryan barked, then smiled to himself. They gave him a few more precious inches of space now. "These old paperbacks are waiting—hard-hitting, hard-boiled masterpieces of murder and mayhem from the past. You guy's ready?"

"Yeah, Ryan! That's good to hear!" Ernie Cigarettes chanted. "So good to hear!"

Ah, Ryan thought, true pulp fiction!

Then Ryan saw it! The book he'd wanted for so long. It had been on his "want list" since he'd come out to Mars. At first he wasn't sure what the title might mean, it proclaimed it all so boldly in black print on the cover. Then he knew. *One Lonely Night* by Mickey Spillane! Hard-boiled private eye Mike Hammer fights a cabal of deadly and devious communist spies and undercover agents in the Old America of the 1950s United States. Over one hundred years ago! The book that got Spillane hated by the Left of his era because he dared have his hero enter the fight against the evils of Soviet imperialistic Communism. Reagan's "Evil Empire" incarnate! More importantly these days, the book was still very much forbidden because it chronicled Mike Hammer's personal fight against agents of what was looked at as an earlier manifestation of a worldwide "totalitarian authority." That rang too close to the truth of the present-day worldwide governmental Authority, which was as totalitarian as could be. The result was obvious. The book had been banned for almost a hundred years.

This one book epitomized the struggle that Ryan and all Marsmen were fighting today against the Department of

Control and the Earth Authority. It was hard, stark poetry by a master craftsman of pulp action from a past age singing out boldly to free men everywhere. It was even more valid today, here on Mars. It was a gorgeous old Signet paperback edition in the rare first printing, with cover art by Lou Kimmel showing Hammer tied up and menaced by a gorgeous bad-girl femme fatale with a gun. She was luscious but deadly. It was a reversal of most cover art images of those old times. Here the girl had the masculine hero tied and helpless. Usually on the covers it was the other way around. Ryan quickly stuffed it in his pocket without saying a word to anyone. He'd sneak away tonight and try to read a few pages.

It just didn't get any better than looking through all those old paperbacks. The guys back then really knew how to write, they knew how to tell a story full of action and meaning. No, they weren't great literary stylists, they never said they were. For the most part they never tried to be either. They were pulp writers, telling a pulp story of action and adventure—and often deeper meaning. But they knew how to do that with perfection. They did it so well, that sometimes it even approached art. The old paperbacks oozed pain and hardship and the heroes in them spoke the truth as they had lived it back then, today spoken to a future that had lost all hope and truth decades past.

CHAPTER TEN
MARS NEEDS WOMEN!

When Ryan got home to his place he took out the copy of *One Lonely Night*, and as he did with each copy of any Spillane book sent to him from his brother on Earth, he turned to page one hundred, and delicately extracted the tiny microdot. It was all so very low tech, so entirely obsolete, but still effective. The kind of thing the enemy would think much too old hat to be of use any longer. Ryan set the dot down on a slide, then put the slide under the microscope and took a look.

Now Ryan smiled. It seemed his brother was on the ball. As usual. This was invaluable information to the Resistance. On the face of it, it was just a list of the new pioneers, settlers, émigrés, sent out to Mars from Earth. However, it also told which of these new émigrés were spies and paid agents, informers, sleeper cells, assassins. Who was working for what Earth government department or agency. Which secret police, espionage outfit, organized crime cartel, underground cult, or various political groups of every stripe they were affiliated with. All men that Mars did not need. Men that Earth kept on sending out to Mars nevertheless. Men who could now be watched once they got here. Men who would discover they had no input to the system here either.

Some of these men would have sudden and very fatal accidents after they got here. Hey, Mars was a dangerous place! The accident rate could be high, sometimes. Others were guys who would just disappear. It happened, men often were detailed to work in remote areas that caused them to lose touch with Earth once they got out here. These men who would be Earth's eyes and ears on Mars—spies—were now known before they even got here. They would immediately be confounded and controlled from the minute they landed. Of course, their holo image would always dutifully send back a report in their name created by the Resistance. A report full of phony, misleading, useless information. There would be enough lies, distortions, garbage, and dangerous disinformation to make even an old-time Soviet *apparatchik* gag in dry-heave disgust.

Ryan knew the main thing though, was the names on that list. It wasn't the usual list of men only. Though gender specific names had not been in vogue since LastCen, there were still enough first names listed to indicate that most, if not all, the new émigrés had to be *female!* That was unheard of! It was glorious, yet Ryan was immediately suspicious. It appeared the men on Mars were getting something that they had wanted for decades. Not only books, but women!

Mars was getting women!

Mars needed women!

Ryan could hardly hold back his joy, his sheer delight and whooped aloud, knowing how happy the men would be when they heard the news.

Then he saw the last name on the list.

He immediately froze with fear and a sense of dark doom overtook him.

The name was listed in a special amendment. It said that one of the new émigrés could be this person. It was the one name he never wanted to see again.

It was a name that could not be compromised or controlled by the Resistance like any of the others.

It was someone who could never, ever have an "accident," be bought, or turned over.

It was someone on a mission no Earth agent had ever had the guts or desire to go on.

Ryan realized that it was *her!*

It had to be!

She had actually come out to Mars!

A cold chill took control of him. Why? Why was she of all people coming out here?

Obviously to see things for herself.

That was not good. Not good at all. It placed them all at terrible risk. It placed everything at risk. All his plans....

It placed hope itself at risk.

Ryan felt a cold chill roam throughout his body. A deep chill that went right into his bones and froze him into stillness. His eyes looked at the name on the bottom of the list once again.

It had not gone away. He had hoped the name would just disappear. Like an illusion. Like it had not really been there at all and he'd only imagined it.

It had not.

It was still there.

The name taunted him with fear.

It was the name, Arabella Rashid.

It was her.

Herself.

The Supreme Director, of the Department of Control and the most dangerous and deadly person that there ever was.

Arabella Rashid was The DOC's most effective and most vicious leader. She was responsible for extending the powers of The DOC to heretofore unexpected and unexcelled lengths and into many non-traditional areas.

"Tightening the noose" the men on Mars called it. And most shivered involuntarily as they thought of the bestial organization they'd thought they'd left behind them on Earth. Paramount in its activity was media control, mind and thought manipulation, truth re-interpretation—as they called it. Re-education of social and political misfits—all for their own good, you understand. Tyranny with a smiley face—which could get as steel hard and deadly as it needed to be very fast. All to extend tighter control of every citizen

Under her leadership, the DOC rewrote, or revised everything on the digital record. It had all been changed. It was all suspect now. Memory and history under the DOC had become the least truthful, the least knowable of events. Truth did not exist any longer. Freedom was forgotten and had dissolved.

She was the hand behind it all.

Ryan tried to reconfigure his thoughts on the matter. It was not good that she, of all people, had come out here. She'd come out to Mars, of all places! What the hell did she want? What the hell was she after? An historical analogy to the situation entered his thoughts. It was tantamount to the Spanish Inquisition coming to the New World in the 1500s back on Old Earth. Evil entering the Garden. Ryan shuddered at that thought. He knew what that meant, and what it could mean to the men of Mars who were his friends and brothers.

Ryan looked over the list his brother had sent him. There was a coded asterisk at the bottom indicating that all the names were female.

Women had finally come to Mars!

It was a wonderful, glorious event. Ryan, and every man on Mars had waited so long for this day. Earth government had held back for decades on sending women, the reason supposedly being that it was for safety concerns. *Bullshit!* As if women were too delicate to go to Mars! What utter rot! The real reason was that Earth knew that with women, what naturally followed was children. Then a sense of community, a sense of society, perhaps even a sense of "country"? Something the Earth government—and The DOC—definitely did not want to see begin on Mars.

Or did they?

Why the drastic change now?

And why now, Arabella Rashid?

Earth had never wanted the Marsmen to be too independent. Oh, it was kind of all right for them to be a bit on the kooky side, in their own funny male-pioneer-type way. However by Earth holding back on women, they also were able to hold back on the sons and daughters that would have normally come from these men. Mars would remain barren in more ways than one. Thus Earth could control their future, in the ways that mattered. It had worked successfully for many decades.

The Resistance had understood this since the beginning also. Ryan and his associates; his agents and fellow travelers, on Mars and on Earth, had done all they could to make sure every impression Earth received of Mars was of an inhospitable pioneer world full of crazy men who were fanatically loyal to Earth. Men who wanted more than anything else to recant the terrible mistake of their immigration here and return home to the loving and beloved bosom offered to all by the blissful Mother Earth government. Then they could once again enjoy the blessings of a benevolent paternalistic system that truly cared for them—and told them all what to do.

Of course, nothing could be farther from the truth.

The cover-up of what was really happening on Mars had been a difficult accomplishment at first. The tricking of Earth's agents, the false reports, misleading and planted news items, all the phony programs. Then there were thousands of bogus emails and phone calls sent back to Earth relatives and hard-copy letters and photos sent in returning supply ships all full of lies and propaganda. There was an entire office in Marsport that did nothing but do all this 24/7. The Mars Resistance knew The DOC and its agents and co-lateral investigative agencies could not fail to monitor and study this data. The bottom line was that Earth was fed the greatest line of pure, unadulterated bullshit the Universe had ever seen. It was wonderful, consistent and cunningly done, and it made perfect sense. So the Earth masters believed all was going according to *their* plan—when in fact *nothing* at all was going according to their plan!

Nothing was safe or secret on Earth anymore. There was no such thing as privacy. Certainly not where Earth was concerned. Even residential view screens in the private homes of citizens had the power to enable special watchers to look in on the people watching the screen. But who was watching the watchers?

The DOC! They watched all.

The DOC heralded it as a great breakthrough in humankind. They called it *Thinking Made Easy.* The worldwide government held "Thinking Made Easy" events and offered free software. Everyone who was anyone, plugged into it and joined the fun.

Now it seemed that Earth was changing the game.

Ryan wondered, had the plan by the Resistance worked? Perhaps it had worked too well? Or been found out? So many years of hard work, so much effort and expense to mislead Earth about the richness and beauty of Mars. This wonderful elaborate plot, all done to cover up the fact that Mars was a place where men could live free. A place where self-sufficiency—the lack of need for anyone, anything, and especially some Earther big-brother, know-it-all government Authority—shone forth. A place where the absence of, "we're doing it for your own good" by government, made them truly free.

Earth people said they loved freedom—but they hated freedom.

The Authority on Earth always stressed "cooperation," however their definition of cooperation was obedience while their true aim was dependency.

Mars saw self-sufficiency as the antidote, and saw it as a human right. It was the only true road to freedom for the individual in this bleak world that had become their future.

Obviously, there was a serious difference of opinion.

Tyrants always desire to be needed. Tyrants *need* to be needed. If you do not need them, they'll kill you, or have you killed, or create your need for them. Ryan and Mars had played a very tricky game. He just wondered if the cat was out of the bag now?

Ryan also knew if a society is lucky enough not to need a tyrant and able to remain free of a tyrant's grasping clutches, there will still always be tyrants in-waiting. A Tyrant will be there in whatever guise, laying in wait, ready to lay claim to you as his own. It was important for each man on Mars to stand on his own two feet—as a free man—with a free mind and his own ideas. The tyrant Earth government did not want that. Under the tyrant's thumb you become controlled. Eventually, you become only...property!

After time, property with little or no value.

Ryan knew this truth.

* * * * * * *

Now Ryan's mind suddenly jumped back in time, thinking about the old days. The real old days! He remembered when he'd been a kid in what had been called Old America. The United States of America. It was strange to him that his memories went back that far. Was that part of the programming too? It was all so far away, a long-ago dream. He and his brother alone, and hunted, after their father had been killed. That had been in the old Rebellion. Their father hadn't been anyone important. A part-time soldier, some called him sunshine patriot, others Minuteman. It did not matter. He was one of the fighters who showed up in 2025 to try and take Chicago and make it a free city after the meltdown. He was one of the dead afterwards. Body unidentifiable, except by his two sons, who afterwards thoroughly burned the corpse with gasoline in a vain hope the government goon squads would not be able to identify the dead rebels via DNA and then go after their families to exterminate what they termed a pestilence. The wives and children and his own wife, Cathy. At this point in time The DOC was using systematic rape, murder, and torture to squeeze information out of people. All preparatory to the genocide of social and political undesirables and chronic troublemakers. Old time Republicans were hunted down and exterminated. Democrats were next, if they didn't see the light properly and embrace full governmental control. Boy were they shocked! Then the Atheists, Christians, Jews, Muslims, even Agnostics. Anyone who could conceivably oppose anything, for any reason. It didn't matter what it might be. After a while there seemed no reason for any of it. It was just sheer, brutal terror. All they succeeded in squeezing out of people was fear and hatred. And rage.

The rage seemed to ensure there would be a time of comeuppance and revenge, "Someday.... Some-damn-day...!"

* * * * * * *

Ryan's thoughts were back on Mars now. His mind time-tripping back to the present. Those old memories were strange, alien to him. Were they even his own? Were they implanted? He could not be sure about any of it. Now he was an adult again, looking over the list of names his brother had smuggled out to him.

The names were all women!

It was almost too good to be true. Even with obvious subversive agents, troublemakers, paid informers, sleeper spies, terrorists, traitors—and even with Arabella Rashid traveling to Mars under another name, it was still wonderful. It was all so scary but wonderful.

Ryan's brother, who went by the name of Michael, hadn't been clear on that aspect of the situation. It made Ryan wonder if Arabella Rashid was actually one of the women on the list of names he saw printed on the microdot. If so, she lay hidden there among the dozens of names of women who had waited, some for years, to come out to Mars to meet a man and begin a new life.

CHAPTER ELEVEN
SIMON'S REVENGE

As the years passed she began to suspect that Simon, even in death, was still manipulating her mind. The very thought terrified her.

Arabella Rashid feared Simon had played with her deepest thoughts and innermost desires just as he had manipulated everything else in the world. She tried to deny it all, rationalize it away—after all Simon was long dead—but it caused her untold panic and utter terror. Had her memories been tampered with? Changed? Had her personality and thoughts been rearranged? The DOC had the power and technology to do that easily, surely, and Simon had done it to everyone who worked under him. That included the clones and all his subordinates.

Had Simon done it to her too?

Arabella Rashid vainly tried to wipe away the sweat of panic that drenched her in cold fear. Knowing Simon, she realized it was not only possible, it was probable.

She tried to remember the man who had helped her dispose of Simon's body so long ago. Had it been Ryan? Funny how she could barely recall his image now. It had been twenty years since she had murdered Simon and begun her own phase of his Janus Project—but something had gone terribly wrong with her plan.

She looked over the reports and the messages sent by various DOC field agents and spies. A pattern was emerging. She correlated them with her own private records. These had been sealed long ago and were Top Secret. It seemed to be some type of diary. Perhaps letters to herself to be read in the future? Something to warn her, or remind her?

But of what?

She was not foolish enough to believe that all things would stay the same, move perfectly according to plan, or that she would have the same plans and desires as a woman in her thirties today. The Supreme Director of the hated and feared DOC, had begun as just a twig of a girl of thirteen when she'd taken Simon's life and all his power.

Now she realized something had gone wrong sometime after that time.

She called in Jenkins, her most trusted advisor and confidant. He was an old man now, approaching octogenarian status, and had been with her for almost twenty years acting as her servant and chief secretary. He had been tried and tested by the DOC and implanted with loyalty programs that had tested him many times. He was 50% synthetic and replicant now, almost half-android, as he'd lost so many parts in her service over the years from tests of his loyalty.

"Well? Did you find anything?" she asked.

Jenkins bowed, he was always so obviously full of joy to be in her presence. Not all of that emotion was the result of his programming. "I think I have. I combed all projects begun soon after your ascendancy to the Directorship as you asked me. Many are still secret, most are shrouded in mystery with most records having been wiped away."

"Yes, the DOC is nothing if not thorough," Arabella Rashid said softly. Then hopefully she began, "But you said you found something?"

"Well, there seems to be something, but I can not make anything of it. It makes no sense, really. The only reason it came up at all in my search is that it is still a viable program."

"It's still in operation?" she asked incredulous.

"Yes, it was begun about twenty years ago, soon after your ascendancy," Jenkins said slowly, carefully, "and because it is still in operation, that is the only reason there was some record still available. But it is very secret, For Your Eyes Only, upon pain of death."

"What is the name?" she asked.

"Big Brother, or more properly, the Big Brother Project," Jenkins replied.

"Big Brother?" Arabella Rashid said softly. She'd never heard of it. "And what does it do?"

Jenkins sighed, shrugged his shoulders, "Well, my lady, that's what has me so confused. What I have discovered about this project, makes no sense at all. At first, I thought the plan was some very subtle DOC scenario to obstruct all discovery. But I have delved deeper into it and it is just what it appears to be. That's the weird part."

"Well, out with it, Jenkins!" she said impatient now.

"My lady, it seems the sole purpose of the Big Brother Project is, and I am quoting here now from the prime directive file, 'to ship out old mystery and hard-boiled crime paperback books to Mars.'"

Jenkins held his head low, sad that he may have failed her.

"Paperbacks?" she asked curious. "What are they?"

"An obsolete and cheap information storage device from LastCen for the distribution of popular fiction," Jenkins explained softly, regurgitating what the history files had told him. Obviously embarrassed at his failure to please his mistress.

Arabella Rashid laughed deeply, "That makes no sense. No sense at all."

"Yes, my lady," Jenkins stammered.

He *had* failed her.

"What does one box or case of these things have to do with Mars, Jenkins?"

Jenkins stood his ground like the valued and loyal retainer he had proved to be for so many years—or that he had been programmed to be. "My lady, it is not just any paperbacks, but apparently only certain types, and it is not just one or two contraband boxes or cases. Shipments have gone out to Mars on every supply run to the planet. They have gone out under special DOC seals. In fact, thousands of cases and crates have been shipped out to the planet this way over the years, the decades. There was also a secret closed shipment. I believe that many years ago an entire obsolete library of these hard copy "paperback things" was secretly shipped to Mars."

"What the hell for!" she demanded. "What is going on here!"

"I don't know, my lady," Jenkins replied carefully.

"Then find out!" she ordered the old man.

"Yes, my lady," he replied and was about to leave when she beckoned him closer.

"And what of the other files?" she asked timidly, almost afraid of what he might tell her now.

Jenkins cleared his throat nervously, came closer to her. She was beautiful, but terrible. He feared her, understood her great power, but felt pity for her as well. So many conflicting emotions surged within her. For Jenkins knew she was a woman lost within herself, not at all the person she appeared to be, and now what he had discovered verified it. And he dreaded to tell her the truth.

"Well? Are you going to tell me?" she insisted, then she smiled benignly. It was difficult for her to be harsh with him. "Come on, Jenkins, it can't be that bad. Can it?"

The look on his face showed her that it was.

She waited bravely, insisting.

Finally Jenkins nodded as if coming to a momentous decision, and began. "I found some old records on the Janus Project. There are discrepancies. They indicate that twenty years ago it was you who set up what has become both a contrary plan and the concurrent plan."

"Contrary and concurrent plans!" she whispered.

"Yes, it is incontrovertible. I have found the records, the proof of it. It shows that as the new Director you set into motion a secret part of the Janus Project to sabotage the initial DOC project originally begun by Simon."

"No, that cannot be," she said firmly.

"Yes, and there's more," Jenkins added, sadness clouding his face at his words. "You not only set the plan in motion against the Janus Project, you set it in motion against the governmental Authority and the DOC. You planned a future...rebellion."

"Jenkins, that is impossible! I am the Director of DOC!"

"You really don't remember, do you?"

"Remember what, Jenkins?" Arabella Rashid asked softly, nervous now, wondering about the past and Simon. My God, what else had he done to her!

Jenkins sighed softly, said, "Simon. I am afraid he did more than just use you sexually, my lady. It appears he had you secretly programmed long ago to carry out his plan, and that programming kicked in twenty years ago. You know how such things work. It's based on a secret DOC trigger. At a certain, preordained time, or hour, it just happens. You go to sleep one night as one person—then wake up the next day a totally different person. Since that day you have been doing his will, my lady. Not your own."

"Jenkins that is impossible!"

"No, my lady, it is entirely possible. It happens all the time," he replied simply, then added softly, "Does the name Moses Sage mean anything to you?"

Arabella Rashid shook her head, "Of course not. Where did you ever pick up such a preposterous sounding a name?"

Jenkins stood silent. What he had found out could rock the Department of Control to its very core and surely be a sad end for his lady and himself. It would be a shame if it ever got out. A sin against Her. He had to do something. There had to be another way.

"You realize what you have said, Jenkins?" Arabella Rashid said, understanding fully the implications and the danger perfectly. "You have just given me a death sentence."

"No, my lady." Jenkins said carefully, "that is not to be... because I will never divulge anything I know."

Arabella Rashid was surprised by his words but she knew she could trust him. Jenkins had been—created is not the proper word—but he had been well prepared by the DOC scientists. Specially implanted and programmed to be supremely loyal to her, and her alone. In his mind he could never betray her and continue to live.

Arabella Rashid smiled at him, "So now what?"

Jenkins had been thinking about that for some time, since he had found out this information. Now what, indeed? There was one idea that came to him, daring and bold, dangerous and likely to fail, but he had to offer it. "I believe you when you say you have never heard of this Moses Sage. But DOC records prove otherwise. How do we explain the discrepancy?"

Arabella nodded, she knew now, "Simon. It had to be Simon. He had my mind programmed beforehand, some time before his...death...and soon after his death the new programming kicked in. His death must have been the trigger. Sneaky bastard! He trusted no one. When I awoke the next morning...I was different...."

"The next morning or the next week, or month, it makes little difference. The change was made. You would not remember much—from before. It seems the only explanation, my lady," Jenkins offered, then he added, "I am sorry."

"So am I, Jenkins. Simon has had his revenge, the monster. He was a genius. He probably had some suspicions or it was just his natural preparation for the possibility that I might take his place some day. I was the only one who could get close enough to him to do it."

"It seems likely," was all Jenkins said in a whisper.

Arabella Rashid had hardly heard him, she had hardly any awareness of her surroundings at that moment. She spoke in a monotone, like a machine, like a programmed thing. "He did it to me. This was his revenge. He knew I might take over and so he had my mind tampered with. And I know how now, with his own engrams, with his own damn thoughts and personality! He set me up, so he could possess my mind and spirit even after his own death! I can feel him inside me now, making decisions. I have been running the DOC just as he would have done. I have done terrible things, Jenkins. Oh my God, there is great evil, I have much to atone for. A fine revenge, indeed!"

"I am sorry, my lady," Jenkins mumbled uselessly, but his emotion and obvious care, touched her deeply.

"So am I, Jenkins, so am I. I have been a monster—I am a monster! And I don't know where the truth lies anymore," she was, crying now, desperate.

Her situation tore Jenkins apart, it was killing him to see his lady in such pain.

"What do I do now?" she asked hopelessly.

Jenkins dared speak up, for his lady, and said, "It's the paperbacks, my lady. They are the key to the plan that you set in operation twenty years ago. The key to that past you can not remember but must unlock. The paperbacks offer the key to your lost self."

Arabella Rashid nodded, Jenkins was correct, "Yes, these paperbacks? And they were shipped out to...?"

"To Mars, my lady," Jenkins offered.

"Mars? There's something about Mars, Jenkins," she said as if in a dream.

"Yes, my lady, there very well may be."

Arabella Rashid nodded, looking over at Jenkins with the old determination back in her eyes.

"Then I shall go to Mars," she said firmly.

CHAPTER TWELVE
MARS GETS BOOKS, WOMEN, AND BEER!

Arabella Rashid hunkered down in her tiny berth in the cramped hold of the Earther spaceship *President William Jefferson Clinton.* Of course, no one knew her real name, even her most trusted lieutenants, advisors, and agents did not know of her travel plans to Mars. Nor her intentions once she got there. That would be crucial information for anyone back on Earth to know. None of them needed to know any of it. It concerned Arabella Rashid quite a bit as well, because she was not all that sure what her intentions were at this point. In fact, there seemed no reason for her secret mission at all. It was most perplexing.

Mars was known to be coming along well, everything working out just as planned. Everything going along as expected. All The DOC projections and extrapolations regarding the planet, its colonization, and the men chosen to settle there seemed to be running exactly according to The DOC plan. Arabella Rashid shook her head. Every-damn-thing seemed *so* perfect. She knew something *had* to be wrong.

She just knew it!

* * * * * * *

Time passed.

Arabella Rashid put down the paperback. She'd been doing a lot of reading on her trip out to Mars and she'd read dozens of them on the long run out. She took a minute and examined the book carefully. She looked over each one of the old quaint books she'd read so many times now that she felt as if she knew them like old friends. They were such strange old relics. Odd curios from LastCen. She wondered where these particular books had come from. She'd found them all in a box under her bed her first night after the lift off from Luna.

Some lunatic moonman had probably put them there, she shrugged. It didn't make any sense. Maybe he had forgotten them? It was known the crazy cannibals of Luna, the Lunatics, pulled all kinds of strange stunts. And yet, it was unusual. Everyone knew Lunatics couldn't read. In fact, they were all damned wireheads, so juiced up on junkware they barely could think coherent thoughts. No, someone had left the old paperbacks for her on purpose. But who? And more importantly, why?

Arabella Rashid knew the only place where they actually read books anymore—old paperbacks, the reports called them—was on Mars. As she had apparently set the planet up that way decades ago.

She felt there was some other connection between Mars, her and the paperbacks though. Yet even as she considered it, she could hardly believe her own thoughts on the matter. What possible connection could there be? Logic told her it had to be insignificant at best, or perhaps some silly coincidence, but her gut feelings and the old paperbacks themselves seemed to tell her differently. Wheels within wheels? Boxes within boxes? Or just more meaningless bullshit? Coded messages within coded messages?

What were these Marsmen up to?

Arabella Rashid was the Supreme Director of the Department of Control, and she saw things getting out of control now. Not yet. But soon. Somehow. Some way. She could almost smell it coming. Was it just paranoia? Or was it the same intelligence and insight that had enabled her to rise so high to become Supreme Director in the first place? And remain in control for over twenty years. She wasn't sure. Not yet.

Arabella Rashid sat down to read a bit, then put the paperback down and thought about what she had just read. She'd never really read anything—fiction, that is—like this stuff before. Certainly none of that really old stuff from LastCen. It was all forbidden. Most of these books had been collected and burned by the firemen. The ones she had here were so old. So time worn. And yet, there was something special about them. Something that grabbed her. Down deep. It wasn't really the crime story or even the private eye investigators—that last was a silly outmoded concept. She wondered if Earth and Old America had actually had PI's once. What bothered her was something else. Something deeper. It was about truth. The books spoke something real to her. It was life and love and blood and sweat and people stepped on all over but then getting right back up again, and again, to fight back. And sometimes they even won! As the Director of The DOC she could relate to that. After all, she'd been one of the ones doing most of the stepping-on for too many years.

Except, today the people on Earth didn't fight back like the people in these old paperbacks did. The people on Earth didn't even know the difference anymore between freedom and sheepdom. They didn't know what was real, what was fake, what they thought, or what they were told to think. They had no concept of what they should fight for, or against. Or why? It was pathetic. A world of sheep. They had become all useless dependents and eventually only...parasites.

The people of Earth were just what they had been created to become. She hated them all. For none of them knew what they had lost, too few had even a vague feeling of comprehension about their world. Some felt they were missing something, but most were not capable of understanding what it was or how to make things better. Decades of senseless vids, brain links and plug-in implants had turned off and ruined the thinking capabilities of the masses. Citizens were confused, totally brain-locked, they weren't capable of doing much more than what their masters told them to do. The professional classes, the so-called "intellectuals," were worse. College professors and "great thinkers" who were merely overly-educated politically-indoctrinated morons. They had made of themselves perfect slaves. Slaves who loved their slavery. And cowardly sheep. Sheep who reveled in their sheepdom.

Why, most citizens these days were just plain useless. No one worked. Few were even able to hold a job, or had any desire to work. They weren't even good slaves, not even worthy sheep. No good to themselves, or anyone else. Useless. They had become a drain on everything and everyone. They created, built, contributed—nothing.

The DOC had done its work too well.

It had controlled all the life and passion and individualism out of everyone.

Arabella had seen it all her life, but now it was getting worse on Earth, Simon's society was crumbling, dying. That was good, but what would take its place? The human mind was starving to death on garbage.

On Mars it might be different, or at least, something was different. And these old paperbacks? Research had told her the stuff had been called 'mystery and hard-boiled crime fiction' in the old days of LastCen.

The paperbacks were definitely a part of it. Whatever *it* was.

James Ryan was another part of it. Memories of him flooded back to her now. She saw his image in her mind from the old days long ago and wondered about him. Where was he now? What was he doing on Mars? She remembered she'd sent him there twenty years ago. Implanted, programmed, like all the others, and paperbacks had been a part of it. But it seems to have all gone out of control somehow. And Arabella Rashid was after all, the Director of worldwide systems control. Control should never go...out of control!

* * * * * * *

The *President William Jefferson Clinton* landed at Marsport and Arabella Rashid debarked, towing a brace of luggage. Inside she had a sealed box filled with old paperbacks. Her baggage rode a small dolly through the carry-off ramp, then to the main gate.

At the gate there was a backlog. Of course. The women were being checked, and then placed in a holding area. Everywhere were men, gawking like they'd never seen a real, live woman before. In fact, some of them never had. Most of these men hadn't seen a real flesh-and-blood woman for over twenty years.

Arabella Rashid knew what was next, the swearing-in ceremony to the Earther government. To the Authority. The loyalty oath. Digitally recorded, of course.

She did not speak to anyone as she moved forward. Neither did anyone speak to her. It was almost an Earth custom, never to speak to another human being. It was all so tense. You could feel the fear because the eyes of the watchers were always watching.

One woman, a girl really, smiled at her. She was going to speak, but Arabella looked away, her DOC training interfering with her human compassion. It was the basic reaction, and it irritated her. She felt so constrained. Constrained by her own self.

It was not Mars. It was she that was the problem.

There were dozens of young women now coming forward, the first load of new wives for the men of Mars. She wondered how many of the women were spies from Earth, maybe even from her own DOC? Maybe they were even here spying on her? She smiled. It was a strange world, Earth or Mars, and stranger things could happen.

The swear-in ceremony had all five dozen young women lined up—like for a firing squad, she thought with a grim smile. They were going to be recorded as they stood to repeat the words some old Marsport bureaucrat was told to say to them, by some other Earther bureaucrat.

The guy who was going to administer the oath was a real relic too. He stood up tall and straight, thick white mustachios

waxed and pointed upwards, old eyes glittering with apprecia-
tion and some amount of lust at the evident charms of all these
young women standing so boldly before him. He smiled at the
women, obviously mentally cataloging each of their assets or
charms, and said, "Ladies, ladies, young ladies, a very heartfelt
welcome to you all to Mars. It is truly wonderful to have you
all here as our guests. Each one of you are a joy to behold. Well
now, on to business, on to the swear-in ceremony. As required
by Earther law. Then we'll process you and take you to your
new quarters."

There was a quiet murmur of approval and some excitement as the women looked around at the new environment. The
low buildings under the domes, the blood-red sky and rust-red
mountains far in the distance.

The old man began, "Please repeat after me: 'I hereby swear
allegiance and total obedience and subservience to my home
world of Earth and the government for which it stands. Forever.
Amen.'"

Everyone said the words. Loudly. It was all being recorded,
Arabella knew. Then it would be transmitted back to Earth.
Studied. She'd managed to hide her face from view, even though
she knew the work she'd had done to her face before she'd left
Earth should render her unrecognizable. Nevertheless, you had
to play along with the swear-in whether you believed it or not.

Especially, if you did not!

The next step was something that totally surprised her. The
procedure she'd seen in records sent to her from Mars had shown
that at this point in processing new émigrés were dismissed.
Then allowed to go through the gate where they had their papers
stamped, meet their Watchers, and then were escorted to their
new quarters. All under very strict security. Instead, the old
man said with serious formality, "Now, will you all please stand
for the World Anthem of Mars."

Arabella tried to hide her utter astonishment.

Mars did not have any World Anthem!

Arabella Rashid and the other young women stood and

looked at the old man. He slipped a disk in a wall slot. A song suddenly began playing over the speakers. Loud. It had a good melody, a hard-driving pop-rock tune, one of the old classics from LastCen.

Arabella didn't know it. It wasn't popular today. Even among the oldies. She was sure that it was not on any of the approved lists.

She realized that it had to be an underground recording! And it was being played here now, and out in the open! That was amazing arrogance. And so dangerous.

It was a good song though. Arabella liked the melody and the voices harmonized well together. It was a powerful, inspiring tune. However, some of the words, the ones she could make out, sounded very individualistic, even subversive. They were so very incorrect. Yet, these same words touched her heart, her mind. They made her upset. They made her think and yearn.

Yearning was allowed, but thinking was always dangerous.

On the way out of the gate she asked the old man, "That anthem you played? What was the name of it?"

The officer eyed her approvingly. He knew she liked it. So did he.

Arabella Rashid smiled back. Working her charms on the old fellow.

He said, "Missy, that's an old, old song, a real dandy ain't it? It was originally written by a real-music band way back in 1977, something called Fleetwood Mac. Strange name, eh? Don't know what it meant. Anyway, the song is called, 'Go Your Own Way'."

"It's a nice song," Arabella said, absently thinking about the title. It was most definitely subversively totally individualistic.

The old man nodded, then said curiously, "And it ain't just a song, it's the World Anthem of Mars. That's what it is. That's enough for us."

Arabella Rashid walked away. Strange old coot. Where did he get off acting like he was someone? Like he had some kind of mind and thoughts all his own? Like he was a person who mattered.

Then she checked herself—that was Simon talking.

Not her.

She hated his voice in her mind and would ignore it all she could.

It was all very confusing and even scary.

Then she noticed that the old man had a battered old paperback stuck in his back pocket. She was able to make out the title as he walked away from her. The title said quite plainly, *Kiss Your Ass Good-Bye*. She was astounded. When she caught up with him she could see that it had been written by someone named Charles Willeford. It had a nasty cover showing an angry and ugly face of a very dangerous-looking man. And that title! It was so mean-spirited! Actually in-your-face defiant and full of anger. Maybe even rage? She realized there was a lot going on out here on Mars. A lot that needed looking into, and she was just the person to do the looking.

Arabella Rashid couldn't help thinking again about that song on the walk to her newly assigned quarters. "You Can Go Your Own Way?" No, not a question. It was a declarative sentence, a declaration. A declaration of, like, independence? You *Can* Go Your Own Way, it was proclaiming, bold, free, true. But not on Earth. No not there for shit-sure. And not here on Mars either. Not now, with Arabella Rashid and the Department of Control breathing down your grimy rebel necks.

* * * * * * *

Alvy called the meeting to order. He saw Ryan in the front row, nodded, then said, "Three items of business, gentlemen. First off, a new group of paperbacks has arrived on planet in the latest supply ship from Earth. Ah, and how's this for a good joke, the name of the ship is the *President William Jefferson Clinton*."

There was a riot of laughter, and a lot of knowing nods from the wiser heads in the crowd. Someone in the assembly said,

"It's typical. They probably renamed the old *President Richard M. Nixon*!"

"Yeah, one con man to another!" someone added.

Alvy got back the attention of the crowd with a hard fist on the podium. Everyone shut up, all eyes shot to him up front, "Thanks, ah, gentlemen. That's better. Anyway, Ryan here has the new paperbacks, and five new Price Guides full of bibliographic facts—and even better—many color photos of rare book covers. They are from the last year of issue in 2020. These will all go up on the auction block in thirty days. All proceeds to go to the Resistance. This package contains primo stuff gents, the hardest-ass stuff you'll ever read anywhere, plus the five rare reference volumes. So bid high and bid often!"

There was general clapping, talk, deal-making. Alvy got their attention back after a few moments, said, "And now on to the other two items on this red-letter day on Mars."

"Yeah, how about it!" a heckler demanded.

Alvy nodded, continued, "We have caused to be shipped out here, through certain channels which I shall not divulge, a certain Old Earth alcoholic beverage. It is called beer. Some of you may have heard of it? The Resistance has imported two hundred cases of this fine old beverage. Rumor has it the brew was liberated from the last underground survivalist bunker that had been sealed and froze shut solid since 2040. We also have numerous cases of a certain "Old Number 7" which is said to be a very excellent Tennessee sipping whiskey by the name of a *Mr.* Jack Daniels. These will be parceled out to our people deserving of such obvious honors and comforts and to others so as to obtain certain concessions from the Earther blockhead, bribe-taking, brain-washed, lackeys of the Authority. Who we all can't stand and have no damn respect for."

There was a rousing cheer. Alvy could be a rabble-rousing bastard when the mood was upon him. He toned it down however, when Ryan gave him a sharp look. So it was back to business now.

Alvy continued, "Of course, ah, we will be passing around a

taste to everyone here. Just to wet your whistle, you understand. Your choice, gents, a long neck bottle of ice cold Bud, or a head-banging straight up shot glass of Jack Daniels Old Number 7. Either way, it will put most of you in the mood for more and grow hair where you don't have any left. And it will get you ready for what is to come next."

"You're damn right about that!" a guy named Too-Tall Tom shouted, rubbing his massive stomach in obvious anticipation. Homemade spirits on Mars were never as good as the quality Earth stuff. That's one thing the Earthers hadn't forgotten—how to make good strong booze with a mighty righteous kick to it.

"Okay, so have a drink on us, and quiet the hell down."

Bottles were passed out. Shots were poured and glasses handed around the hall. Toasts rang out everywhere and on every subject. Finally the talk quieted down a bit and everyone's attention was directed to the stage when Alvy came back up and began again.

Now it was time.

"And now we have our third and most important subject to discuss. I saved the best for last, gentlemen. I am proud to announce Mars now has—*women!* That's correct. Women have come out to Mars!"

The silence was breathless. All was quiet. Utter stillness for a heartbeat. You could hear a pin drop. Some guys even froze before they upended their beers. Then suddenly there were wild shouts and cheers of joy. These soon became catcalls, and hoots, hollers, and all kinds of lusty words. Some words were savory, some not. Some were hot, some not. Some were horny, and some even hornier. They were men, after all. Men who were not ashamed to be men. And for the first time in their lives they were feeling like men.

Now Alvy really had a hard time quieting them down. Eventually, the volume of laughing and talking in the room receded to the point where he could be heard with the sound system cranked up to the max. "These women are the first batch of a stream of new settler wives. That's good. We need women here!"

"No shit, Alvy!" Manny barked back. He'd just downed a shot of Daniels, with a Bud chaser.

"So let's treat them good," Alvy barked. "I got your promise on that, men? Respect them! They're here for us! They're on our side!"

The men quieted down. It was time to get serious—and these were nothing if not serious men.

"It's going to be good, but we have to be careful. The Resistance has to be careful. Some of these women are certainly spies. Earth puts a few in every batch of new settlers. We know they do it with the men. What makes us think they wouldn't do it with the women? But we'll find the few bad apples, we always do. Then we'll neutralize them. Make them harmless and ineffective. Except this time it's different. There's something else."

Alvy looked serious now, even scared. That made everyone there get attentive real fast too.

There was quiet now. All eyes on Alvy.

Some men even put down their drinks.

Alvy said, "You all remember having been told about a woman named Arabella Rashid? She is the Director of the Department of Control. Well, our informants tell us she is hidden among the 60 new women who arrived here today."

This was not good news.

This was terrible news!

There was a barely discernible gasp and frequent guttural mumbles among the crowd. You could feel their fear ooze out of every pore in their skin. They looked around the hall nervously as if expecting an attack any moment.

Alvy continued, "Of course, she is under assumed identity. One that cannot be broken or discovered. She can be any one of the sixty women who arrived today. The DOC is nothing if not thorough. Control is their main...I guess the only word for it is... obsession."

"Yeah, that's for shit-sure correct, Alvy!" a fellow known by all as the One-Eye Geek shouted back.

"Right, Geek. They're bad, and we all hate them, but why are they here? And why *her* of all people?" Manny asked.

Alvy said, "We don't know."

Ryan stood up, "Gentlemen, the Resistance is under the gun now. Mars is under the gun. We know who some of the spies are in this shipment, and they'll be taken care of. Isolated. Sent out to Little Siberia, on Olympus Mons. There no one will ever hear from them for a few years. Until they have an accident, or wise up."

There were general nods of agreement. A few years out in Little Siberia could work wonders on even the most dedicated Earth agent or spy. By the time those women came back they'd be different, changed. If not, they'd go right back out to Olympus Mons for one more year of vacation in hell until they understood the point was to cooperate with what was going on here. It might be harsh but it had to be done to keep up security.

Ryan looked at the men, he knew they were waiting for his words. He took a deep breath and began, "Arabella Rashid is another matter. We have no lead on her whatsoever. No one knows what she looks like. In fact, there are no records on her at all. We can't even be sure if she is really a *she*, or if that is in fact, her true name. I kind of doubt it. But she's dangerous. We don't want the Earthers to figure out our plan here, especially now when we are finally getting what we want most, women on Mars!"

There was a glum nod and moan from the men. They were scared now.

Ryan continued, "We now have women, for wives. We can have families, children, build ourselves a real society, still free of Earth, but now it can live and grow. Women! Wives! My friends, the women will ensure these good things happen. We need the women, we need them to join us, but we have to be very careful. Arabella Rashid is blood poison to our ideas, a danger to our most sacred hopes and dreams. We've worked so hard for so long to deceive the Earthers. We have them believing we are eagerly sucking in all their lies and propaganda. Fooling them into believing that we are totally under their power, even so damn very happy to be. Well, Earth has no power here! Never did! Never will! We are freer than they will ever know. We will be even more free of them some day soon!"

There was applause and shouting. It grew from anger and fear. Members of the audience held up their paperbacks shouting, barking, growling out a mouthful of words, cheering, yelling, chanting over and over again: *"We Are Free! Don't Order Me! We Are Free! Earth Don't Mean Nothing to Me!"*

Ryan wondered how long it would all last.

CHAPTER THIRTEEN
MARS DON'T NEED NO GUNS!

Arabella Rashid sat alone in her private quarters immersed in a horrendous propagandistic virtual reality news show from her small personal VRPod. The blood and bullets whizzed by her like she was in the thick of the action, the charred flesh smell assailed her nostrils. It was disgusting and she soon turned it off. She opted to watch the room vid panel instead. Interestingly, there was no direct link with Earth, or the official government stations, from back home. It was strange. The signals were certainly beamed to Mars, reception was indicated back on Earth. However she now realized the shows were never actually *shown* on Mars. They were never seen here at all! In fact, it seemed absolutely nothing was shown on Mars. She was astonished to find that the vid screens here were all blank. At first, she thought it was just her luck that she'd received quarters with a malfunctioning vid. However, she soon realized the truth. Even as reports and surveys by her agents through other DOC means, all indicated that these vid shows were always very heavily watched. Ratings were reported to be very high. Surveys said Earth programs were very popular and influential, and actually loved by everyone on Mars.

"Bullshit!" Arabella Rashid said out loud.

She turned off the blank vid. She picked up a paperback and began reading where she'd left off.

She stared at the cover of the paperback she'd been reading. It was something she couldn't get out of her head, something called, *Only The Dead Know Brooklyn* by some guy named Thomas Boyle. It was an oldie from way back in 1980-something. Far in the past. Way before she'd ever been born.

Cloned, she corrected.

Arabella Rashid thought about her own past. Thinking back on it now was difficult. Strange. She recalled how at such a young age she'd become the mistress of Simon; the 100-year-old bio-reconstructed Director of the DOC who had been dead now for twenty years. She remembered when at just thirteen years of age she'd set up the Director for the long hard fall, then took over the entire organization. How just hours later, Arabella Rashid was fully ensconced with all the power, privilege, and fear of the Directorship of the dreaded DOC. Back then, no one knew anything at all about her, other than her name. It was a name that caused very real fear. She was the person—rumor had it, a mere slip of a girl just entering her teens—who had taken down the evil Director, Simon the Monster. Then she had taken his place to destroy the world. Or bring it screaming down to its knees.

Arabella Rashid smiled. She remembered Simon. She thought of his old hard hands touching her, the evil ways he'd used her. Then she thought of the book she'd just been reading. The DeSales crime novel by Thomas Boyle. Part of the story concerned children at something called a "Halloween festival" in somewhere called The Neathermeade in a place called Prospect Park, in a long-ago city called Brooklyn. It had been somewhere in Atlantic coast Old America, Eastern Security District, she knew. The book sang to her soul about abused children. It made her think back, on how Simon had used her. Ill-used her. And all his other children. All those he called his "special children." Most of them were dead now. She couldn't remember any of the names. Except she did remember two of them, even after all these years. Vague memories of them stood out. They were the two brothers. They had been clones also.

It was all so distant and vague now. At least one of the brothers was still alive. It was rumored that he might even be working somewhere in The DOC, of all places. He was said to be under secret orders. No one could ever know who he was. As with herself, all agents and officers were forbidden to know anything at all about the Director. And the Director knew little about members of the Board and other areas of The DOC which were under secret orders. No one knew of the existence of anyone else. They were not supposed to know. Everything was secret. Erased. Or never existed in the first place.

Then there was the other brother. Lost. Probably killed and long dead by now. Arabella remembered him. He was smart, and good, and bold, but so long gone now his face had drifted into the dust of her forgotten memory. He could be anywhere, of course, even out here on Mars for all she knew. Another of the children Simon had collected, to be trained to become his next generation of agents. Killers so stone cold nothing could stop them. Agents of evil and oppression Simon had specifically created for his needs. But like her, they had been used by Simon. Or so it was rumored. Nothing could ever truly be known for sure.

Arabella remembered reading another book. The title of this one was, *Nineteen Eighty-Four*. A LastCen horror novel. Actually, political horror. She realized that if George Orwell, the author, saw Big Brother as a big black boot upon the face of man—forever—then Simon's children were the people the Director had in mind to carry out that evil upon the human race. Forever. Personally trained and raised by Simon and The DOC, they would take over the world someday and make it scream.

Arabella smiled at the fact that Simon was no more. He had looked so good dead. Better than when he had been alive, she mused. At least in death the monster was harmless. But his creation, the DOC, went on without him. She had tried to control it, make it less brutal and deadly but this Frankenstein's monster had a mind and will of its own. It ran rampant, an out of control juggernaut of pain, fear and death.

Arabella still remembered the surprise on Simon's old face when she set the beam on kill, and then fried his old plastic body to molten slag on the floor of his so very exclusive high security office. Or so she wished. She had an implanted memory to that effect. But it was false.

Actually, she had stabbed him in the neck when she was kissing him. It was just like one of those femme fatales on the covers of the old paperback crime novels. Was that mere coincidence or something more?

She felt Simon would understand, if anyone would. She had, after all, achieved his goal. She'd taken over The DOC, as he had told her he wanted her to do some day. She'd just done it a few decades earlier than Simon had anticipated.

Or had she?

After Simon's demise, the 'War for Control' lasted only a week. Arabella and most of Simon's teens easily killed off the old pros, quickly rearranging the department structure as she saw fit. It was a new order. It became worse than ever!

Of course, they took over in secret, in this most secret of places. Consolidating power and position until they could not be removed and they were in complete control. Even a hint of resistance or opposition meant instant removal. Quite a few key people simply vanished. They were declared *persona non grata* and never spoken of again. Their names instantly erased from all files and the digital record. They not only disappeared; they had never existed in the first place!

Arabella Rashid couldn't remember the name of the two brothers. She'd accessed her infobank before she'd left Earth and found out that the file had been wiped clean many years ago. That was certainly strange, but not out of the ordinary at The DOC. Most personnel files had been deleted or "revised" during the War for Control. A lot had happened since those days. She knew now that her own memories were not her own and she feared for what Simon had planted in her mind. It was obvious to her now that at least one of the brothers must still be alive and was hidden deep somewhere within The DOC bureaucratic infrastructure. Somewhere in the never-ending snake-like bureaucracy and hierarchy. Somewhere. But where? And why?

Who was he? And did this have anything to do with Mars and...
paperbacks?

* * * * * *

James Ryan said, "No guns. We don't need them."

"Come on, Ryan, we got no choice here," Manny said, egging
on the crowd. He pulled out a copy of *The Godfather* by Mario
Puzo. "Now this guy knew his stuff. What we need here is a
Luca Brazzi."

Ryan smiled, what he needed was a few Tom Hagens. Guys
with brains. Good and true *consigliori*.

"Listen, guys," Ryan said. "I know how you feel, but there's
no way in hell we can go up against them shot for shot. More
guns won't help us. More brains will. You know what I've
always said, and it's damn true and it has worked. The only way
we can beat the Earthers and The DOC is to be smarter than
they are. We can never out man them, never out spend them,
never out gun them. The way we win is if they do not suspect
even for a moment that there is a Resistance. As far as they
know, it does not exist. Don't let them suspect any hint of what
we are really doing. What we are really about. We can do it! It
has worked for over twenty years!"

"Yeah, Ryan, but that was before this Arabella Rashid witch
stepped foot on Mars!" Alvy said. 'The Witch', as she was
called by those in the know. Those who had serious reason to
fear her and The DOC. She scared the hell out of Alvy and most
everyone else in that room. She was said to have been just a slip
of a girl when she'd taken over DOC, but she had grown into
a totally unprincipled amoral monster with unlimited power. It
was a devastating combination of ruthlessness and power that
spelled danger any which way you looked at it.

"Why's she here, Ryan?" Manny asked nervously.

Alvy said, "I been digging around all over the Net on her,
and what I see is all the expected crap, and a lot of propaganda.
More lies of the Earthers, the usual PC party line bullshit! You

know, you really gotta read between the lines with them. She is very bad news. *Puta! Mala loca!* A crazy evil. Bitch! Whore!"

"I agree," Ryan said with a bit of a smile. He wouldn't have put it exactly that way but the truth was the truth. He'd never seen Alvy so riled up before.

"Then what do we do, Ryan?"

Ryan sighed, "We do what we've always done. We wait. We work. We be patient. We plan."

Faces fell. They were expecting something more. Action. A fight. Something grand they could all sink their teeth into. Something stupid that would feel good, but get them all killed.

Ryan looked intently at each and every man there. A thousand faces hungry for freedom, champing at the bit, dying to stand up tall and shout: "Dammit! I'm a man! I will fight for my freedom!"

Ryan smiled, he knew what they wanted but he knew the truth too. They'd all be cut down so fast they'd never know what hit them. And they knew it as well.

Alvy repeated more softly, "So what do we do now, Ryan?"

Ryan looked at him, then into every face there. Finally he said, "We do what we have always done, gentlemen. We go our own way!"

It was the words from their anthem.

But they were not mere words.

Those words had meaning to each man there.

The crowd looked up. They nodded. They were determined. They wore grim smiles. These were serious men after all. Fists were being raised. Eyes grew sharp, angry, focused, more determined than ever.

"We go our own way!" Alvy shouted.

"We go our own way!" a thousand voices repeated.

"We go our own way!" Ryan barked, drowned out by the throng.

"We go our own way!" a thousand gruff voices repeated, standing tall, raising arms with clenched fists—determined, strong, united, willing now—to play it the right way. The smart way.

The only way they could play it.

And win.

Their way.

* * * * * * *

Arabella Rashid put away the old paperbacks in a secret hiding place. Carefully. Almost lovingly. She realized that she loved this stuff, these old crime and police novels. The murder mysteries. The private cops and detectives. The attitude. The down-right guts of the people in these books. The men and the women. You didn't meet people like that anymore. It was such a pity.

Arabella smiled sadly about that. So be it. Earth, she realized now, was doomed. On the road to being a brain-dead sewer inhabited by mindless sheep. Mars? Mars was different. Strange. Difficult to pin down. Inexact. A little lonely. Somewhat sad. Dangerous for sure. Cruel. But also bold, and full of life. Exciting. There were real possibilities here. And there really was freedom. You could feel it. Taste it. It was like medicine, it made you feel better, made you strong and healthy. Just like in the world of the old paperbacks. Just like the old paperbacks said it should be.

It was about a little thing called hope.

Arabella Rashid realized something else as well. It was amazing, incomprehensible, unthought of, but there was real resistance here to Earth. Serious resistance. And it had been successful! Quiet, oh for sure it was so very, very quiet and absolutely undercover, but very successful nonetheless. Quite amazing, actually. It was an organized resistance. It was at the gut level. Instinctive. Deep. In fact, the more she thought about it, she realized this Resistance was actually the controlling force on Mars—not the Earth Authority, and not The DOC!

Now, that was serious. What was she going to do about it?

CHAPTER FOURTEEN
PAPERBACKS AND FREEDOM!

Ryan said it plain but true, "Loyalty, people, goes from bottom to top, but it also must go from top to bottom. When there is no longer any loyalty from those at the top to those at the bottom—when loyalty is expected only from bottom to top—then there is no loyalty at all. There is only tyranny, or slavery. Then rebellion can never be far away."

As Ryan said those words, he realized they seemed to come to him from so long ago it was like it was from another life. Perhaps it was.

Ryan told them all again. "We don't need them any longer, my friends. Earth, the Earthers, all their damn rules and laws and orders. The DOC! It's all no good—*NG!*—from today on. And admitting we do not need them, or anybody, or anything— is the freedom we crave."

Alvy stood up, shouting, "I would rather go hungry than take the scraps they leave us. I would rather starve then eat their bread!"

There was a cheer, growing into a chant.

It was time.

Alvy unfurled the banner. It was the secret flag of the new independent Mars Republic. A red circle in a field of black stars, and surrounding the planet like the rings of Saturn were the words "We'd Rather Starve Than Eat Your Bread!"

There was an uncoiled snake that ran across the bottom of the flag, thin, lean, menacing. The words written upon the coils of its sinuous body in serious warning proclaimed: "Don't Tread On Me!" On the top of the flag were the words, "Go Your Own Way!"

Alvy waved the red flag of Free Mars and the men cheered themselves hoarse. They embraced as warriors, hugged and cried as brothers, shed tears of anger and pain, and then as planned beforehand, they each left to their appointed duties.

The Revolution had begun.

Ryan watched, waited.

Wondering when it would come.

The betrayal.

Who would sell them out? Would it be his best friend? Or his supposed brother Michael back on Earth? The brother he did not remember. Or maybe himself, even? Ryan knew he was not above caving in at the right pressure. The DOC knew nothing if not how to apply proper "pressure" to get what it wanted. Then what? Would DOC storm troopers swoop down on them and kill them all? They'd done so on other Earth cities before. Many times. He'd seen it in the Old Earth vids. They made no secret of it. They were proud of killing enemies of The Authority. Ryan figured he was sitting pretty high on that list right now. So must his brother. So were Alvy, Manny, Ernie and all the others. And what about Arabella Rashid? Who was she? Where was she? What was she doing here? What was she doing right now?

Ryan sighed, it had been a good twenty-year run out here. A hard life, to be sure, but to live as a free man meant everything to him. It was especially important if you'd never lived like that before. And the paperbacks were a joy to read. Such wonderful stories and heroes.

It was all so delightfully strange.

So unreal.

And yet that's the way freedom should be.

* * * * * * *

Ryan thought about the message he'd received from his spies.

The Resistance was everywhere on Mars. It was every*one* on Mars. People told him things. One of the things he heard was about the woman on the *President William Jefferson Clinton* with the old paperbacks in a box under her bed.

She'd been seen reading hard-boiled crime fiction. She had a box of paperbacks. Apparently, she had also been reading them on the trip out to Mars from Luna.

Ryan knew the books were not hers. They just could not be. He wondered where she'd gotten them. He thought about it a while. It was most interesting. He seemed to see his brother's hand in this. Somehow. He couldn't quite figure it, but it was the only thing he could come up with.

But why?

Another message from his Earth brother, perhaps more subtle this time? Perhaps the paperbacks would lead him to Arabella Rashid like a bloodhound to a fox? However the paperbacks could also lead Arabella Rashid to James Ryan. And to the Resistance!

It was a two-way street, a double-edged sword.

Very dangerous.

Ryan wondered who was being led to whom.

Was this the betrayal he knew would come? Ryan shook his head. He had no way of knowing. He got together a bunch of paperbacks, including a prized copy of Howard Schoenfeld's *Let Them Eat Bullets!* This was a wonderful one-shot Gold Medal hard-boiled crime novel classic by a one-shot author and wartime conscientious objector. A brave man who paid his dues with prison time but stood his ground for what he believed. Ryan packed the paperbacks away in a small canvas bag. Then he decided to pay a call on a fellow paperback reader. See what she had. See if she wanted to do any...trades.

CHAPTER FIFTEEN
MARS AIN'T LIKE NO PLACE ON EARTH

Mars is so cool!

Not temperature-wise, she thought, though that also was true this time of year she was told.

Arabella Rashid visited all the outposts and towns, the factories and mines. She looked in at the centers of Marsport, and she had to admit it—she liked the place. She liked the people. And they seemed to like her.

Mars really was cool.

When she got back to her cube she saw the message from James Ryan on her screen. There was no visual though, which she thought odd. She called down to the desk, told the clerk she needed her screen repaired.

The clerk told her, "Sorry, ma'am, the screen is not broken. All the visuals on our screens are set on blank from the main center."

"They're off?" she said incredulously.

"Yes, ma'am, the guests and citizens like it better that way. Privacy reasons, you know. The caller can't see you, and you can't see your caller."

"Well, that's not the way they do it back on Earth," Arabella Rashid said testily.

"Exactly, ma'am," the clerk said noncommittally, so practiced it really seemed like he was not committed to any opinion at all. "Will there be anything else?"

"No," Arabella said. She cut the link and sat down on the edge of her bed. There were real problems here. "Privacy" was such an outmoded concept. There was no such thing as privacy any more. Privacy was actually subversive. Why would a person want to keep anything private from anyone else? By what right? And certainly not from the Authority or The DOC! The audacity! Mars was a world that seethed unruliness, hard-headed opinion and resistance to anything Earther. She saw a dangerous determination here that could easily breed an attitude for rebellion.

She wondered about that. Was it really possible? Rebellion? Here? Nonsense! Such a thing was unimaginable. Nevertheless, she smelled it everywhere, even in the way the people walked out on the streets. Their very posture and body language oozed independence, pride, and worse. Defiance! And here she finally did see the influence of those mystery and hard-boiled crime paperbacks. A world of outlaws! Rebels! It was all pretty clear, it was hard-nosed, hard-boiled attitude of such intense self-sufficient freedom-lovers it practically screamed to Earth and the DOC—I don't need you!

Get Out Of My Life!

Get Out Of My Way!

Leave Me Alone!

And then there were the paperbacks she'd found under the bed in her cube on the *Clinton*. Who the hell had left those there? Or put them there? And why? Was it some kind of message? A joke? A warning? Perhaps a marking? And this book person, James Ryan? Coming here in half an hour, making an appointment with her, for of all things, to trade paperbacks? What the hell was that about?

It was all so crazy. James Ryan. Did she remember that name? She seemed to know it from long ago. Another life? Even before Simon! Or maybe it was just after Simon?

Arabella Rashid shook her head, took out the box of old paperbacks and placed them on her bed. She sat down and read a few pages from the latest one she'd just begun. This was a fast crime caper novel, Mike Black's *The Heist*. She read it, and she waited for this James Ryan to arrive.

* * * * * * *

When James Ryan got to Arabella Rashid's cube, she buzzed him right in. She was surprised to see a youngish-looking man, but with more age than first appeared. There were many years of experience in those eyes. And she could tell that not all of it was good. There was something else. Arabella knew this man knew things. He knew a lot of stuff. Arabella could almost smell the scent of secret knowledge on him. She wondered, just how much did he know? She was determined she'd find out—one way or the other.

Ryan smiled at the youngish woman before him. She was about 10 years his junior but you'd never know it by looking into her eyes. For while her face was soft, youthful, almost girlish— it was her eyes that betrayed her. Those eyes glittered with life and intelligence, but they also showed an intensity and depth Ryan had not seen in anyone since he'd left Earth twenty years before as a young government agent.

What Ryan saw in her eyes was raw and naked power. It ran deep, and dark, and deadly because it was combined with the will to use that power to whatever advantage she desired. It was a devastating combination.

Ryan smiled, a bit forced though, and he tried to relax. She was very attractive. Even though his natural built-in alarms of danger rang loud and clear, he liked what he saw in her.

She was tall and lean, dark and bright-eyed, long glow-green hair, the latest Earth fashion. She had full red lips, nice legs, athletic. It was all the good stuff he liked in a woman in all the right places.

Arabella Rashid smiled back hesitantly. She had no idea what this man wanted. She did like the look of him though, even as he moved closer to her weapon stash under the pillow at the head of her bed. A knife at the right end, a small silenced hand gun at the other end. Just in case. She noticed that Ryan was carrying a small canvas case. It didn't appear to be too heavy. She wondered what was inside. She wondered where his weapons were hidden. Was he carrying explosives? A bomb?

They kind of circled around each other for a moment, kind of like human vultures doing a death dance over the dregs of a corpse. Or pretty damn near it. Though they'd certainly not describe it that way.

They were both professionals.

They both knew it now.

"Hi," Ryan said, with his best boyish smile this time. "Name's James Ryan. I work out at the Olympus Mines, engineering, my specialty, and other odd jobs."

Arabella Rashid smiled back. She knew just what that 'odd jobs' meant. Trouble-shooter. A yellow caution light went off in her mind. "My name's.... Well, you know my name, Mr. Ryan. You're the one who rang me up on the screen to ask to see me."

"Yes," Ryan said. "That's right."

"To trade...paperbacks?" Arabella said, incredulously.

Ryan smiled back. He expected this. "I know it seems kind of silly, but a lot of the guys here collect these old books."

"Indeed. Do they read them too?"

Religiously, Ryan wanted to say. Instead he shrugged, replied, "Yeah, a lot of them do. Sometimes."

"Do you, Mr. Ryan? Do you actually read these old books?"

"Ah, yes. Some of them. The really good ones. As many as I have time for."

Arabella Rashid smiled, she could see he was holding back. Now she understood. She took out her small box, spreading out the old paperbacks on the bed with the covers face-up in front of them.

His eyes lit up. Actually lit up and he smiled as he looked from the cover of one book to the next intently, then back to her.

She sat down on the edge of the bed, watching Ryan examine the books. She was examining him as he examined the books. He was very interested. He took a quick look at each one carefully then holding it up, looking it over front and back. He smiled, then nodded.

Ryan then opened up his own canvas case. It wasn't explosives or a bomb at all. Instead he took out a dozen or so old paperbacks of his own and laid them out on the other end of the bed next to her.

"You want to...trade? Really? Just that? Is that really it, Mr. Ryan?"

"Yes. If you're interested. I usually come across dupes, duplicate copies. Then there's books I've already read but didn't especially like. I—a lot of us—trade our paperbacks to other guys for their paperbacks. I know it seems kind of childish, but that way everyone gets something they want. Like that Mike Black novel you have over there. Or even the two Don Winslow novels. His stuff is so good it hurts! Or those William F. Nolan Black Mask boys private eye novels."

"I've just begun the Mike Black book," Arabella Rashid said, picking up her copy of *The Heist*, looking it over. This one was an old Leisure paperback. She handed it to Ryan to inspect. A bit reluctantly.

"Like it?" Ryan asked.

She nodded. "It seems to be a good book, a fabulous story. Of course I haven't finished it yet. Just begun it, in fact."

Ryan nodded, put it down and looked at her book stash, examining each paperback minutely. His eyes suddenly starred noticeably when they zeroed in on a copy of *Green Ice* by Raoul Whitfield. This was a hard-boiled gem if ever there was one. It was by an underrated and original *Black Mask* writer, a buddy of the great Dashiell Hammett. Hammett—'The Man' himself! This edition was an old and incredibly rare *Avon Murder Mystery Monthly* digest, and it was in pretty decent shape for such an old and delicate paperback. It screamed out to Ryan—"Read me, Baby! *Read me! Now!*"

"Now that's a great one," Ryan said. He carefully picked up the delicate old copy of *Green Ice*, and he examined it lovingly for a moment.

Ryan handed it to Arabella Rashid. She looked it over. It was such a thin volume, hardly seemed like a real book at all, "This is good to read?"

Ryan smiled. "It's a classic, very best hard-boiled, high in body-count. An outstanding Depression Era out-of-control crime, graft, and caper involving missing emeralds. The green ice of the title. It's old, but it's, oh so good."

Arabella Rashid looked at the copyright date. It was written almost one hundred and fifty years ago! Incredible! This particular edition was over one hundred years old itself. She shook her head, "It's such old stuff."

"There's no age limit on quality," Ryan said matter-of-factly.

Arabella Rashid looked up at him, nodded, then put *Green Ice* on the table beside her bed to read next.

"So why did you really want to see me, Mr. takes-care-of-odd-jobs Ryan?"

CHAPTER SIXTEEN
TRADING PAPERBACKS

"I don't believe it. I can't believe it!"

"Believe it," Ryan said, serious, but smiling a bit. It was, after all, kind of downright silly. Totally unexpected.

"...to trade paperbacks?" Arabella said.

"Sure," Ryan said, then as if to prove his intentions he began, "To start off, I'd really like to trade you for that copy of *Green Ice*. I can let you have something very nice for it. I don't know if this will appeal to you, being a woman and all, but I've got a great copy of *The Black Echo* by Michael Connelly. It's the first Harry Bosch novel, a hard story about a cop who as a kid saw his mother murdered and it effected him for the rest of his life. It's a story similar to what actually happened to a young James Ellroy. Ah, if you want to trade, I'd also like that old Bantam edition of John Fante's *Ask the Dust*. That is a tough one to find and a cult noir classic. In fact, Connelly even makes mention of Fante's book in another one of his Harry Bosch novels, *The Closers*. You see, there's a lot of history in these books, not only in the stories themselves and the characters, but with the authors, the cover artists, even some of the editors and publishers."

He stopped for a moment to allow her to digest his words. He knew he was blathering a bit. She smiled, she still seemed interested, so he continued.

I've also got something else really special, it's in plastic to protect it. *The Hound of the Baskervilles* by Arthur Conan Doyle, the only Sherlock Holmes full-length novel. This one is a beautiful paperback edition from 1952 published by Bantam Books about 125 or so years ago! Rare as hen's teeth today. The only copy like it on Mars!"

"Sherlock Holmes?" Arabella Rashid said, turning the name over in her mind. She liked the sound of it. She thought she'd read something about him once, long ago. Before Simon. "I've heard of him. It's not really hard-boiled crime, though, is it?"

"No, not really, but it's like they say, the great classic stuff lasts forever. True quality writing, or great heroes and stories, always stand the test of time. This novel was originally written in a place called England. It is as good today as when Doyle first set his pen to paper to write it more than two hundred years ago."

She looked back at Ryan oddly, "You really like this stuff. You even seem to like the people who wrote this stuff—and the people in these books too."

Ryan smiled, "I feel like I understand them, I guess. They're kinda, almost like, real to me. It's hard to explain."

She didn't ask him to explain. Ryan wondered if that was because she herself understood, or if it was just because she didn't give a damn. He found that he really hoped it was the former and not the latter.

Ryan shrugged it off, "In the old days, before computers, before typewriters even, people wrote books by hand. Pen on paper."

Arabella Rashid smiled emptily. She knew all the histories, public, private, secret, and even true. She knew all of that. Why didn't she say anything about it? Why was she playing so dumb? She didn't quite know herself, except that she liked Ryan and liked talking to him. She even liked listening to him talk. Which was pretty amazing for someone like her.

They talked books the rest of the afternoon. Authors, characters, cover artists, the various designs and formats of product put out so long ago by defunct forgotten publishers no one had hardly ever heard of, even when they had been publishing in their own era. They were remembered now by no one at all.

Except Ryan.

It took in a lot of ground. A lot of thoughts and ideas. Except political ideas. They both steered clear of politics. It was not always easy.

Arabella began to realize that she was more than physically attracted to James Ryan. She was attracted to him in a very real and refreshingly intellectual sense. And the fact that they didn't agree on things—often not agreeing on much at all—rather than being annoying was actually stimulating. It was exciting. She was excited. She saw Ryan as a character cut right from the heroes of the books he read. The books she read now too, she thought.

The books they shared and enjoyed.

She also knew he had feelings for her. She could tell, the way he looked at her was unmistakable. She found herself hoping they ran deeper than the merely physical. She knew people, knew men especially. They were all such fools, such little boys really, except those rare few. There were men of character and substance, who had real depth, hard-headed no-nonsense serious types, who were special. Arabella Rashid felt that Ryan was of this type. He was serious. You'd never know it, talking paperbacks, flirting, shooting the breeze. They talked, laughed and joked around, but he was a serious guy. She liked that. She liked him. She did not want to have these feelings. She did not want to have any feelings. She did not like having feelings, nor did she trust them. She thought they'd all been drained out of her by Simon. Apparently they had not.

Arabella felt that for Ryan to be such a serious man was not always a good thing for him. He could be too damn serious sometimes and that could be a bad thing. A dangerous thing. Ideological and hard-headed-serious. That could spell trouble in a political sense. It could even become revolutionary. He could be a man who would dare to say, what a man wanted to say. Or worse, dare to do, what a man wanted to do. Those men were rare today, at least among the social non-predatory, non-criminal type. The unincarcerated. Even the politicals down on

Earth had become mild and meek. Scared all the time. Ryan was not like them. He had strength, character, integrity, a brain. He was bold. He had, she realized...honor.

She was drawn to it, drawn to him like a magnet. The realization made her feel woozy almost. She knew he was drawn to her too and the thought excited her all the more. She knew he wanted her. A serious hungry wanting. But not just because she was the best damn woman he'd ever seen. The best he could ever have on Mars or anywhere on Earth. That was not it. He'd passed up better before, back on Earth. Women like that didn't worm their way into men like James Ryan without a reason.

Arabella Rashid blushed as she looked over at him, watching him look at the books, hiding her glance so he did not know she was looking at him. It was a rare feeling for her. She realized that Ryan somehow saw into her, into her most private area, her most private thoughts and feelings. He saw even into her deep, dark, and ugly places, the places she knew were there and that she was so adept at hiding. Ryan saw it all and never even flinched. Instead he smiled. It did not bother him. He did not fear her. He saw her the way she was, the total, entire woman. She felt a powerful connection with him that she could not deny.

She felt naked before him and she loved the feeling.

Arabella Rashid was awed. She traded paperbacks, she talked authors, she listened to his substantial knowledge on books and other topics. Always she asked questions to keep him talking. She even made a few jokes to watch him laugh. She asked for more information on this book, or that author, even tried to engage him in politics....

Ryan just laughed and talked about a town called Poisonville in a book by Dashiell Hammett called *Red Harvest*, in an early Dell edition he had called *Nightmare Town*. And she wondered if she would end up turning Mars into a nightmare planet once she found out just what was going on here.

* * * * * * *

Ryan was alone now. In his cube. The copy of *Nightmare Town* by Dashiell Hammett lay open on his chest. He dozed. He dreamed. His mind time-tripping back. Back to another life. Another reality.

Back a long time ago.

It was on another planet.

It was another world.

Someone was talking to him so he knew he wasn't back in solitary confinement.

The voice said, "So what about all the cons in prison who trusted you? You planned an escape, a damn revolution. They all believed in you and you sold them out. Got them all killed."

"That was my job," Ryan heard himself reply in the dream, moving his lips silently along with the images going on in his head.

"Some job."

"Yeah."

"So how does it feel?" the voice asked Ryan.

"What?"

"To be a Judas Goat. You know you sold a bunch of suckers down the river. To die. They believed in you. At least they trusted you. You were their damned leader! Why, you're no better than the hated Authority. They also believe loyalty only runs from the bottom to the top. Never from top to bottom. But it should. It damn well should! You sold them out, Ryan. You're a perfect Judas Goat, you're a low-life piece of shit, and a double-damned rat without any honor at all."

"It was my job."

"Sure."

"And now what? Are you going to sell out Mars? Sell out your friends? To her? The DOC?"

"No!"

"Yes you are, Ryan. I know you. And *you* know *you!*"

Ryan shouted to the ghost in his head, "You've done worse, Macky!"

Macky just laughed and walked away.

He was thinking of her again. He couldn't help it. He didn't want to, and he knew that he shouldn't, but he had no choice. There was something within him, something that made him think about her all the time now. He saw her face in his mind's eye and it made him smile. It made him want her, and it said to him that he needed her. He did not like that. Ryan did not like to need anyone. He knew this could be his ruination.

Or his salvation.

But which one?

Ryan wasn't scared.

He knew what he had to do.

He had to find out.

* * * * * * *

When he saw her the next day the first thing she did was kiss him and say, "You know, you were right about *Green Ice*."

Ryan held her close. He didn't want to let her go. He knew she was potential dynamite to his plans, poison to him and all his dreams, but he knew he had to take the chance. For himself. For her. For them.

But she was dangerous for him, he understood that too. If anyone could turn him, she could. He knew it. Deep. He'd lie for her, steal for her. He was scared. He might even sell out the revolution to The DOC for her!

Was that why she was here?

But he knew he had to take the chance. A chance for happiness. To do that, he had to find out the truth for himself. That would entail considerable risk. It might endanger Mars, but danger was what Mars was all about. Taking chances. Fighting the odds. Finding things out for yourself. Standing on your own two feet. Going your own way!

He took her around the planet, showing her what sites there were, and some of the mines. They 'coptered out to Olympus Mons up to the very pinnacle over a dozen incredible miles high to a point that was the top of the world. It was breathtaking.

Many miles higher than Everest in the Himalayas back on Earth. They drove across endless deserts of red clay, with pockmarked cratered surfaces, deep into the ruts of the old Mars canals. Across the horizon were the twin moons of Deimos and Phobos, chasing each other in a mad rush across the dark starry night sky.

It had been breathtaking. It had been a wonderful day.

That night they traded more paperbacks. They talked books once again, then talked about life. Then about love.

Then they made love.

CHAPTER SEVENTEEN
PAPERBACKS AND POLITICS

She said to him afterwards, while they were still in bed together, "Politics...?"

"I know," he said.

"It's tricky. You have to be careful. Like out here. You would not believe it. When I got here a few days ago some old coot played over the spaceport PA system some damn song...."

Ryan smiled, "Old John McGregor. Did he play the Mars World Anthem?"

Arabella Rashid looked at Ryan carefully, said, "Yes, he did, but...."

"I know...."

She said, "Look, James, Mars does *not* have any anthem, no World Anthem, or any other kind of anthem."

"I know," Ryan laughed lightly. She didn't like it. He didn't appear to be taking this serious. He was a serious type guy and this was the most serious thing there was. He only smiled, nodded.

She liked his face when he laughed though. It was so healthy, so hearty. So full of life. It infected her, made her smile too. But she wished he would take these things more seriously. Be more careful.

"It's subversive," she told him, serious herself now.

He just smiled again, "I know."

"You seem to know a lot."

"I'm Mr. Takes-Care-Of-Odd-Jobs, remember? That takes in

a lot of territory."

"But with politics..?"

"Yes?" he asked.

"It's tricky," Arabella Rashid said again.

"I guess it can be."

She looked at Ryan. "You have to be very careful," she said, wondering about him, concerned for his safety, all kinds of thoughts entering her mind now.

He didn't say anything in reply, he didn't want to confront her.

Finally she shrugged it off. She'd get no straight answer out of him on this topic she realized, just as he'd get no straight answer out of her. Nothing at least, that she didn't want him to know. It was an impasse. She finally said, "Tell me about Mars...."

"And what else...?"

"Well, about Mars...and paperbacks."

Ryan smiled, "Why don't you tell me about what's going on back on Earth first?"

Arabella Rashid thought that one over for a moment. She couldn't very well say what was *really* going on back there, but she did want to talk about some of it with him. She felt she needed to talk about it with Ryan.

It was a terrible breach of security, a breach of the highest order. It went directly against her own guiding philosophy and rules, but then again, they were *her* rules. She had made them. She could break them. Anyway, she was way out here on Mars, in secret identity, so what did it matter? What did anything matter? Earth was so far away now. And when she thought about it, Arabella Rashid kind of liked it that way.

She looked over at Ryan, watching him watching her.

What a strange, fearless, contrary, exciting, intelligent and damn exasperating man. She'd never known one like him before and she realized now that while she'd known many men in many ways, she really had never known a real man before. Certainly no one like Ryan. All the others may have been fine, some were fun, they were all certainly male, but Ryan was a man. He brought out the woman in her and she loved the feeling. The awakening of it all.

He was quiet, waiting for her.

Arabella said, "There's not much to tell."

Ryan laughed deeply. Almost mocking her. She was almost sure of it and it surprised her. But she deserved it. It was like he knew something about her, for sure. Not her secret identity—but her secret inner self. For her to get angry and sensitive about it would end up telling him more about her than she should give up. At least at this time.

"You're so damn sure of yourself, Ryan!"

Ryan shook his head, "No I'm not. I take chances, you know how that is? It can be dangerous. It can even be fatal these days."

Arabella Rashid, sobered, nodded. She knew he was right. She wondered, did he suspect who she really was? The enemy. His worst enemy imaginable come to his happy, free world, now right here with him in bed! Arabella Rashid and the DOC!

"So?"

She nodded, "There's some news that's kept strictly under wraps, a war brewing on Earth. A cyborg replicant by the name of Moses Sage has united all the Underground peoples and forced an alliance with renegade warriors from the top world Authority...."

"The nanotech super warriors? I'd heard of them. I thought they were just rumors," Ryan said softly.

Arabella hesitated, nodded, said nothing more.

"I thought the rumors of their existence...I mean, I'd heard stories, but.... So they are real? There really are these super warriors?"

"Too real," Arabella said. "A group of them in one of the Security Districts that make up one of the LastCen nations—something once called the United States of America—well, they have joined Moses Sage. Now his Underworld people are at war against the Authority...."

Arabella Rashid stopped, she'd said more than enough. More

than anyone had a right to know.

"The Authority," Ryan mused, "run everything on the Earth. All the former nation-states, all the biz-conglomerates, the media and world net is under their control. But who controls them? We both know it's the Department of Control that...."

Arabella Rashid leapt at Ryan, covered his mouth with her hand. She held him down firmly, whispered, "Be quiet! Are you crazy! Don't ever mention that name! We are not to know of such things. We are not to talk of them. They can...."

Ryan threw her off him.

She was astonished. She had tried to save him, "The walls have ears...."

Ryan said, "This is Mars! Not Earth! The walls do *not* have ears here. We still have privacy here. Now I have to leave...."

She said, "Ryan? James? What did I do?"

He got up to go.

She watched him get dressed.

He was leaving her? Just like that!

Her stomach fell to her knees.

She grew angry and silent and cold.

She began to think of revenge and spite.

She said, "Where are you going?"

He said, "I have to leave."

* * * * * * *

He thought about the paperbacks again. Only the paperbacks are true, real, always there for you waiting to be picked up, waiting to be read. So many authors speaking their truth directly to you. Personal. To you only. Like you are someone special. Like the author really cared about letting you know his own special truth, the real inside dope within him or her. It's the true story, and it was good. So fine. Not like some people that live and cheat and play their dirty little games.

Paperbacks have always been, they always will be. So he hoped.

Ryan thought about that one special book, from some memory chip lost back in his mind, something called, *Mars Needs Books*. He knew what Mars really needed was women. More women like her. He knew who 'her' was now. Arabella Rashid. There could be no doubt. He was also in love with her. He also knew she loved him. Though she probably would never admit it. He was also sure she was hell-bent on the death and destruction of all his plans and dreams. Not to mention his life. She was probably working on it all right now. Planning it all very precisely.

He knew only too well what she'd do if she had her way here on Mars.

She'd make Mars *scream!*

Everyone would be rounded up, tortured, brain-wiped. That would not be the worst of it.

Ryan shook his head. He tried not to think of her but he couldn't get her out of his mind. He finally decided. He had to do something about her. He had to take a chance on her.

He took out the box. It was his box of insurance. It had been hidden so many years ago, when he'd first come out to Mars. The box with all the dust on it.

The box with the gun inside.

CHAPTER EIGHTEEN
I DON'T NEED NO DOC

It was a day later.

On Mars, a day late and a dollar short was a way of life. It was part of the hard-boiled attitude that spoke so truthfully to the tough miners and construction workers who had built this world and struggled on a day-to-day basis to make it work. They worked and lived under the worse conditions imaginable. They thrived without any help from Earth.

The only thing the settlers and pioneers on Mars received from Earth were problems: excess regulations, stupid rules, unjust laws, spies, bureaucrats, terrorists, subversives, mind-control mechanisms of every type, all to keep them slaves of Earth. All to increase the control of The DOC.

It always came back to The DOC, Ryan thought. To The DOC and Arabella Rashid.

He decided he'd have to kill her.

But he couldn't do that.

So he decided he'd have to tell her.

Eventually.

The secret war on Earth was real, she'd let on to him about it. She'd told him about it, even mentioned Moses Sage, finally brought his name out in the open.

It was valuable information. Now he owed her.

He knew what he had to do for the first time now.

Something he did not want to do.

He had to trust her.

There was something he wanted to show her.

He knew he'd have to show her the secret place and hope that she would understand.

Then maybe she'd listen to him and their personal war could end before any fatalities.

Otherwise, they'd all be doomed.

Then all of them would be very dead, very soon.

So he was okay with it all now.

He was sane. He knew it. Better.

He was sure of it.

But this was all just so damn crazy.

He knew they didn't have no doctor for what was bothering him.

But to show Arabella Rashid their most secret place was infinitely dangerous. The kind of thing he'd need a shrink for. Or a firing squad. But not the shrinks they have today, like the ones down on Earth. Not those political shrinks. They were evil. They were all collaborators with The DOC. There used to be honest head doctors in the old days. Even if not perfect, at least they really did try to help their patients. Sometimes their advice even worked. Not likely today.

He didn't need no doctor. He needed some guts. He needed some serious guts because if he showed Arabella Rashid the secret library of Mars and he got the wrong response from her— if it appeared she would use the information to move against Mars, against the Republic and the Resistance—then love her or not, he'd have to take care of it.

He just hoped he had the guts to do what needed to be done.

He knew that he didn't, but it was his job.

"I am 'Mr. Takes-Care-Of-Odd-Jobs'. That's what I told her. That's what she called me. And it's true. I know it and she knows it. And 'odd-jobs' takes in a lot of ground. Too damn much ground sometimes."

Ryan looked at the weapon in his hand. He had not made use of it since before he'd come to Mars. Now he might have to use it one last time.

On the woman he loved.

Ryan was the 'odd-jobs' man. The revolutionary. The killer. The traitor to the cons long ago, the fink according to Macky, the liar, the rat—the warrior against Earth freedom. He was also the keeper of the Secret Place, but he knew the less said about that now, the better.

Some spoke of making him king.

But he knew what he really was cut out for.

Ryan.

James Ryan.

Fool.

And.

Knave.

Ashamed of himself.

Some called him a man of honor.

He knew better.

There is no true honor....

...that is not born of dishonor.

He had been there....

...and back again.

He put the gun away.

He hoped he would not have to use it.

He prayed he would not have to use it.

He could always strangle her, or blunt force trauma would work in a pinch.

It made him sick to even think about it.

He imagined the cold steel pressed against the soft flesh of the temple of Arabella Rashid's head. He could see himself pressing that trigger. If he had to. He could see her dying in his arms. If she had to. And with her, all his hopes and dreams dying too.

Or would she get the drop on him? He was weak. Perhaps she would trick him? It had happened before. He knew all about such treachery. From both ends, from both sides in the struggle.

If she won—if The DOC won—then that would be it for him and Mars and everyone on the planet. DOC would investigate, she'd see to that. The DOC was nothing if not thorough. They'd find the truth soon enough. What they would discover is that the entire planet, and everyone on it, was a dangerous nest of revolutionaries that needed to be neutralized immediately. Serious hard case Authority problems. They'd have no choice according to their own twisted version of truth and correctness. They would eliminate the infestation and that meant killing all human life on Mars.

A secret order would go out on a planetary scale.

KTA!

Kill Them All!

Ryan figured Arabella Rashid might start with him. Or maybe, if her DOC training got the better of her, she'd save him for last. A special case. Watch him. Gauge his reactions. Try to turn him. Scare him. Make him beg. Cry. Cause him to die inside little by little as his friends all around him, and his world, were slowly destroyed before his eyes.

Such was The DOC way.

They so enjoyed their work.

He gave her a call and told her," There's a place I'd like to show you."

"I've seen all the local tourist traps, Ryan. There's not all that much to see here on Mars, that I haven't already seen," she said a bit stiffly, still bristling from the other day no doubt, but trying not to show it.

"This is different," he told her.

"How is it different, Ryan?"

He said, "It's cool, kinda revolutionary, if you know what I mean."

She perked up. "What is it?"

"It's one of the best spots on Mars. You have to see it to believe it. There's nothing like it on Earth at all. Not anymore," he told her proudly.

"Not another tourist trap?" she said. She couldn't resist busting his chops one last time for the way he'd left her yesterday. She still felt the hurt, was actually surprised by it, but not really angry.

"This isn't anything any tourists will ever see. Not now. This is something special and I want to share it with you, show it to you."

"Is it some kind of secret, Ryan?" she asked in a conspiratorial whisper.

"Yes," he replied mysteriously.

Arabella Rashid smiled her most winning smile. It was delightful to see, except Ryan could not see it. She said, "Ryan, I really like secrets."

"I figured you would."

"So how many people know about it...?"

He didn't say another word. He pressed the time and coordinates code that showed her where and when they were to meet.

Then he broke the link.

CHAPTER NINETEEN
THROUGH THE MARTIAN DESERT

She was there early. Naturally. Waiting. Looking impatient, a bit tense, perhaps somewhat angry. But she softened when she saw him approach. Angry at herself that she had made it evident she was so happy to see him. Upset especially that she had made her feelings transparent to Ryan. But that was okay. Ryan returned the feelings, returned the smile. His eyes drinking in her loveliness and warmth and reveling in it.

She was a vision, he thought.

"So how many people know about this secret place, Ryan?" she asked him as they walked through the Mall and over towards the North Gate. There they'd suit up, get a land buggy and drive out to the crater.

"Not many. It's a secret, like I told you."

"What kind of secret, Ryan?" she insisted. She knew she was being difficult but so was he. Nevertheless she was enjoying baiting him.

"A very big secret," he laughed.

She smiled, he *was* playing with her. Yet, instead of making her mad it made her happy. She was also playing with him. So the feeling was mutual.

She just looked at him and shook her head. He guided her to the North Gate. She acted obstinate, but wasn't. She was more curious than any cat ever could be at that point. She knew Ryan knew something about what was going on here on Mars. Now, for some reason, he had decided to show her.

Of course, she knew it could all be a trap. He may have discovered her true identity and was taking her outside the port to eliminate her. In fact, she knew that this Ryan might not be a Marsman at all. He could be a DOC agent acting on orders from someone back on Earth to eliminate her. She'd just have to wait and see. But there was something unique about Ryan. She liked him. She felt she could trust him. And then there was the other thing, she thought she was beginning to fall in love with him. The thought surprised her but also delighted her, she had to admit. She was quite astonished, but found out she actually liked the feeling.

"So where are we going, Ryan?"

"You'll see, soon enough."

She said, "I guess we're going outside?"

He nodded as she tried to keep up with him.

"Where?"

He directed her to Joe's Place. They rented suits and helmets, as a precaution. Then they rented a land buggy.

They got dressed fast. Got in the small vehicle and drove out of the North Port Gate into the Martian desert. They drove on the bleak red, pock-marked surface, on dry rock and around small craters.

They were quiet for a while. He was thinking. Nervous.

She looked thoughtful as well, apparently looking over the arid lonely landscape.

There was a lot on their minds.

Paramount was which one of them might end up killing the other.

He noticed that in her pocket was an old Pocket Book edition of *The Maltese Falcon* by Dashiell Hammett. He'd given the book to her to read the other day. It made him happy to see her with it now, to see that she cared enough to read it and to have it with her today.

"How is it?" he said, pointing to the book.

She looked at him like he'd spoken some incomprehensible language. She'd obviously been in some very deep thought, on a world a million miles away from him. And from Mars. Far away. On Earth and back at her desk at DOC most likely. That was not a good sign he thought....

"The book," he asked again. "How do you like it?"

She gave him a short laugh. "I just finished it while I was waiting for you."

"And?"

"What a great story!"

He said, "Did you like the ending?"

She said, "Yeah. I really understood it. When you have a job to do, you just have to do it. Isn't that right, Ryan?"

He thought that over a moment. A very short moment. It didn't take him long. It was a no-brainer. He knew how it was. She knew the score too.

He shrugged. "Sam Spade's a lot tougher guy than I am."

"But he's not at war with the world like you are, Ryan. He's not at war."

"I'm not at war. I just want to be left alone. I want to be free. I can be free here on Mars. I want to stay free, that's all. Is that too much to ask for? And we don't need no DOC to come out here and try to control our lives."

"Nor any Arabella Rashid, either?"

He looked at her sharply then. He'd said more than he'd ever intended, but she'd said too much as well. She'd mentioned her real name, dropped her trump card.

So it was her.

It had to be!

It was a fact! An incredible fact that she was here on Mars. Here now with him!

Now she had admitted to him that she was here on Mars! It had to be her, unless she was lying to him and playing some kind of game. He didn't want to think about that and had no idea what *that* might imply. It was the first time she'd ever mentioned her true name to him. She'd all but given him her secret identity. On purpose, it seemed. But why?

He knew that he should have killed her right then and there.

It would have been the by-the-book thing to do. Even according to Old Earther rules and DOC rules for this sort of thing. But this was Mars. Mars was not Earth. Thank God! He did not ever want it to become like Earth. Mars was different. And it should stay different. Always.

He said, as calm as could be, "Actually, I figured you for her all along."

"But you weren't sure. Were you, Ryan? Not one hundred percent sure?" she asked confidently.

"No. It was all too unbelievable," he sighed.

She said, "Ryan, are you all right? You look a little pale. You're not going to faint on me, are you? Do you want me to get you a doctor?"

He smiled, said, "No, I'll be all right. It's just a shock. The Department of Control here on Mars. Really here! And you, so open about it all. You are Arabella Rashid, here with me. You're her! I can't believe it. I'll be all right. I don't need no doctor. I need a reality check. I'm just wondering how come I'm still alive, that's all."

"I might ask you the same thing," she replied, a sparkle in her eyes surrounded by hardness.

He just shook his head.

She said, "You really do look like you need a doctor, or else you sure need something."

"I need some of that old number 7 Jack Daniels Tennessee sipping whiskey. A lot of it."

CHAPTER TWENTY
MARS AIN'T JUST A STATE OF MIND

Mars does things to your mind. It forces reality and it's real tough, that is what it really is. Real nasty too. It takes a real long time to get out there from Earth. The trip out takes almost an entire year. A long solid time of loneliness and solitude and thinking. All kinds of thinking. There is also the very real danger of death alone out in space. That means there is a lot of time for reflection, thought, planning—for reevaluation of your life up to that point. It's a very natural human reaction to the time and stress factors involved.

Mars was a new beginning for most. People who left Old Earth left all the old problems behind. It was a new world. And if they were smart, they left a lot of the crap learned on Old Earth behind them too when they came to Mars.

Mars changed people.

Most people.

It had changed James Ryan for sure.

Now Ryan hoped it had changed Arabella Rashid.

It was in one of his dreams.

The fact that she had told him her true identity was a start. The fact that open warfare had not broken out between them, quite astonishing actually, was another check on the positive side of the ledger to his way of thinking. Sure, they were in love with each other. They must be. That had to be it.

But so what?

Love was not everything. To some people love meant nothing.

When you were the type of people Arabella Rashid and James Ryan were, too often love was just another useful weapon in the arsenal of warfare to be used against your enemy. Sometimes even being your most effective weapon.

Or so it had always been down on Earth.

* * * * * * *

The vehicle approached the crater now. The place was unmarked, not on any of the charts. It was in a desolate area, but there was a road of sorts that lead into it. Most strange, Arabella thought, and she asked Ryan about it.

"You ain't seen the half of it," he replied with a smile and she was sure of that.

"Are we there yet?" she asked, as if an eager child on a family trip.

"Yes, just about. It won't be long now. A short walk outside, we have to get to the turbo, go down, then de-suit. Then I'll show you something that Earth has not seen the likes of for over a hundred years."

She said, "I can't wait, Ryan."

"There's just one thing you have to promise me, Arabella," he said, using her real name for the first time. He decided he liked the sound of it, and she decided she liked the way her name sounded when spoken by his voice.

She said, "What's that, James?"

"This is a secret. So you have to promise me not to tell anyone. All right?" he asked, not smiling now, stone-faced, calm but unreadable to her. He was dead serious.

She just watched him in amazement.

"It's like the honor system," he added. "Do you promise?"

She said, "Yes, James, I promise."

"No matter what it is?" he asked incredulously, wondering already if she was lying to him. She probably was, after all. Was this the big betrayal he'd expected, what he'd been waiting for?

Or was she being true? Had she changed? Mars could do that. Mars could perform miracles on the human soul and spirit. He knew that was true.

"Yes, James, I promise. No matter what it is."

He smiled at her. He did not move his hand toward his gun. He knew he could never take up a weapon against her now.

Arabella smiled back, but she knew he was armed now. So was she. She relaxed a moment. She knew now he would never take action against her. She did not want to think about what she would have done were she in his place. At least what she *would* have done if she were back on Earth. But Ryan was correct. On Mars things were different. She forgot about her own weapon, and instead concentrated on the man walking next to her. Dreaming wonderful dreams with him as he spoke to her.

Ryan said, "Come on. We go in through here. Then down six levels. The place is all hollowed out. It was said to have been the home of some pre-human aliens. They're long dead and gone now. Early astronauts did some archaeology long ago but DOC closed it down once they took over on Earth. Then it was to have been a secret missile base. In fact, that is just what the DOC and the Earth Authority think that it was originally. A secret missile base built by aliens, later to be used as a secret missile base by The DOC. But we've put it to better use."

Arabella Rashid was impressed. She'd struck the mother lode all right. The inner-secret of Mars and the rebel Resistance. And Revolution. It was here and thriving all right. She realized now, "revolution" was exactly the correct and proper word for it. Subversion and revolution. Just the thing The DOC hated and strove so hard to crush. They would crush it in every way, shape, manner and form in which it appeared. Wherever it reared its ugly head.

On Earth! *Crush it!*

And now, here on Mars as well.... *Crush it!*

She sighed sadly, it was all so inevitable.

"Are you all right?" Ryan asked her.

"Yes," she looked back, wondering why he was showing this

all to her, knowing who an what she was.

"Then come on, it's right over here," he said, leading her toward the opening.

The building was enormous, a huge underground cavern, reinforced against all manner of attack, hermetically sealed and with fully functioning cyber security, ventilation, and climate control.

This had to be it! The secret base of the rebels!

They de-suited in an outside chamber before they entered the main hall and then Arabella Rashid had her breath taken away by what she saw.

"It's our secret. This is it."

"What is it?" she gasped.

"The secret Library of Mars," Ryan said, proudly. "I'm the, ah...Chief Librarian."

The hall was enormous and it was flanked by row upon row of shelves, all packed tightly with every kind of book. Mostly all paperbacks. It was incredible. She realized almost breathless, it was even quite lovely. Beautiful and wonderful.

Arabella Rashid looked at Ryan incredulously. "Chief Librarian? And to think, I thought you were just the leader of some...Revolution?"

Ryan blushed, "Actually not a Revolution, a Resistance. There is a big difference. We are resisters. We resist Earth's ways, ideas and interference. We're resisters."

"And some day revolutionaries," she said confidently, "and eventually... enemies...."

Ryan took a deep thoughtful breath and replied, "Perhaps. Some day."

She shook her head like it was all so crazy.

And Ryan knew that it was, but he wouldn't let that stop him.

"Come on, let's go inside and I'll show you around. I'm sure even Arabella Rashid of the DOC has never seen anything quite like this before."

* * * * * * *

Once inside, Ryan proudly explained to her, "The thing is, the books here are in a hermetically sealed, and preservation-secure environment. Here they can be protected for centuries. They were each plastisealed back on Earth before being sent out here. In fact, the books, I just got and all others were also plastisealed for a hundred years before being shipped to me. That is how they were able to stay in such good condition after so many years. They came from secret private collections. These books are the real treasure of Mars. This is the treasure Earth decided was too dangerous to keep on Earth. And yet, they are too important to destroy totally. Knowledge is treasure after all, but the greater treasure here is truth that comes from human stories."

Arabella Rashid nodded, amazed at all the books shelved so neatly. It seemed there were miles and miles of books everywhere she looked.

Ryan continued, "Of course almost all the books here are non-fiction. History, politics, biographies, philosophy, so much more. Those are the most important books we need, the crucial ones, books with information, all published LastCen. Even before the Authority came to power. Before the DOC took control of everything. Real books in original hard copy, undoctored, unabridged, uncensored, and not subject to any PC monitoring whatsoever. There is no reevaluation, no reinterpretation, no revision of any of the text. What was written was printed, just as it was written. What was printed, has not been changed in any way. Not at all like what's in the digital record, which is changed, updated and rewritten every day to conform with current fad, fashion, political policy, agenda, and propaganda.

Arabella Rashid let her eyes rove over the seemingly endless rows of high shelves. It was awesome. She'd never seen anything like it. Never had she imagined something like this could even exist....

Ryan continued, "The books here are the information storage devices of human truth in print, at least the truth as it was originally written by the original authors, without any changes to their words. The hard copy form is unchangeable without tell-tale signs of that change. They're from the unpolluted old days, before brain programming, from days when such things were unethical and unlawful. It was a time when the control we take for granted today was in its infancy. A time when disinformation, reevaluated facts, and revised conclusions were *not* PC. In those olden days it was believed to be wrong, unethical, certainly immoral to even think of doing such things. It was book blasphemy."

Arabella Rashid listened to his words but she thought her own thoughts and he could not tell what they were. What they might be or mean for him and Mars.

Ryan continued, "That was the old days, when for the most part, results were based on facts and evidence. Not when facts and evidence were used to ensure pre-ordained results. Today our sources of information are constantly changed, doctored, corrected, revised by the government on Earth—or by the DOC!"

She nodded, she knew all about that. It was all true. Ryan had even left out a lot of the more horrendous ways the government and The DOC controlled the masses. Mind-altering drugs in the food and water supply, hidden messages in disks and manipulated software, subcutaneous implants that most people did not even know they had imbedded within their body. VRB-Virtual Reality Brainwashing. Nanotech monitors capable of triggering subject death once that subject thought the wrong thought! Of course The DOC controlled all forms of all media, and in doing so controlled all forms of thought on Earth.

But not here on Mars!

Ryan added, "There are no disks here, no brain implants, or mind-computer links. Nothing that could be doctored or changed. Here we only have the original hard copies, only books. It is just pages, paper, covers, words printed on paper. A book you can hold in your hands. Real. Full of facts. They may not always be correct, but at least they're a galaxy away from the lies and distortions of your controlled media, links, implants, and *everydamnthing!"*

"Calm down, Ryan!"

"I'm calm," he said tersely.

"You're not like any librarian I've ever heard of. Even in the DOC. They're usually kind of...."

"I know. Meek. Mild-mannered."

"Yeah," she said. "Like, what the hell happened to you?"

"I'm sorry," he said softly.

She just laughed, "Don't be sorry, baby."

"Come on, then, there's more to see in the Fiction Section."

"How the hell did you get all these books out here?"

Ryan shrugged, "A few at a time. I have a contact who buys them up by the ton on Earth. No one seems to care much about them anymore. He gets them usually in more backward third-world districts and sectors where people have been using them for fuel for the last few decades."

"Fuel, you mean they burn them?" she said, shocked.

"Yeah. They need to keep warm, so they burn them. They can't read. They don't know or care about books. They don't understand what they really are. Some people are scared of them. And the Sector and district governments, the DOC, all encourage them to burn them."

She looked at him, "It's all right, I know all about it."

"...The DOC, the leaders, keep everyone uneducated and illiterate except the elite. Most Citizens on Earth can't even read anymore. Oh, they recognize a few words and symbols here and there, but they can't actually read a complete book. They're even scared of them now. They think books are dangerous. It is an idea given to them by The DOC. People are terrified of the ideas in books that they don't understand. But that fear doesn't stop them from putting any kind of government-approved software into the slot in their head. Or taking the latest fad-drug. They'll do that and love it as they get themselves more deeply programmed and controlled than the reading of any mere words on paper could ever do, and they don't even know it. But they're scared of books. Imagine that? You have no idea how it was out here twenty years ago. The literacy program, I had to begin from scratch...."

"Did it work, James?"

"Too well. Now I've got a damn planet full of know-it-all scholars and cynical literary critics, avant-garde political theorists and cranky social engineers who argue bibliographic theory. Damn annoying—and damnit—it's just great!"

She smiled.

"So many books!" she said in awe.

"Yeah, it is a lot. Over a million. We smuggled them out here shipload by shipload. Crates that say 'vids' and the latest 'brain-implants'. What crap! Instead the boxes were full of old paperbacks from LastCen. Paperbacks were sent because they are much lighter to transport than heavier hard covers and much more common. We took all the great old stuff, all genres, and all the non-fiction and fact books we could find. The entire knowledge of our species. The history of our race, Arabella—the human race! It's all here, at your fingertips just for the asking to be looked at."

"How do you access it all?"

"Computers. Yeah, we're not Luddites here on Mars. But we use the computer as a tool, it is a productive servant like it was intended to be and like it was used LastCen. It's not the master on Mars, like it is on Earth now. It has its limited uses as a file system, a roadmap to where any book on any topic by any author could be found anywhere in here. Title, author, subject, and more, all indexed and cross-referenced a hundred ways."

She said, "It's all pretty impressive, James. You're right, there is nothing at all like this on Earth."

"Not anymore," Ryan said, remembering. "Once there had been thousands of such libraries worldwide in a hundred different languages."

Arabella Rashid looked at Ryan carefully.

Ryan looked back at her and thought, how sad she looked. She looked so very sad. She knows. He thought: *She's going to do it. She's going to sell me out. I've failed.*

Suddenly Ryan felt very tired. The gun in his pocket weighing heavier and heavier in a physical sense, but also in a mental and emotional sense. Meanwhile the seconds passed into minutes quietly. Slowly. Both of them savoring the time. Savoring being with each other. And thinking. What would they do next?

They stayed there the rest of the day and slept over that night. The library had accommodations for visiting scholars and researchers. A large and fully automated cafeteria, stocked with the latest in pre-processed and hi-tech manufactured foodstuff. It even tasted like the real thing if you weren't too particular. Scholars on a research bender weren't that particular about food anyway, they just wanted it to be hot and substantial enough to keep them going. They usually had better, bigger things on their minds than food.

Ryan understood; still and all, he enjoyed his meal with Arabella Rashid.

After they'd eaten, they went to bed and made love all night, then slept in exhausted slumber. They slept late to wake next day and shower in the mid-morning.

Ryan figured he'd done what he came out here to do, shown her what he wanted to show her. She'd seen what she had come to see. The Secret Library of Mars.

Big deal!

It would probably all be blown up with tactical nukes soon enough, if Ryan knew the DOC like he knew he did. But he'd done what he'd set out to do. He proved to her that he trusted her. He had foolishly opened himself up to betrayal.

For her.

Now it was all up to her.

"We might as well get an early start back to the port," he said softly.

Arabella surprised him when she said, "James, we don't really have to go back right now, do we?"

"I guess not. What do you want to do then?"

She looked back at him almost as if he were a simpleton, "I've done a lot of thinking. I don't want to leave here. I want to stay. And...look around with you. Can we do that? Look around? Together? Read some of the books? Maybe read some of them to each other?"

Ryan was astonished but very pleased, she seemed genuinely interested. He'd expected secret shock troops from some hidden DOC battleship orbiting the planet to burst in and arrest him any minute. Or perhaps some kind of action taken against him by Arabella herself. Like a bullet in the head. She was certainly capable of such action.

"What do you want to do? Really?"

"Look up some of the books in the file. There are some things I'd like to read about. Some truths I want to discover. Or rediscover. If it's not too much trouble."

"You want to stay here for a few more hours, I guess. "

"Well, yeah, but actually I was thinking, why don't we make a day of it. I wouldn't even mind a day after that, or even a week out here. But only if you want, baby."

Ryan nodded. She had called him 'baby' again. He smiled. He liked that. No woman had ever called him that before. He said, "Sure. What's another day or two, or three...."

Arabella Rashid said, "A day or two, or maybe three, James. It's not a big deal."

"Yeah, Arabella, it's no big deal now."

"Thanks, James."

He put the doom that was hanging over them out of his mind for the moment. They had two-three days—and they'd make the most of it damnit!

He smiled, "Come on, then, I'll show you how the files are configured. I set it all up myself years ago. You'll be able to find anything you want and the servo-robots will bring you the correct book every time. They'll bring the book right to your desk, room, or even to your bed if you like. Or you can go hunt for it on the shelves yourself. Sometimes that's even more fun, but I warn you, it's easy to get sidetracked."

Arabella said, "That's real service, Ryan. Come on. Let's take another look around first."

He thought he had to be dreaming it all. She was back downstairs now, looking up essays on "Noir" and the originators of hard-boiled crime fiction, of all things.

* * * * * * *

He'd just showered, shaved, and was getting dressed. He took the gun and deposited it in the waste chute. Goodbye, weapon. He had to take his chance. He'd taken that chance. It looked like he had won. It looked like Mars might win too. A lot of things looked good to him at the moment. But that's the way things always look, just before things turn bad. He wondered about that. Mars ain't no state of mind, it's a real place and ugly reality has a nasty habit of reasserting itself at the oddest moments.

CHAPTER TWENTY-ONE
MEMORY WILL ALWAYS PLAY YOU

It was cool. Arabella Rashid and James Ryan at the secret library. Talking and enjoying themselves, looking through and reading all kinds of fascinating things during the day—having all kinds of fascinating fun and games at night.

The days passed wonderfully.

It was a good time for both of them.

A free time.

Away from it all.

Away from politics.

Away from duty.

It was too short a time of course, but neither of them would ever forget it.

They talked a lot about books. She wanted to see one of the rare book rooms. The one with all the hard-boiled vintage era paperbacks.

"Come on, James," she said, leading him down the hall, hand in hand. She wore a short mini- dress, she'd told him it was the latest rage-style back on Earth. All very sexually and politically incorrect these days. "You like the way I look?"

He loved the way she looked. The fact that she'd dressed that way for him was almost too much for him to believe. He didn't say much about it, but he thought a *lot* about it. Her. Finally he said, "It's very nice. You look great."

She smiled, she knew it only too well. She said, "You know, it's not on any of the approved clothing lists."

Ryan laughed, "Only on Earth would they have approved clothing and unapproved clothing. Of all the damn stupid things. Do they actually have...?"

She nodded back to him, "Oh yes. There are laws and they enforce them. Rigorously. It's been the law for a long time almost as far back as LastCen. Today it's become mostly custom and fashion. Approved fashion, of course. Unapproved fashion is dangerous, it can lead to a prison term. Or worse. You could be labeled a trouble-maker or an "incorrigible." That can lead to a Brain-wipe. Reprogramming."

Ryan shook his head.

She told him, "There was this girl, she was a low-level secretary in one of the hundreds of DOC agencies. I didn't know of her. I certainly did not know her, but I heard it all afterwards. She'd been involved in some kind of clandestine sexual relationship. Actually, it was worse than that, it was a secret marriage! Can you believe that? And in The DOC with another DOC worker. I mean, the guy wasn't just a Citizen—he was DOC. I think he set her up for a promotion. Then he betrayed her!"

"Marriage is still outlawed?" Ryan asked.

"Official DOC policy, and it's frowned on in the general culture also. And we all know the general culture always follows the lead of the elite's," she said in a matter of fact tone.

He nodded, not surprised at all.

She continued, "But back to this secretary. She ended up getting secretly married. Some of that kind of thing goes on among citizens and lower-level workers. They know they'll never rise high no matter how hard they work, so nothing matters to them. They flout the rules. Of course, with good sense, only up to a point. This girl went too far.

"She was found out, betrayed. She talked of having children. And raising them herself! The general Earth culture frowns on sex. Except for procreation only by the elite, of course. Citizens are the workers and they're job is to work. And obey. They're not allowed time for children and raising families. The girl was taken away. Never seen again. I heard later she'd had a complete brain wipe. But the process didn't work right, it fried her mind. Killed her. Such a waste."

Ryan asked, "Did you have anything to do with her disappearance?"

Arabella Rashid sighed, said, "No, darling, she was so far below my level, you know? I never come into contact with *those* people. But it was taken care of under my watch. I was essentially responsible."

He said, "But could you have done something?"

She said, "What? Even if I had known. What could I have done?"

He repeated, "You could have done something to stop it, to help her. To save her. Maybe change the rules?"

She looked at Ryan, "Darling, I'm the one who makes the rules. I am there to ensure these rules are carried out. DOC's function is to ensure obedience to those rules from all citizens."

"I know," he said, "I just thought I'd ask."

She looked at Ryan closely. She saw his disappointment. Her face was a mask. But inside, deep inside her she felt pain. Such hurt. She was so sorry.

* * * * * * *

They reached the Rare Book Room and a sign that said: "Hard-boiled Paperbacks." It was the biggest RBR in the secret library. Ryan had made it the best of the lot. It was his personal thing. It had one copy of every damn paperback he could find, buy, beg, borrow, steal, smuggle, transship, grab, grope, get, weasel, intimidate, or cajole for his library. Here he displayed, filed, researched, stored, shelved, or collected as much of the classic hard-boiled fiction from LastCen as he could find. Old Baxter Moneybag's collection simply paled by comparison. Had Baxter but known....

There was a lot to look at.

"It's very impressive," Arabella Rashid said, looking over a near complete run of rare 1950s Lion paperbacks. There seemed to be only a couple missing, one was #99, and allowed a wry grin. She knew that book well, but she stayed mum about it all for now.

The books lay shelved with their colorful, garish spines shown in all their wondrous glory. Many were also displayed face-out so the covers could be viewed. "They're really beautiful books, James. Little pieces of art, like posters. The women.... They're so...."

"Vibrant, vivacious, alive," he said. "Like you."

She smiled, actually blushed. He could barely believe such a thing was possible. Or was it just an act? Even now?

She said, "And the men, they are so strong, so hard, so intent. Just like you.... Just like you were last night, baby."

Ryan smiled, said, "You keep talking like that and I'll end up keeping you awake all night and we won't get any sleep tonight either."

* * * * * * *

Memory really can play you. Sometimes Ryan wondered what was real and what was fake. What was a lie and what was true? These days it was impossible even to ask those questions. You're bombarded with government lies and propaganda, your mind and thoughts influenced, if not downright controlled. Sometimes brain implants full of syntha-prop begin in the womb. Inputs are surgically implanted into the fetus. The baby is plugged into supposed "education" software while still in the womb. They don't waste any time. By the time an Earth child is born he or she is *not* brainwashed actually—one would wish their techniques were that primitive! By birth the newborn's mind has already been so conditioned and programmed, charted and controlled, that they are made into the perfect Citizen. Brain dead, accepting, harmless. And helpless, just the way The DOC likes them. And if there's ever a flaw or problem, bio-link implants and neural chips filled with government approved reinforce womb programming kick in.

It works only too well.

Ryan shuddered. That had never existed on Mars and never would while he was in charge. He saw to it that all of that stuff had been reversed and deprogrammed over the last twenty years here. Mars was an entire planet of self-sufficient, in-your-face, angry, independent, free-thinking, incorrigibles with bad attitudes!

It was wonderful.

It offered hope.

But the mind could still play you. The DOC was all-powerful. They played mind games that were mysteries to all. Sometimes Ryan wondered if he really was on Mars at all. Maybe he was lost in some secret DOC virtual program. Was there really a secret library or was it just a thought, a fantasy, from the corner of his mind that Arabella Rashid and The DOC had caused to be brought up to play him? Was there even space travel to Mars yet? Wasn't he really still back down on Earth? Back in solitary confinement. Naked and alone in the dark. Mumbling to himself. Clutching a copy of that old paperback to his stinking hide and trying to read the words printed on the old dirty paper.

Now what the hell had been the title of that book?

He remembered it now.

Mars Needs Books.

Yes, that was it. Macky had told him once that hard-boiled fiction held in it the true seed of American individualism, culture and freedom much like the earlier era represented by western fiction did. That mirrored the attitude that made a country and people great once.

Ryan had laughed then and told Macky, "There is no America anymore."

It was long gone by then.

A memory now, but Ryan could hardly remember it.

America had been cut up, divided, walled off. Some states had seceded, other states secluded themselves, cities became Security Districts. The Underpeople, the refuse of the Earth who were too poor and useless to society to bother to brainwash, came to be eventually led by some replicant. Not even a human-being truly, but some pseudo-robo-bio cyborg. His name was Moses Sage. Ryan remembered what Arabella had told him about it. The secret war back on Earth. Moses Sage, and nano-tech warriors that he had thought had only been a rumor. Like The DOC was a rumor. The interesting thing was the revolt. It seems that some of the nanotech government knights had defected and had joined Moses Sage in a scheme to free the Underworld.

Was it true?

Could he trust Arabella Rashid?

Or was he being set up?

Of course.

It had to be a set-up.

But why?

More importantly, by whom?

If it was not Arabella, if it was not The DOC, then who the hell was behind it?

Ryan had an ally on Earth. His only ally. His brother.

Was his own brother the person setting him up?

Ryan's brother—who was not his bio-brother, not his true brother at all who had died in the war—shipped him boxes of paperbacks, or so the story went. Over the last twenty years hundreds, if not thousands of boxes of paperbacks had been sent out to Mars. Ryan would trade them with the miners and other men of Mars. There had been many huge crates with tons of paperbacks marked "mining supplies." These were separate and had been the basis of the secret library.

They—and Ryan was not sure who *they* might be—seemed to be allowing him to indulge his paranoia and fantasy here. But why? It seemed that they didn't really want to destroy the old books, the old knowledge, the truth it all held. Maybe what they really wanted was to get it all off-planet. Off Earth. To keep it safe. Somewhere else. Away from the people who would destroy it. To keep it all somewhere where the masses couldn't get at it. Where only the elite could get at it. Like on Mars, or maybe where the government and The DOC wouldn't get at it? Which was it? Why the secret library?

Ryan shook the thoughts around in his head. Was he being played? Acting out parts and plans that he thought were his own, but were in fact orders he had no knowledge of from secret masters? Who was pulling his strings? It had happened before. With him and with Macky. It happened with many millions more down on Earth every single day.

If so, then why not here on Mars?

Memory can always play you.

And so can the DOC.

Memory can always be played with also.

And the DOC loves to play with your memories.

And so can Arabella Rashid.

Maybe Ryan should have killed her.

Then again, he loved her and perhaps, just perhaps, she was the one real hope of his world.

The world of Mars.

Unless she was its doom.

Then she would be James Ryan's doom as well!

CHAPTER TWENTY-TWO
THE DOC WILL SEE YOU NOW

He was in a waiting room. It was a doctor's waiting room. It was big and white, stocked with a dozen chairs, a dozen people sitting on the chairs. People of all kinds. Citizens. Gloriously ignorant and confused representatives of the proletarian masses. No one said a word or even looked at anyone else.

There was a table piled high with magazines. They were actual hard-copy magazines from LastCen. No one was paying attention to them at all. That was because all the good little Citizens, the sheep-like proles seated quietly, were each engrossed in reading books.

Books!

They were actually reading!

They were all reading the same book!

It was a paperback!

He saw what the title was.

Mars Needs Books!

* * * * * * *

When he woke up, he was not in the secret library of Mars. He was not even sure he was on Mars at all. In fact, he was not even sure he had ever been on Mars in the first place. To be truthful, he didn't know where the hell he was. Or where the hell he had been.

Things can sure get strange sometimes. So damn science-fictional....

Ryan opened his eyes and saw....

Nothing.

There was blackness all around him.

No sound.

No smell.

No nothing.

Ryan began to get that feeling in his gut when it tightens up like a brick and begins a spiral descent at warp speed through his bowels all the way down past his knees. He began to feel he was back in solitary confinement. Even worse than that, he began to feel that maybe, really, he had never actually left at all!

Then he saw her. Her face slowly came into focus before him. Then it came into view, clear now. He couldn't move. He thought he must be strapped down, or drugged, or held in a stasis field. More than likely he was brain-linked to whatever software she had him hooked into. Some damn diabolical DOC machine!

Arabella Rashid, she was playing him like an old style player piano!

She looked so beautiful.

She was so deadly.

And he'd been so damn stupid.

She said, "I know you, Ryan. Better than you know yourself. Don't. Don't feel so bad about it all. About being tricked. There really was no way you could know. Nothing you could do about it. The programming had been set a long time ago...."

He could not speak but his lips silently mouthed the words, "...since I was in the womb?"

She smiled. She knew. He knew. The Earth demons had everything under such tight control. The DOC was always in control. Of everything. Of everyone. The master of control-freak obsessive totalitarianism.

Ryan whispered, "Like in Orwell. Like in *Nineteen Eighty-Four*, a boot on the face of humanity...."

"Forever," Arabella Rashid said, completing the quote. Then

she took out a book. It was an old Lion paperback. From the middle of LastCen. Ryan had never seen a copy of it before. It was rarer than rare today. It was Jim Thompson's *The Killer Inside Me*. But not the Quill reprint or any of the others at all! It was the true original Lion edition from the 1950s. Thompson's first book for Lion Books and the beginnings of his career—and a noir legend. It was an ass-kicker of a nasty crime novel. There was certainly no copy of that particular edition of that book here on Mars. Ryan had heard tell of the book, of that particular rare edition, he had even looked for it, but he had never seen an actual copy. Even old Baxter Moneybags didn't have a copy of this particular edition. Nor the Secret Library. Ryan had never even heard of a copy available. In any collection. Where had she obtained it? How had she obtained it?

Arabella Rashid showed him the book, smiled. Then she put it away in her back pocket. She came closer, whispered in his ear, "The boot on the face of humanity, forever, Ryan. Forever! That was the...original plan."

He looked at her carefully. He didn't understand this at all. Then she seemed to have more to say.

He wasn't going anywhere so he decided to listen.

She was having some trouble saying it.

Her eyes drifted away from his, said, "We've all turned into such monsters. We have all become the thing we hate the most, Ryan."

He could not reply.

"*The Killer Inside Me*, The DOC, The Authority, all the sickness and deadness on Earth. It all has to change."

Ryan looked at Arabella Rashid astonished.

"I planned the revolution, Ryan. Years ago. I was the one who began the program. It was DOC sponsored. Do you understand? But I changed it. Simon wanted to revitalize the species. He chose Mars for the laboratory. I chose you as the guinea pig. I programmed you. Used you. Made you what you are. The DOC hurt you and filled you with hate and anger—and the lowest guilt and shame. Then we set you loose on Mars, and sent you all the worst incorrigibles from Earth; misfits, troublemakers, and crazy wise-guys who think too much and can't keep their big mouths shut. Fools and crackpots all. We programmed them, each and every one of them. We programmed you all to *love* to read, to *need* to collect the old hard-boiled paperbacks of LastCen. And we thought that if you all didn't kill each other, then some day you'd revolt against Earth and then we'd come and make war upon you. Kill you all and revitalize the species. A holy war, Ryan. Kill off all the Marsmen! Kill off all *your* people. Even though they were *our* people too. Originally. In doing so the big brains like Simon thought the Earth would be saved. The species revitalized. A good little war can sometimes do that, clean out the gene pool, survival of the fittest and all that crap. I didn't think so. However it seems to have been a staple of human history since before history was even being written."

He still couldn't talk, he could barely think straight anymore. He'd been so ill used he could not comprehend it all yet.

Arabella Rashid smiled softly at him, she patted his arm. He felt like some kind of pet. "The thing is, Ryan, you came out here to Mars, and on the way here you discovered something. You changed. Not a lot at first, just a little, but that little was enough. You put down your rage and hate, you read your books and you learned from them. You taught the others. They learned. And you had a plan."

"I was a man with a plan," he whispered. "Once."

"It was a plan The DOC gave you, Ryan. And don't you ever forget it!"

* * * * * * *

He closed his eyes. Wishing he was any place in the world but where he was now. When he opened his eyes there he was, and there was Arabella Rashid, standing in front of him, waiting for him to come back to her.

"What do you want?" he asked.

"That's not the question, Ryan. What I want to know now is, what do *you* want?" she countered.

He looked at her carefully. More confused than ever now. Grasping. Wondering. Wired. In more ways than one.

"What do you want, Ryan?" she said almost angrily now. He didn't like her to be angry with him. "Tell me. We don't have much time."

He looked at her, "I don't understand."

"Yes you do."

"No. No, I don't!"

"Yes. You. DO!"

"What do I want? What do I want!"

"Yes, Ryan. What the hell do you want?" She took out another book, a copy of *Little Caesar* the gangster classic by W. R. Burnett. An old 1950s Avon edition. Ryan remembered he had a copy in the Rare Book Room of the secret library. "You remember this one? Rico? Remember Rico? What did Rico want, Ryan?"

He remembered now. He said, "Rico wanted...more. He wanted more! He wanted it all!"

"Yes, Ryan."

He said, "Like the DOC?"

Arabella Rashid smiled, "Yes, Ryan, like The DOC."

"I don't want that," he said softly.

"Is that so, Ryan?"

"Yes," he replied.

"So, Ryan, just what the hell do you want?"

He shook his head trying to clear it.

"Wealth?" she asked.

He said nothing.

"Power?"

He shook his head.

"Fame?"

Ryan laughed at that one.

"Me?" she said.

Ryan smiled.

"You're not answering me, Ryan."

He said, "Not under these circumstances."

Now it was her turn to smile, "I quite agree."

"I just want...," he said.

"I believe you now. You just want what you've always wanted, Ryan. You just want to be left alone. And not be hurt and used any more."

"Yes," he said, and began to cry.

And then he heard her say, "Go back to sleep now, Ryan. When you wake up you'll forget all about this. You'll forget all about the fact that there is a war on, all about the fact that I am your commanding officer...and the woman who loves you. I'm sorry I had to do this but I had to look inside your mind, to be sure that you had not been tampered with by Simon, or by his evil son—and your supposed brother, Michael, or another DOC officer. I had to erase some of your programming. Now it will be all right, better. I promise you."

He shook his head.

"Ryan, how old do you think I am? How old, Ryan?"

He tried to focus his eyes with all the effort he had left. He looked deeply into her perfect face. Perfect form. Watching it all slip away from him as the trance took hold and he drifted off. He said, "Thirty, maybe thirty-five?"

The last thing he remembered before he went under was her perfect smile as her lips silently formed the words, "I am a clone, much as you are. I am one hundred and forty-seven years old, James."

Then he was asleep and all those bad memories were erased and gone forever and he was whole within himself again.

CHAPTER TWENTY-THREE
LEAVE NO ONE BEHIND

Next morning Ryan said, "You know, I had the weirdest dream I ever had in my life last night."

"Really?" She asked showing mild curiosity.

He looked at Arabella. Careful. She was so cool. Perhaps he should have killed her when he had the chance. He felt so sad, so betrayed, so played, he felt like crying, or killing her, or making love to her. He loved her so much. So he just took a deep breath and did nothing. That was always the safest course when dealing with someone like her.

He said, "the dream...."

"What was the dream like, James?"

He shuddered, "I don't think I can talk about it."

"It was so bad, that you can't talk about it?"

"Yes," he said.

She said, "Was I in it?"

He shook his head, "Were you ever!"

She smiled, "Do you know what I really like about you James? You're an agent, a killer, but you're smart. Even better, you learn from your actions. You also learn from the actions and mistakes of others. You learn from your mistakes, you learn from the books, you learn from life, from me. You learn, James, and that's...priceless today."

He shrugged, not knowing where the hell she was going with this. He allowed a playful grin, "I always figured I was a price-less kind of guy."

"And you have a good sense of humor, usually. Though that last remark.... And one more thing, James, when presented with a problem you restrain yourself from acting stupidly. You know? You don't do stupid things, like days ago when you had that stupid gun. What were you going to do with that gun? Shoot me? Kill me?"

"I thought about it," he told her, taking a slow, deep breath, "I love you, you know that, but I couldn't let you destroy everything, everybody here on Mars."

"But you restrained yourself."

He nodded.

"And in doing so put yourself and everything here at risk." she said thoughtfully, waiting for his answer.

"Yes," he replied finally. "It was stupid."

"But you restrained yourself, James."

He did not reply.

"Why?" she asked.

"I don't know."

She shook her head. "James, you damn-well know. You're the best killer the DOC has ever produced. Our most special agent. You could never, ever restrain yourself because your programming is too powerful. Your natural order of action on Earth would preclude such individual independent behavior. Why did you restrain yourself out here on Mars?"

"I don't know."

"You know."

"You were ready for me?" he asked.

She smiled, "Of course, but you did not know that."

"You know so much why don't you figure it out for yourself and then tell me!"

"James, you're being a real hardhead!"

He said, "Maybe I know something that you don't?"

She looked at him carefully, softened her gaze, said, "James, I love you. These last few days here with you have been.... But you just don't understand what's going on. The secret war. It's in DOC itself. It's deep. It's serious now. That's why I am here."

"I had a bad dream last night, Arabella."

"James, it wasn't a dream."

He looked over at her, chilled now to the bone. He mumbled, "It wasn't a dream?"

"No, James."

He shuddered, shaking now like some wirehead junkie. She came over to him and held him in her arms, stroking his forehead softly, "Baby, baby, I've been so rough on you. I'm so sorry. I never thought it would come to this. Simon did things to me too. After I killed him, I thought...I thought it was all over. I thought that I had won and things would be better. When I took over DOC I didn't realize it was just the beginning of Simon's revenge. His real power over me was *inside* me. I never knew that. Last night you insisted on helping, you even insisted on the brain-wipe and the reprogramming. We can still get your old self back if you want it and get rid of this new self—this new Mars-created James Ryan...."

He stopped shivering. The cold left him almost as quickly as it had entered him.

"You want to know what made me change?" he asked.

"I know what it is, now, James. It's the long trip out here. It's the seclusion, the loneliness, the amount of time. One year to be able to slow down, rest, think, reflect, reevaluate."

He nodded, "It has a certain mind-opening effect."

She held him and kissed him, and he kissed her back.

"I love you, James Ryan. The new you. The better Mars you. The new man—not the old DOC killer agent. And you've changed me too. At first I couldn't believe it. I thought Simon's vile spirit had been locked inside me forever, making me do terrible things I can not even talk about, but his programming has been breached, or corrupted. Or it somehow deteriorated. I began to realize that there was something else involved here. Something none of us had ever anticipated. It was Mars. The trip out here. And what's written in all those old paperbacks. A change came upon me. It wrought freedom. Life. Love.

"Freedom from Earth."

"And the Department of Control."

He smiled at her. "That's a very subversive statement."

She said, "It sure damn-well is, James."

"So what's your game?" he asked. "Why did you come out here? What do *you* want?"

Arabella Rashid smiled, brushing the long hair from her eyes. She said, "It's the secret war. The DOC. Mars. You. You didn't start the revolution out here like you were supposed to do. You changed. You got smart. Started a resistance instead. A damn smart and strong one too. A real brotherhood. And it worked. And it screwed up the DOC's plans for Mars."

"The DOC?" he said. "Not you?"

"No, not me, James. Not anymore."

He kissed her. "We can do it."

"Fight them? It won't be easy," she told him.

"Freedom, liberty, life, love, the real big, important things are never easy," he said.

"Listen, James," she went on. "I have something here I want to show you. It's a paperback. An old paperback. From LastCen."

She placed the book on the table in front of him, face up. He looked at it. He thought he was back in the dream. It was that same rare Lion paperback of *The Killer Inside Me* by Jim Thompson.

"Nice book," he said nervously, remembering it from the dream—that had not been a dream. It was incredibly old. From 1952. Way back LastCen.

She looked at him closely, said for the first time, "You don't remember, do you, James?"

He said, "Remember what? I remember the dream, I think, but...."

"Not the dream, James! Before. Don't you remember anything from before? I mean from before your previous personality and memory, before we did the brain-wipes and all the reprogramming. Before you came out here to Mars. You don't remember anything else about this book, *The Killer Inside Me?*"

He shook his head. It was all a blank.

He said, "Actually, I never read the book."

She said, "James, you *are* the book."

"How?"

"In the book there's a sheriff, Lou Ford, a nasty psycho, but he's also a master of camouflage. And that's you, baby."

"I don't know what you are talking about."

She sighed. "James, you see this old Lion paperback from 1952, from LastCen? That's your book. You purchased it. James, you purchased it when it was *new*. Lion Book #199. You bought it off the newsstand in that little candy store in Des Moines, Iowa, in the old USA in 1952! I know, because I was with you when you bought it. Before I ever become Arabella Rashid. In the old days of LastCen, when my name had been Kathleen Ryan. Remember, honey? I was your wife. Your child bride."

She was twisting his brain into a pretzel now.

He didn't remember any of it.

She explained, "We, us here now, are clones of those previous selves. The people we are today were created from DNA, memories and personalities we were given by Simon. They can do that with clones, not only replicate the structure and DNA of any subject, but include memory and personality also."

He did not think that was possible. Then he realized it was just too freaky and screwed up not to be true. He looked at her closely and said, "That would make you, what?"

"One hundred and forty-seven years old, James."

"And me?"

"James, you are one hundred and fifty-seven years old. You were always ten years older than I."

"But we look...I mean, you can't be more that thirty-five.... And I'm...."

"Don't you understand? The DOC can do anything. The DOC has done it all. James, I came out here because I need an ally. Your so-called loyal and harmless little book scout of a brother back on Earth doesn't really exist. It is a secret DOC department making a power play to take over control of The DOC. Nothing is ever what it seems to be. They have to be stopped!

The leader, Michael, is not your brother, he is Simon's clone, his son and successor-in-waiting. He's Simon's wild card. You see, Michael was never a part of Simon's Janus Project. He was a sleeper mole deep in the DOC. He was Simon's fallback. Simon programmed me to take his place in the event of his death. That was Simon's revenge on me. If that didn't work, and now it is all unraveling, then Michael was programmed to make his play for power and control from me.

Ryan didn't know what to say. He couldn't even put a face to his supposed brother now.

"Michael, your brother, was in fact, the manifestation of The DOC's original intent in the flesh. You know what that is?"

"Orwell? The boot on the face of humanity?"

"Forever, James. Forever!" she said, "and he would become Big Brother in the flesh, and the very worst manifestation of all that means."

He nodded, he had heard of all that but...still....

"That's what they want. Not mere control anymore. They can destroy. They can create. They can program. They can reprogram. They think they are gods now!"

"And they can do it?" he asked.

"Honey, they can do anything they want if we lose. Simon had the plan, and now Michael will carry it out. I came out here concerned about a power struggle at The DOC and I was looking for answers because my own memories had been compromised because I was changed by Simon's programming. That's all different now. I changed. I want to fight them now. Really fight them, like I was meant to do before Simon doctored my mind. I want to beat them. I want to...."

"I know, now. You want to be forgiven for all the bad you've done? You want to make up for it?"

"Hell no! I can never be forgiven for the terrible things I've done, James. Even the terrible things you've done, under my orders. What we can do is try to set things right. This time we do it right and leave no one behind!"

CHAPTER TWENTY-FOUR
TERMINAL CASES

They were meeting in the secret library. Ryan had called together all the leaders of the Resistance. The men of influence, bosses, workers, miners, readers, big brains, the judge, bartenders, all the big-mouths, fools, angry, loud, too-smart, shifty misfits, fighters, and the various wounded of all kinds. He brought them all together. It was one hell of a motley crew.

Alvy called them all to order in the huge meeting room on the lower level. There were hundreds of men. The leaders of Mars—and the leaders of the Martian Resistance.

"The bar is closed! Now come to order! Ryan wants to say a few things and then introduce someone I'm sure you'll be most interested to meet."

There was shouting, cat-calls, demands for beer.

"Shut up and sit down, will yah!" Alvy shouted. "No beer until after we talk!"

They didn't shut up. They were true-blue Marsmen, after all. Marsmen never did what anyone told them to do. Every one of them was a first-rate PITA—pain-in-the-ass. Each was a damn troublemaker to boot. But they eventually quieted down a bit, out of respect for Ryan.

They damn well fell silent when they saw him walk out with a woman at his side. She was hot and lovely and had every man's juices flowing just at the sight of her.

Ryan didn't mince words, he stared down at the crowd looking intently at each man, recognizing each face, each story that went with it. One by one, with that magnetic eagle-eye gaze of his he demanded their attention. And got it! It was a rough crowd to be sure, prideful hardheaded individualists and die-hard trouble-makers. Crazy-minded bastards and crackpots too tough to die here on Mars, too honorable, ornery, or serious about liberty and independence to live on Earth any more. He was one of them. These were his people. He loved every one of them old, ugly, cantankerous sons-of-bitches!

"Gentlemen!" Ryan said, "and I use the term *very* loosely."

There was laughter, but it was nervous laughter nonetheless. All eyes were looking up front, but they were not on Ryan now, but on the woman at his side. She was surely beautiful, but that wasn't it. She stood there very business-like, very serious, almost cold. Yes, maybe, very definitely cold and...dangerous.

That's what concerned them about her.

Everyone wondered who she was.

They didn't know who she was yet. Ryan didn't want them all to panic, so he'd have to ease them into who she was.

"Okay, guys," Ryan continued. "We've come to it now. It's crunch time."

There was a murmur among the crowd, rapid and rapt, mostly fueled by speculation about the woman. Murmurs and whispers flowed from dozens of voices. Who was she? Why was *she* here?

No one had yet imagined the truth.

Was she an ally?

Or a spy?

Ryan said, "We've come to a fork in the path of our resistance against the oppressive policies and laws of Earth. There are two pathways we can take at this point in time. One of them is to accept what the Department of Control has planned for us all along. Hardly any choice at all. The other path is one we have planned for ourselves as free men seeking a free Mars."

"Then we fight?" a voice shouted.

"Revolution!" another barked triumphantly.

"We should declare our independence and fight for our

freedom from Earth!" another shouted from the crowd and....

The flag of the Mars Republic was unfurled and waved. They stood up and cheered.

Ryan tried to stop them. He tried to quiet them, seeking to shout them down, to shut them up. They were losing it. They were going the wrong way, down the wrong path. He had to stop them before it got crazy and he lost all control! How ironic!

"No! Stop it! You're wrong! You're doing the exact thing The DOC wants you to do!"

Arabella Rashid stepped forward. She pulled out a small caliber old style handgun, pressed the trigger, and a bullet shot into the ceiling over the heads of the crowd. It brought down a fine mist of plaster and white dust. The report was an ear-blasting cacophony in that massive cavern-like hall.

There was immediate shock and quiet. Every face, every eye, immediately transfixed upon her now.

She said, "That's better. Now sit down and shut up. I have some news for you that you all need to hear, unless you all want to be killed. Then it doesn't matter one damn bit and I personally don't give a fuck!"

That quieted them.

Ryan said, "Come on, sit down, guys. It's going to be a long night and we have a lot to discuss and vote on before we're through."

* * * * * * *

Ryan began it. He talked to them for an hour, giving them his report about what the Resistance was trying to accomplish on Mars, all that it had accomplished, and what the plans of The DOC were for them all.

"KTA," Ryan told them, "Simple as that. KTA—Kill Them All! That's what the DOC had planned for us all along, brothers!"

There was rage and ruinous pain burning in each member of the crowd but they simmered down when Ryan told them, "But it's not gonna happen, brothers. We're not stupid. We're through being used and we have an ally here. She is someone I want you to listen to very carefully. She's on our side, brothers, so sit calm and listen. Think and be smart. You may have heard of her. I tell you she's on our side. Just remember that. Her name is Arabella Rashid. She is the Director of the Department of Control."

A thousand blank faces stared back at Ryan, no fear, no anger yet, just total and uncomprehending disbelief at this point. Was this some joke? They all hoped, prayed it might be. Everyone there had heard the name. The fear and anger would show up soon enough. In substantial abundance. It was growing almost immediately—fear, panic, were the shock troops on the way even now!

"Okay, baby, you've got their attention," Ryan told her.

Arabella Rashid nodded, strode forward, said in a loud powerful voice, "We have a plan to free Mars and to outsmart The DOC, but you must listen very carefully. We have to be smart and bold and not be afraid."

There was stunned silence. Slowly the men were coming out of it. They knew The DOC. They feared it to the core of their being. Even though the organization was said not to officially exist, everyone had heard the rumors, had felt the fear, the control, the restrictions all their lives. On Earth. For sure. But not here on Mars. Not until now. Now memories of Earth flooded back into their consciousness and they began to look around them, the old paranoia returning like a flash of lightning. Many expected any moment for Authority shock troops or nanotech warriors, space marines, or some Big Brother-type goons with big boots stomping down on them. Big-Brother with a gun in his hand, and the will to kill.

Arabella Rashid said with calm and determination, "Do not fear. There will be no shock troops, no government goon squads or kill forces. We are safe. For now. Now listen. I need to tell you some things and then you need to talk them over and decide what you want to do about it."

"How do we know we can trust you?" someone shouted.

"If you couldn't trust me, moron, you'd all be dead meat by

now. You know how the Authority is back on Earth?"

Many heads nodded.

"Well, The DOC is far, far worse, let me assure you."

There was silence. Hopeless silence, And fear. Fear to act. Fear not to act.

Thick, syrupy fear.

And anger.

"But I am not here as an enemy. That's what I am trying to get through your hard heads. I am here as a friend and ally!"

No one knew what to say to that, so they didn't say anything.

Ryan said, "Listen to her, my brothers!"

"There was a plan," Arabella Rashid continued, pacing back and forth, making eye contact with members of the crowd as she spoke to them. "The plan has been in operation for decades. The Janus Project. It will be replaced by a new plan. A better plan. That plan will free Mars! Maybe even free Earth! But it will come at a price."

Every eye was on her now.

"The original plan was for the DOC to collect the most incorrigible hard cases, troublemakers, crackpots, religo-nuts, extreme-politicos, Trotskyites, left-wingers, right-wingers, no-wingers, and ship you all out here. Then fertilize you with ideas from books—hard-boiled crime fiction was the initial implant. The stuff oozed crime, sex, action, suspense and violent passion. The stuff of life! Then in time you were all supposed to progress to more political forms of fiction. Each one of you was programmed and implanted for this before you left Earth. I mean really, think about it. You all collect...what?... *paperbacks?* Of all the damn things! There has to be something else involved there. There is, and it was Simon and the DOC behind it all. Eventually you were supposed to turn politically ideological and rhetorically incorrect, organizing secret cells that would soon become an open and bloody revolt. Then you would all be put down like dogs. Every last one of you. It was the perfect set up and you were each programmed for it. You had no choice!

"But it never happened," she continued. "Key components changed in many of you. It was something to do with the long voyage out here. And the paperbacks. People change on the way out to Mars, or Mars changes them when they get here. Whatever it is, something changed you all. It changed me too. So what was supposed to happen, did not happen. Or more accurately, it didn't happen exactly as The DOC planned. Incredible in and of itself. Unbelievable to be sure. But something else did happen instead. Paperbacks happened, some kind of crazy but divine madness. It seemed to create an innate understanding of life and brotherhood you all took from reading the old books. A kind of sub-culture. You all caught it like a virus, or bought into it like some mobsters from LastCen. 'An offer you could not refuse'. Or would not refuse. You get what I mean?"

The Godfather by Mario Puzo," someone yelled helpfully.

"Luca Brazzi," someone else shouted. "He was a kick-ass, super head-breaker!"

"And just the kind of person you do *not* need now!" Arabella Rashid shouted back. The man sat down. Quelled for the moment.

"We—every one of you, Ryan, myself, all of us—we are all fighting for freedom and liberty. However, to keep the fight going, we have to survive. First. You know how the Authority is? The DOC is much worse. They would not think twice about authorizing the liquidation of every person on Mars, and they'd carry it out with a cold-hearted efficiency, speed, and completeness if they thought it would get them to their goal."

No one said anything in reply. They knew she spoke true.

Arabella looked into the crowd. Into every face. They were wary of course, suspicious, but expectant too. Waiting. Wondering what her game was. She wondered about her game as well. It was so bold, so crazy. Would it work? Or would it destroy them all?

She told them, "For the last twenty years you have been wise. Don't blow it now, people. You have won a considerable victory. It was by default, because the Authority and The

DOC does not suspect what has been going on here, but it is nevertheless a victory. It's a great and proud accomplishment. You've managed to keep yourselves free and survive. I need not remind you that the graveyards of Earth are full of free *dead* men. You've not had the Authority on your back or The DOC breathing down your neck every minute of every day. Not yet! Mars was founded as a settlement world but The DOC wanted to turn it into a planetary penal world that would revolt and be purged in a holocaust. You prevented that. You saved yourselves from death. By being smart. By playing the game. Your game, not *theirs*. By pretending to be utterly loyal you survived, and so you have won the first round of the game. Against all the odds. You survived. Now we go to break the bank!"

There were cheers. Nervous. Tentative. Curious, with reservations, but cheers nevertheless. They were fighters after all. And they felt she just might be on their side now.

There were expectant looks forward.

"They are waiting," Ryan whispered to her.

"Give them another minute. I want their undivided attention. And yours, James. This is it," she said carefully.

Ryan nodded. He knew. It was crunch time.

Arabella Rashid's voice, bold and powerful, began, "The bottom line is this: Earth, The Authority, The DOC, are all aware that something is going on here. If I could see it, they could too. I have little doubt. I have come out here but Michael, Simon's successor, must also know I am here by now. It will not take him long to put it together. Even now his own programming may be kicking in to cause him to make a play to take over the DOC. However we can stymie them again. We can do that by giving them just what they expect. They expect a revolt. You must give them what they expect! But *not* the *way* they expect it!"

There were some nods, but also a lot of blank stares. Fight? Don't fight? What was she saying? Fear was creeping into questing eyes now at the realization that the enemy knew all about the Resistance and the revolt brewing here. And about them.

That was scary.

"Earth and The DOC are expecting a revolt. Let's give it to them! But fake it. We fake it all. Fake the news. Fake the vids. Fake the reports. Fake the police and military transcripts. Fake the whole damn rebellion! We can even fake executions! It doesn't matter because we can send false images back, file reports that mean nothing, give them all the flimflam they can eat! Validate their plans and procedures. Yes, there was a revolt. It was quickly put down. Almost everyone stayed loyal to Earth. We all "love" Earth, love The Authority, of course—and everyone is terrified of The DOC."

There was cynical laugher from the men. Hard. Biting. She continued, "Those few involved in this dastardly plot will all be caught, of course. The revolt quickly put down, all violators executed. We can give Earth evidence of hundreds of bodies, or even thousands of summary executions. They'll get their holocaust. They'll be expecting it all neat and tidy and they'll get it all fully documented. Of course, it will be all faked, but they'll never know the truth and they will not find out until it is too late."

It was possible. They had after all, manipulated similar images and sent them back as reports to Earth for decades now. They had fooled the Authority, even the DOC.

It could be done.

There were nods, whispers, cheers, some claps, more cheers; they liked the idea of sticking it to the Earthers. Making them look like fools. Screwing with the head of the hated Authority. Taking a piss in the eyes of the dreaded DOC. There was general agreement. This was good. It might even be fun.

"We can give them everything they want, everything they expect. Trick them big time, and we can get away with it. By making them think they have won, they will turn their attention elsewhere, hopefully within and against themselves. We can win this!"

There were wild cheers now.

Arabella Rashid raised her hands. "There is more. Listen carefully now, brothers. It will not be all that simple or easy. Earth and The DOC are not to be sated that easily. They will require the leadership of our revolt to be brought back to Earth for 'questioning'. We all know what that means. Horrendous and painful torture, brain- scanning, memory-drain, and finally some form of public execution. This 'leadership' can be reasonably limited by us to just one man. The DOC will buy that, but that man must become a willing sacrifice to save Mars and its people. There is no other way to make such a plan work. The DOC will require their pound of flesh in the form of the leader of the revolt transported back to Earth. We must find the right subject. Someone who loves Mars and is willing to be destroyed for what he believes in. Someone who will lie to the interrogators even as they drain the last drop of blood and life from his living body and never give them the truth. Someone willing to go through hell so that Mars, its people and freedom, can live!"

There was quiet now, but confusion too.

One man stood up, looked around at everyone, said, "Lady, we don't really have any leader. We are our own leaders. Each one of us. That's what Mars is about."

Arabella Rashid nodded, "That may be true. That's why this place is so special. So important. Why each one of you is important."

"Then what do we do?" another man asked.

She said, "I've thought about this on the long journey out and talked it over with Ryan, Alvy and some others here. Do you know what we are, people? Do you know what each and every one of us is in the eyes of The DOC? We're terminal cases. Nothing more. People who are waiting to die, or to be put to death. Except it won't be any mercy killing. I can assure you. Terminal cases! Every one of us! Does that give you any thoughts?"

They were thinking it over. They got the connection of a sacrificial lamb—the man who was the leader of the revolt on Mars, a man who had proclaimed himself the King of Mars!

That last idea, King of Mars, was one touch the Earthers and The DOC could never resist falling for.

"The King of Mars!" Arabella Rashid said. "Only our King will die for his people—so that they all may live. So they can survive. So in time they will secure their liberty!"

Ryan came forward, kissed Arabella on the cheeks, then spoke to the throng pressed close around them. "This is what we're going to do, find a willing terminal case, pass him off to Earth and The DOC as our new King, the leader of the revolt. Then sacrifice him like a lamb to the slaughter. It's horrible, but it's the only way to trick the Earthers. It's the only way we can convince them. They expect a strong charismatic leader. It will be tough on the chosen one. He can not be implanted or reprogrammed with any kind of material, nor brain-wiped. He will have to memorize an enormous amount of material to feed them all bogus gobbledygook that looks legit, but that will be nothing compared to the interrogation he is sure to receive from The DOC. Then he will be tortured. Painfully. Horribly. Finally he will die at the hands of Earther and DOC scientists, but that death shall not be in vain!"

There was silence in the huge hall.

Arabella Rashid had checked again and again, all the med-reports, scans, all the files and computer extrapolations. She knew who she wanted.

She looked at Ryan and said, "I'm sorry, but it cannot be you, James. I know you want to do it. I know you'd willingly sacrifice yourself in a minute for your brothers here, and for Mars, and for me, but you cannot be the one. The DOC would strip your mind apart. You're already so programmed and implanted, they'd have a field day with you and eventually learn too much information we do not want them to learn. It would put everyone here in terrible jeopardy. James, you have to stay here on Mars and help lead the people. I have to play my part and go back to Earth with the leader of the revolt, this so-called King of Mars, in chains as my prisoner. Then I have to orchestrate his torture for information while the members of the DOC Board and Michael, look on. Evaluate. If a way can be found I will try to murder the man, to save him from further pain. It must be a helpless, innocent man, James."

Ryan could see Arabella was sickened by it all. But it had to be done exactly as she said. It was their only hope. It was the only way they could deceive the Earth Authority and The DOC. Give them what they wanted. Give them what they expected. Verify all their assumptions and expectations. Feed them what they wanted to see, hear, feel. They'd suck it all in, greedily. Then all their plans would be rendered impotent.

Ryan knew who she was after. The perfect candidate. A loner and mystic—or nut some said—a guy by the name of Iron Mike. Marsman Iron Mike. He was the biggest, blackest, ugliest, most contrary son-of-a-gun Christian-zealot, recluse, that there probably ever was. He lived alone. He did not talk to anyone. Ever. He did not quote scriptures. He did not proselytize. He did not complain. He said nothing. He never read paperbacks, he only read the Bible. To himself. Quietly. He was the only man on Mars who had not joined the Resistance and the only man whom the Resistance did not fault for not joining. Such was the respect felt for the man by even the hardest of these men. Iron Mike had been here years before Ryan or any of the newer settlers. Some said he had been born on Mars. But that could not be possible.

Marsman Iron Mike was a living legend on Mars. A living legend everywhere on the planet since he'd saved a dozen men from a mine cave-in.

Ryan remembered it, twenty years ago when he'd first come out to Mars. They'd worked in the deepest, darkest tunnel of the old Olympus Mons Mine #12. They'd called it the Mine of Death in those days, and with good reason. They'd been down over sixteen hours, bone-tired, worn-out, a full twenty-man crew. They'd been ready to go up top at shift end when the cave-in suddenly began. The titanium shoring splintering and cracking like kindling, rending in loud screams, the men screaming even more loudly. The only way out, a tunnel twenty yards away looking like it was about to come down any second and trap them all in a terrible death. No hope in sight.

Then they saw Iron Mike, standing in the tunnel, all six feet six inches of him, 300 pounds of bone and muscle and hard ass attitude. By himself he was holding up the splinters of the shoring with his bare hands. His arms outstretched like a great black Jesus on the cross, his blood dripping down his body as he held up the tunnel with bare muscle and grit, with only will power and his faith in His Lord. Like a modern Martian Samson in the Temple, he held the roof of the tunnel up so that all his brothers could run toward him and escape under the protection of his huge arms, and make their way to safety.

To life.

Twenty men would have been goners for sure. Long dead now. Suffocated or cut to pieces, and covered by tons of Martian soil. Those men included Ryan, Alvy, Old Manny (back when he had been Young Manny), Ernie Cigarettes, even Baxter Moneybags. He'd not been called Moneybags back then because he was a dirt-poor miner like everyone else. Those and fifteen others had all been saved by Mike. All of them would have been dead, had not Iron Mike saved their sorry asses. And that was just the beginning. Iron Mike didn't stop there.

Iron Mike saved dozens of settlers when one of the Marstown bubbles burst years back. In fact, there were half a dozen instances where the Marsman, as he was often called, always seemed to appear in just the right place at the right time. He just seemed to be where he was needed most.

Marsman Iron Mike was a legend on Mars but he never spoke about any of it to anyone. He never talked about anything. He never gave interviews. He never said a word about anything to anyone on any subject. People said he had the spirit of old Mars within him. The spirit of the Old Ones who had been there before man had ever come out to the planet. Others said he was surely full of something—they just didn't know what and wouldn't say!

"Marsman Iron Mike is the man we need, James," Arabella Rashid told Ryan.

James Ryan shook his head, "You'll never find him, and if you do, he won't talk to you. Even if he does, he certainly will never agree to help us. I don't even know if we should ask him. He would never agree. He's never embraced the Resistance, or anything else for that matter. There is also the fact that you and I know what is going to happen to him on Earth. How could we ask that of anyone...?"

Ryan was going to say more but he was distracted by some confusion at the opposite end of the huge hall. There was a mob and some turmoil. Someone was entering the hall and the crowd suddenly all stood. Silent. Watching.

At first Ryan thought...could it be? Betrayal! Had Arabella somehow tricked him? Were the shock troops now beginning their attack?

But no, upon further examination it wasn't that at all. In fact, it seemed it was just one man entering the hall. Alone. A tall black male. Some thought him ugly as sin, others that he was just big and mean-looking. He boldly walked up to the front of the room where Ryan and Arabella Rashid and all the others watched him in surprise and awe.

When Iron Mike finally reached them he said, "I'm your terminal case. No more than a year or so to live. I'm your man, Ryan. Let's do it."

"Mike?" Ryan asked astonished. He had not seen his old friend in almost ten years, but he looked as though he had not aged a day.

"Are you sure?" Ryan asked.

"You know that I am."

Arabella Rashid said, "You know what it means, Mike? Torture. Terrible torture like you cannot imagine. I promise you that. And that's not the worse. The physical part, I mean. What they do to your mind, to your very spirit, will be much worse."

He only nodded, "I understand evil."

She continued, "I'll have to take you back to Earth as a prisoner—where you will have to play your part—to the death."

Marsman Iron Mike said simply, "I am ready."

Iron Mike stopped by Ryan as he walked off saying, "You'll know where to find me when you are ready to leave."

Before he left Ryan asked him, "Mike? Why?"

Iron Mike just kept walking away, then suddenly stopped, slowly turned and looked right back at Ryan and said, "I go where I am told, by My Lord."

You could hear a pin drop in that huge hall, each man's breath stopped. Each man's thoughts turned to Mike and the implications of his words. Only a smattering of men there were religious, but while most of those were from so many different and conflicting sects, all of them had heard what Mike had said and understood in their own way. In their own heart. And many wondered. Some suddenly felt tears run down their cheeks.

Iron Mike walked away and was soon gone.

Ryan looked at Arabella, "Was he ever...?"

"No, James, I swear. He was the only one. He was never programmed, he was left untouched on purpose. He is another wild card. You can forget about him being brain-wiped or implanted. Did you get a look at his neck? He doesn't even have an input slot for a disk. I don't know where he is getting his orders from, but it is not from me or the DOC. That's for sure."

CHAPTER TWENTY-FIVE
MARS IS FREE AND SO IS WE

She didn't think of Ryan now. Or Mars. The long voyage had changed her more. Hurt her. Hurt her for what she knew she must do.

Of course, Mike made it all so very easy for her. He never complained. He never even talked to her. She was not able to get to know him. This made it easier for her and she was sure he did it for her sanity. As a gift to her. He never left his cube. He never said or did a thing on that long voyage back to Earth. He just prayed. Then he studied his part from the guidelines she'd given him. Preparing to play his role.

He was...The King of Mars!

It was all so ludicrous and sad, but Iron Mike was set to play his part, a part that was meant to be played, to the death!

Arabella Rashid wondered where Mike took his orders from? It was not from the Authority. Not from any government agency. Certainly not from the DOC. But he certainly took orders and they came from somewhere. The fact that he said they were from His Lord, apparently from God Himself, just made things more curious. A hell of a lot more curious!

It was strange.

Could it be?

Could it be as Mike said?

Or was he the maddest madman of them all?

Mike really was a terminal case. Some kind of cancer had set upon him almost as suddenly as he'd decided to become the needed sacrificial lamb for the Mars revolt. It was progressing at a rapid rate, the Mars doctors had told her. They said he had less than a year left. Coincidence? Or was it something more...?

Now was the time Arabella Rashid dreaded. All the questions had been asked. It was all recorded, all so meticulously filed, documented, witnessed by hundreds of DOC specialists and Board members. Michael and his evil little minions made a special visit and showed intense interest. The records were on DVD, vid, holo, sensory media, every word, mood, meaning, nuance....

When that was all done...it was still not finished.

Now came the hard part.

Now came the torture.

The quest for information.

For *all* information.

It had to be done. The DOC required it.

The DOC monitored it. Closely, intimately, you could almost say, lovingly.

The DOC always got what it wanted just the way it wanted it.

Arabella Rashid, Director of the DOC, knew the organization was a huge, evil, out-of-control monster that existed just to feed. It fed on people. It fed on the innocent. She led it, but she did not really control it. No one could really control it. In fact, the reverse was actually true. The DOC controlled her! And now she knew that it had been that way all her life.

And she hated that. Blamed it all on Simon. However, now she had to face a grim truth. She was the DOC and the DOC was her. She was to blame and she knew it.

That was why she was fighting so hard against it.

That was why she knew she would win too.

The DOC could never win.

Battles, yes, it had certainly won many battles.

But the DOC could never win the war. It could never be victorious in the final struggle. That was because if people like James Ryan, Arabella Rashid and Iron Mike could fight against that system, with someone like her as its darkest and most powerful advocate and enforcer, such a system could never prevail.

But that system could sure do a lot of damage.

It was doing that now to the 'King' of Mars.

And it had done it for far too long on Earth.

So DOC would win its battles.

Ply its treason.

Run its betrayals.

Enjoy its holocausts.

The murders, the killings, all the death....

But it would lose in the end.

* * * * * * *

They were ready now.

Arabella Rashid looked down at Marsman Iron Mike. It was sad to see him lay there so calm and helpless, waiting to be taken apart by the best specialists of torture and pain the DOC had on their payroll. These were monsters in hospital gowns with rubber gloves, creatures who called themselves doctors. Each now anxiously awaiting the command from their Director to get to work. The work they loved to do so well.

Then Arabella Rashid gave that command, though it broke her heart to do so.

She looked at Iron Mike and knew he would win his battle soon, and his war as well. He was a very brave man. She only wished she could comfort him, hug him, wet his dry, swollen lips with soft kisses. Of course she could not. She could not cry for him, nor set her life down in exchange for his, all she could do for him now was silently pray that all played their parts to perfection and that it would all end soon....

All he had asked her to do was to pray for him.

So she silently prayed for him, and herself, for what she was allowing to happen to him was tearing her apart.

She saw his eyes look up at her for the first time.

He smiled. It was a beautiful smile, there was only love and forgiveness there.

It lasted for only a second.

Then Iron Mike closed his eyes.

Arabella wished she could do something for such a good and noble man. Perhaps even a holy man. Instead, she could do nothing. She had her own part to play here too. It had to be done correctly. If she screwed up now then all of Iron Mike's pain would be for nothing. She had to steel herself. Hers was a terrible part, but it must be played, and played well with conviction and originality. She sighed quietly to herself, thought of James Ryan back on Mars and wished so much that she could be there with him. Far and away from here. Well, maybe, some day.

Now she said impatiently, "Come now, doctors, stop wasting time. Let's get on with it!"

"Yes, Lady Director," said the man they called Chief Specialist Rhom, but who in reality was the master torturer of the DOC. Care must be taken here now, for Rohm was one of Michael's most intimate creatures.

"What would you like to know first?" Head Interrogator Androix, asked the Lady Director and the members of the DOC Board who were viewing it all via hologram.

"I want it all," she said plainly and firmly. "Peel him open, down to the core. Drain him dry. Take out everything there is within him. I want his mind, his heart, his soul. The Department of Control requires it—and we all know the DOC gets everything it wants."

Rohm smiled and nodded, then he got to work.

* * * * * * *

It had been going on for days now. They had all kinds of devices, drugs, diabolical machines, the latest and most incredible nanotech equipment to keep a subject alive. They could make this last for months, if necessary. Making the subject receive the most extreme forms of torture, while experiencing the most excruciating pain. It was horrendous. Rohm believed he had actually attained some form of higher art in this area and Head Interrogator, Androix, quite agreed.

Arabella Rashid watched it all with the most evident detachment and analytical interest. To all intents and purposes she was just another viewer, as all the DOC specialists, researchers, division directors, sector heads, Board members, executives, commissioners, and other big shots who watched. Calm. Curious. Evaluating. Collating data. Without any feeling inside them at all for the helpless victim. Dead souls with dead spirits viewing with fascination the dying of the only real human being in the room. They were deader than Marsman Iron Mike would ever be once his brave heart stopped beating. They had been long dead before Mike would ever be buried deep in the ground.

All of them were like that, except Arabella Rashid.

She was calm as ice on the outside, just like everyone else.

But she was crying like a child on the inside at what she was forced to witness.

Her spirit was bleeding on the inside with what she saw them doing to that poor man.

But she played her part well.

Her *goddamned* part!

And she gave the DOC what it wanted.

What it needed most.

What all totalitarian systems need most.

An enemy.

A victim.

A reason to exist.

And Marsman Iron Mike played his part brilliantly.

Like the true hero he was.

He'd studied his script.

Knew it well.

Iron Mike played it all with an energy, a rage, a strength that could never be mere acting. It was, like real, actual truth and undeniable. It was like all of mankind, the very spirit of the human race was pulling together, to push the damned boot heel of totalitarianism off the face of humanity. Then to shove it up its owner's own damn ass!

Marsman Iron Mike!

Sure, they could hurt him.

They could even kill him.

But they could never win against him.

Marsman Iron Mike was a man in a long line of fighters.

Not all were always heroes.

Not all were always winners.

But they could be. They might be. Surely they were sometimes.

He was like those heroes in the paperbacks on Mars.

Arabella Rashid and James Ryan had read about so many of them.

And now there was Marsman Iron Mike.

Sure, the DOC could hurt him.

Hurt him bad.

And the DOC could kill him.

Any time it wanted.

But the DOC could never win against him.

Because he saw through the DOC and all it was. He saw that plain and simple. Marsman Iron Mike would never give in.

He would fight them always!

The DOC could never win against such a man.

And the thing that drove all the specialists and planners and executives at the DOC so crazy was that they each began to realize it too!

They were just relieved their plan had worked and they had stopped him before it was too late. King of Mars, indeed!

* * * * * * *

More days passed.

The grim work proceeded.

They took him apart piece by piece now. Psychologically, emotionally, and physically. But still, they kept him alive, probing deeper for more information.

Arabella Rashid forced herself to watch it all. To remember it all. Iron Mike deserved that much. It was important that at least one person who was on his side, someone whose heart was breaking for all his suffering, should be there. To see it all. To remember. To be there for him. So that Mike knew, that of all the hundreds of cold and evil faces watching and analyzing and questioning and surmising, there was one there...who cared.

They'd been so thorough. So perfectly bestial. Rohm had actually shone. There would certainly be a promotion for him in this. Maybe others as well. Careers were being made.

They'd pumped Mike full of drugs and later nanotech implants. Drained his mind. Synapse by synapse. Cell by cell. Like cleaning out the rooms of some big old dusty mansion. Bit by bit. Byte by byte. So methodical. Finally there was nothing left. His mind was sterilized. Like before a baby in a womb. Empty.

Except for the fear.

They left him with the fear. And they left him with the brother of fear. Pain.

And when they'd taken all he had in him, all that was left for them to do, there was simply the end. The execution.

DOC scientists administered the lethal injection. It was slow. And very painful. They wanted it that way. Even here his end was being monitored and recorded and simultaneously broadcast over the worldwide Net. It had garnered a stupendous 90% ratings share over the popular month-long series. Education and entertainment for the masses of Earth, par excellence. There were even toys produced, action figures, torture tie-ins. For the kids.

Meanwhile, Mike was dying. It was happening slow, on purpose. After all, there might be the possibility of a death-bed confession. Perhaps some grand pre-death panic, or recriminations, begging, crying, denouncements, something good the media could use. The digital record was ensuring that it was all preserved for later use. Rohm thought that some tears now would certainly be appropriate, or maybe even some good old-time religion, with prayers and all. Calls for mercy, rage, or forgiveness from The Almighty would be a nice touch. It was all good for the show. Grist for the mill.

None of it—*none of it!*—was to be gotten out of Iron Mike!

And then, just before Mike's noble heart beat for the very last time, when the torrents of pain and suffering he'd been forced to endure for so many days finally seemed to be over, he looked up at Arabella Rashid and implored her with his eyes.

She went over to him. She bent down to put her face close to his, placing her lips in front of his eyes. She did it so none of the cameras and vids could see. So there was no way for anyone to read her lips. And she silently mouthed the words to him.... "Mars is free!"

It had been their code to let him know he had been successful.

Then before Marsman Iron Mike died, he silently mouthed the words back to her, "...and so are we!"

He died then with a soft smile.

CHAPTER TWENTY-SIX
GO YOUR OWN WAY

She was one of the new *émigrés* to Mars. She'd come out legally with the latest group of wives and she sure had a lot of boxes. It took her a full year to get out there. The boxes were all full of old paperbacks. Hard-boiled crime and private eye stuff mostly. All of it from LastCen. She'd liberated a case of delightfully tough James M. Cain, W. R. Burnett, Thomas B. Dewey, Gaylord Dold, and James Hadley Chase paperbacks.

It was her final trip out to Mars. She was there to rejoin her husband. She had come home. Finally.

She was here now as a new settler.

James Ryan met her at the port.

She stood at attention, with her hand over her heart as old man McGregor made sure the Mars World Anthem was played. Loudly. Proudly.

She saluted the Mars Republic flag.

It blazed with stark warning, "Don't Tread on Me!"

It proclaimed with bold pride, "I'd Rather Starve Than Eat Your Bread!"

It said harsh truth, "TANSTAAFL"—There Ain't No Such Thing as a Free Lunch!

That last she had learned was a phrase made popular by a LastCen science fiction writer, of all people. Some guy named Robert A. Heinlein. A man whose work she'd discovered was hard-boiled in its own very special way. She'd brought copies of his *Farnham's Freehold* out with her to Mars. A kick-ass book!

She saw that the spirit of his work all came together in the Mars Republic flag, which told her boldly, you *can* go your own way.

That phrase she knew now was the title of an old song by a LastCen Earther rock band known by the curious name, Fleetwood Mac. Whatever a 'Fleetwood' or a 'Mac' might be?

She passed the new monument to Marsman Iron Mike, it flashed upon the screens. It said, "The King of Mars, we hail our beloved king!"

There was a moment of touching silence.

Then Arabella Rashid saw James Ryan and cried as she ran over to embrace him.

They held each other for a long time. Each luxuriating in the warmth of the contact of their flesh, and the burning of their love.

Finally she stopped kissing him and said, "You look good. It's so good to see you, James."

"You too," he murmured between kisses.

"I read a lot of great books on the way out. And you gotta see the paperbacks I brought out, James. You'll never believe what I got in these boxes."

"Oh, yeah?"

"Yeah, James, paperbacks like you would not believe, I mean, I know Mars still needs books, right? Well I brought plenty. I also have something else very special for you, baby. And it ain't in any of these boxes either."

She was lovely. He smiled and said, "Well let's get on home and see what it is. "

Arabella Rashid said with a wink, "Yeah, baby, let's do just that."

* * * * * * *

The news came to Michael in ultra-secret digital scramble. As new Director of the Department of Control, he looked at the warning carefully and in alarm. This could not be happening! It simply could not be happening!

The message flashed:

Top Priority! DOC Director! Eyes Only!

Then:

DOC Rebels, under the leadership of the treasonous non-human replicant Moses Sage, have overthrown the Director-ship of the Australia Sector and have now come into de facto control of that entire security area....

Authority shock troops have been sent to quell the uprising, but many are in open mutiny....

Untrustworthy! Untrustworthy....

All space platforms have been alerted and targeted strong-holds of rebel resistance for immediate destruction. However, the space platforms have become inactive. No reason for this malfunction has yet been determined....

Authority Leadership will take immediate action to regain control but it appears a general planetary uprising has begun and the rebel forces are....

YOUR TRANSMISSION HAS BEEN INTERUPTED.

THERE IS NO FURTHER INFORMATION....

D.O.C. SECURITY CENTRAL....

OUT....

ABOUT THE AUTHOR

GARY LOVISI is a Mystery Writers of America Edgar Award nominee and Western Writers of America Spur Award winner. His latest books include *Bad Girls Need Love Too* (Krause), a lovely hardcover showcasing the art of the wildest sexy paperback covers and their outrageous blurbs; *Ultra-Boiled* (Ramble House), which contains twenty-three of his hardest crime stories; *Driving Hell's Highway* (Wildside), a hard surreal noir about a lone man driving the back roads of darkest America; *More Secret Adventures of Sherlock Holmes* (Ramble House), collecting three new longer Holmes pastiches; *Gargoyle Nights* (Wildside), in which a horrid monster roams the halls of Oldearth's dead; and *Murder of A Bookman* (Wildside), where Detective Bentley Hollow investigates murder in the rare book collecting world. Lovisi is the founder of Gryphon Books, editor of *Paperback Parade* and *Hardboiled* magazines, and is the sponsor of an annual paperback book collectors show in New York City, now in its 23rd year. To find out more about him his work, or Gryphon Books, visit his web site at:

www.gryphonbooks.com